THE SHTETL

and other Jewish stories

Mark Harris

THE SHTETL

and other Jewish stories

Matador
9 De Montfort Mews
Leicester LE1 7FW, UK
Tel: (+44) 116 255 9311 / 9312
Email: books@troubador.co.uk
Web: www.troubador.co.uk/matador

ISBN 978 1848760 783

British Library Cataloguing in Publication Data.
A catalogue record for this book is available from the British Library.

Typeset in 11pt Bembo by Troubador Publishing Ltd, Leicester, UK
Printed in the UK by TJ International, Padstow, Cornwall

Matador is an imprint of Troubador Publishing Ltd

For Sharon and Emma

Contents

Preface

STORYTELLERS and storytelling go back a long way, as far back as the dawn of Mankind's first communications by means of spoken language. Accounts of bloody hunts, victorious battles against rival tribes and perilous explorations across uncharted oceans and landscapes were spun and imparted by countless generations of narrators. They were men and women whose vivid imaginations and fluent tongues would conjure up, and often embellish, the events - epic, heroic or everyday – of past and contemporary times.

Myths, legends and sagas grew from ancient narrations, told and retold around flickering fires, in thatch-roofed longhouses and at village fairs, their inventiveness enrapturing spellbound audiences. And despite the advent of the printing press, the art of the master storytellers continued unabated. No less so than in the Jewish communities of Eastern Europe and Russia.

Purveyors of the oral word would travel from town to town, shtetl to shtetl, village to village with stories designed to inform, entertain, comfort, enthuse, excite, exhort, influence, beguile or mystify. Religious storytellers would journey through the lands of the Tsars, the Pale of Settlement and the Polish provinces, weaving into their mystical tales a Torah message to enlighten and to inspire faith and observance in, or maybe even to rebuke, the assembled listeners. Stories were related simply, straightforwardly and occasionally histrionically but generally in a way that could be readily digested by the people who gathered to hear them.

This book is intended to follow the tradition of Jewish storytelling but by means of the written rather than the spoken word. Now and then, the reader will come upon storytelling by characters within the stories being recounted, a technique creating a dimensional perspective of time and place that lends depth and credibility to the narrative. Many of the stories (several of which carry a recurring theme of the Holocaust or the Passover, a Jewish festival of freedom and hope) are written in the first person. But that person is not the author, who regards himself merely as a conduit, an instrument through which various fictional characters chronicle their own personal emotions and experiences against a backcloth of authentic scenarios.

The Shtetl

THERE IS little need for you to know the name of the shtetl where I lived as a boy. The name will mean nothing to you, and the village lives now only in the dying cells of my memory. But let me tell you where it used to exist, long before the ravages of evil men swept it from the face of the Earth. Not too far from the western border of the Tsar's limitless empire, a road threaded its way between the cities of Vilna and Minsk. The highway was much travelled by Jewish merchants, who sold the multifarious wares of their cottage industries and workshops to Jew and Gentile alike. Halfway along the length of that forest-flanked artery was a small market town whose name I now forget. Here Jewish farmers, many from far distant agricultural villages, sold the spare produce of their smallholdings. And if they were to make a moderate profit from their labours, they would purchase necessary goods from the itinerant Jewish salesmen.

My parents and their six children lived in one of those scattered villages some 15 miles from the town. Our village was snowbound through much of the long, freezing winters and oppressive during the short, hot summers. But, for most of the year, the Almighty blanketed our village of some 300 Jewish souls with murky, roiling clouds impenetrable to the sun. For the Holy One, blessed be His name, is the Master of the universe and the Creator of all natural things in this world. The monotone pall of gloom that shrouded the sky above us cast a melancholy greyness over the village. From my childhood there, I can remember only greyness … grey wooden houses, a grey square where our grey shul stood, and a grey river crossed by a grey bridge. And my recollection tells me that, in the seemingly endless winter months, even the snow was grey. I often felt deeply sad as a child without knowing the reason why. It was as if my very soul was struggling to find some illumination, an escape to the light from all-encompassing greyness. Though, naturally, I did not adopt that religiously philosophical way of thinking at the time.

Most of the villagers were poor Jewish peasants, barely making a subsistence living from their tiny parcels of land. I never really understood why, but my father owned a larger, though not the largest, holding at the eastern fringe of the village on which he kept milk cows. My mother would make wonderful cheeses at home. Father would take them to the market town on the Vilna-Minsk road in his horse-drawn wagon once a week, except during part of the winter. Market day was on Thursdays, so father would leave home very early in the morning to arrive in time to set out his dairy wares. The tracks from our village to the town, around hills and through woods virtually impassable at times in winter, were rough and stony. From time to time, happily infrequently, the horse would break or throw a shoe; and father would be put to unwanted expense at the village blacksmith.

Although we were all "sleepy-heads", as mother would call us, my three older sisters, a younger brother (but not my baby brother) and I would be awakened (quite willingly, really) at a dreadfully early hour on Thursday mornings when father went to market. We would stand just inside the open door of the house, swaddled warmly in our bed blankets, while mother opened the gate for father to drive the wagon through. In the treacly blackness, my siblings and I could hardly see a few metres in front of our chilling red cheeks. Presently, we could hear the squeak of the gate creaking open on its rusty hinges, the chopping hooves of our faithful old horse and the rumbling rattle of the wagon's iron-rimmed wheels. As soon as we heard these familiar sounds, everyone shouted, "Goodbye, father ... come back to us soon!" I am not sure that father could ever hear us with all the clatter, especially if it was raining hard too. And if he turned in his cloth-padded seat to look in our direction (which I feel certain he would have done), I do not think he could have seen us in the congealing darkness of the night.

After the market gradually petered out late on a Thursday evening, father would always sleep in the wagon overnight, returning to the village by the following afternoon and well in time to prepare himself for Shabbos, the Jewish Sabbath. He was not the only one to sleep, wrapped comfortably in several layers of blankets as well as his day clothes, in the town's principal open space during Thursday night. For it was perilous to attempt the return journey in the menacingly black hours between dusk and dawn. Not only were the rough tracks to the outlying villages dangerously pitted and potholed, but also they continually skirted the precarious rims of treacherous rocky gullies. Although plainly problematic in themselves, these physical hazards were not necessarily the main perils facing any Jewish smallholder or farmer foolhardy enough to travel those parts at night. Lying in wait might be anti-Semitic louts or drunken ruffians, brutal thieves or robbers, who would not stop at mere threats to wrest the meagre takings of a lone and defenceless trader. Doubtless such assaults were also a possibility in the daytime. But they were a much less likely occurrence, because the wagons were then accustomed to move in a sort of convoy along the road, thus affording some safety in numbers.

Yet other fears were harboured by the peripatetic men-folk of the isolated villages. It was not unknown for military pressgangs to lie in ambush and waylay travellers, forcing them to serve many years in the Tsar's army. It could be decades, if ever, before the families of these wretched lost men set eyes upon their abducted husbands or sons again. Though the sorrowing wives or parents might receive the occasional despairing letter from their loved ones to the effect that they were still in the world of the living. This was scant consolation, indeed. In their surreal unreality, the men were barely surviving, soldiering in the frozen wastelands of Siberia or the scorching deserts of the Russian tyrant's eastern territories. But the night's most feared evils stalking the lonely, narrow trails that meandered the dark forests and heavily wooded hills, were merely the stuff of centuries-old myths and superstitions. Or were they?

The wearing of charms and amulets – to safeguard against the ayen hora, the evil eye, and the miscreant spirits that were said to haunt the shadowy recesses of the earth – was common amongst the Jews of the Galus, the Exile. Father was no exception in our village. Around his neck hung a fine chain bearing an archaic, and intricately fashioned, silver talisman. He had inherited it from his father who, in turn, had received it from his father … and so on, back through the mists of time. Needless to say, our rabbi did not really approve of such beliefs and so-called protective devices, declaring from his pulpit that we should place our faith and trust in the Almighty for His deliverance from wickedness. But the minister's words had scant impact on the age-old customs and usages of his credulous congregants.

When father did not come back from market when expected one Friday afternoon, mother soon became frantic with worry. Father was never later than a certain hour … never ever. Her tearful concern was quickly transmitted to my brothers and sisters and, of course, to me. We were always impatient to see father return home because, sometimes, when he had sold every one of mother's cheeses, he would bring us small gifts. He was delighted to see our sparkling faces as we rushed to open the hastily wrapped presents. Today they might seem like humble little packages, maybe containing a ball, a book, a simple toy or a piece of cotton material to make a blouse or a shirt. But to us they were wonderful surprises. Mother would receive something too, perhaps a new Shabbos headscarf or a brooch. It was good having father in the house again, with his big smiling eyes and his bushy, coal-black beard. We felt safe and secure gathered around the Friday night table. The oil lamps cast a warm glow across the white tablecloth, on which were set the challahs and the wine. Mother would light the Shabbos candles and father would make the Kiddush blessing. Then the girls would help mother with the food, while father dandled the chortling baby on his knee and made my brother and me laugh with amusing anecdotes about market day.

It was an hour before Shabbos came in, and father still had not returned home to his family.

"We need to go and see the rabbi," mother said suddenly, looking directly at me. "We must hurry now."

Leaving my eldest sister Rochel in charge of the other children, mother and I hastened to the rabbi's house in the centre of the village. The sky's hue was beginning to transmute from grey to dark grey as the rebbetzen, the rabbi's wife, opened the door. Seeing our concerned expressions, she immediately led us along the narrow, carpeted hallway to the rabbi's study room. Most of the middle-aged minister's house was carpeted, unlike the rustic dwellings of the villagers. But Rabbi Zalman came from a prosperous family and was never a financial charge on our modestly endowed community.

The rabbi was preparing to leave for the synagogue to conduct the Friday night service. He was very surprised to see us.

"Whatever is the matter, Leah?" he enquired instantly of my mother. "Come and sit here, please Leah ... you appear distraught."

Rabbi Zalman beckoned to a chair and mother sat down, her cheeks strangely hollow and her shoulders sagging. Mother's pained demeanour and posture were clearly redolent of her acute distress.

"Joshua ... come sit beside me," the rabbi said, attempting a comforting half smile. I seated myself quickly and the rabbi pulled up another chair. "Tell me what's wrong, Leah."

By now, our kindly spiritual leader seemed as troubled as we were. He reached for the skullcap on his head, plumped up the large black kippah then prodded stubby fingers into his luxuriant, salt and pepper beard. These were actions well known to his congregants as typical worry signs.

Mother explained briefly that father had not yet returned from the Thursday market in the town. With tear-pearls leaving watery lines down her now haggard face, mother stressed that he had never failed to be home at least two hours before Shabbos. The rabbi thought for a while, constantly rubbing his beard.

"If Aryeh isn't home tonight, tell me at the synagogue tomorrow morning," he said finally. "But don't imagine the worst, Leah. Many things could've happened. Maybe the horse went lame and Aryeh needs to remain in the town over Shabbos. Perhaps your husband wasn't feeling well enough to travel today. There could be any number of reasons, Leah. Please don't sob so ... may God give you strength."

The minister turned to me.

"Joshua, take your mother home. We'll pray in shul tonight for your father's safe return."

As we left the rabbi's house, he put a strong yet gently sympathetic arm around my shoulders.

"Remember, Joshua ... you were barmitzvah last year so, in

your father's absence, you are the head of the household. Take your mother home safely. Make Kiddush for her and your brothers and sisters after the candles are lit. There's no need for you to come to shul tonight."

The rabbi glanced up at the sky.

"Hurry now," he urged. "It's almost Shabbos."

I had always accompanied father to the synagogue for the Friday night minyan, comprising the ten men required for prayer. But on that evening, Rabbi Zalman had given me a special dispensation. When mother and I arrived back home, father still had not returned and the younger children were weeping pitifully. Mother did her best to comfort them, although very distressed herself. Then she lit the candles and I made the requisite blessings over the wine and bread. For each other's sake, we all tried very hard to mask our emotions as we sat down for the Friday night meal. It was difficult to keep back the tears; and, from time to time, one or other of us would start crying again. This would set off another chain reaction of wailing around the table, until mother or I would repeat the rabbi's admonition that we should not think the worst. This served to calm and console the children for a while. After eating and bensching, we were thoroughly exhausted and just sat together in terrified silence … thinking the worst, of course, until we went to bed for what proved to be, at least for me, a sleepless night.

In shul the next morning, we had no need to inform the rabbi that father had not returned home. It was glaringly obvious. After the service, the entire congregation flocked around us to express their hopes that nothing terrible had happened to him. Some people's albeit sincere remarks actually made matters worse. I noticed that, after speaking to mother, several individuals placed a personal amulet to their lips and whispered to themselves "Peh, peh, peh!" in order to ward off any possibility of tragedy by association. After the simple communal Kiddush in the synagogue's small hall, Rabbi Zalman took mother and me aside and offered more practical advice.

"Yankele is leaving the village tomorrow with his wagon for Minsk," he told us. "He's carrying out some errands for me in the city. I know that what I'm about to suggest might upset you, Leah. But I think Joshua should accompany him as far as the market town."

Mother shook her head vigorously and grabbed hold of me protectively.

"Leah, remember … Joshua is now a man," the rabbi continued. "You know how tall he's grown in the last year. You must let him go to the town. He will seek to discover what's happened to his father."

Mother began to weep and clasped me closer to her shaking body. The minister called over his wife to assist in soothing mother's anxious mind.

"You must look after your children, Leah," he went on. "Joshua is intelligent and strong enough to look after himself."

I grasped mother's hands. "With respect, the rabbi is right," I said imploringly. "Allow me to go … please. We have to know what's happened to father. I'm old enough to go, mother, and I really want to go. I'm a man now. Put your trust in me … please, mother!"

After a short while, mother wiped her face and began nodding slowly. I hugged her and prepared to take her home. As we left the synagogue, Rabbi Zalman bent to my ear: "Take care, Joshua … there's much evil at large in the world out there. I know that you're a resolute young man and will do your best. I'll pray to the Almighty that everything works out well for you and your family. Yankele will pick you up at dawn tomorrow. Be ready for him. In the town, he'll leave you with a good Jewish family that is well known to me. Yankele will give you a letter of introduction, which I'll write after Shabbos ends tonight. Mr Solomon and I learned together in the Vilna yeshivah many years ago. He's now very successful in business. He'll give you shelter in his home for a couple of nights and will assist you with your enquiries. Yankele will collect you in three days' time. It distresses me to mention this but, as you travel to the town, look out for any signs … You know what I mean, Joshua?"

I pondered for a moment, then nodded solemnly that I understood. The rabbi shook my hand warmly and patted me gently on the back.

"Go now …" he said. "And may the Almighty go with you."

Early Sunday morning, as a dull light struggled through the grey overcast, Yankele collected me in his wagon. Only mother was awake to see me hasten to open the gate and climb aboard beside the village's odd-job-man. Mother had been tearful when, a little earlier, she had kissed me and handed me a small, battered portmanteau. She had said that it contained a clean shirt, some fresh underwear and a gift for the rabbi's friends who would be providing a roof for me. Yankele tapped the horse with his whip and we moved off down the rough track. I turned and waved to mother. She raised her hand weakly then disappeared quickly into the house.

I knew Yankele very well, of course. He was a lanky, unmarried man in his mid-thirties with long and straggly black hair streaming from beneath a grubby peasant's cap. I often thought he looked more like some Romany than a Jew. But he was always very polite and pleasant when he performed the occasional bit of handy work around our house. To put it kindly, maybe he was slightly less bright than most people his age but nobody minded that. However, he did possess one attribute, which did not appeal to everyone. This was a rollicking guffaw, which he used to unrestrained effect when laughing uncontrollably at his own feeble jokes.

As the wagon clanked deeper into the countryside between our village and the town, both Yankele and I kept a vigilant lookout for signs of any mishap that might have befallen father. We spoke little (I was glad to be spared Yankele's pitiable jests) in order to concentrate on our surveillance of deep gullies and ravines along the tortuous route. Traversing the lonely woods and dense forests, we peered carefully between the trees for any indication of an unfortunate accident. We passed neither man nor beast on the deserted tracks; and, as the horse laboured up the rock-strewn inclines, we gazed down into the dim valleys searching for anything that might seem out of the ordinary.

The gloomy heavens brightened spasmodically. Now and again, I spotted one or two patches of blue sky, which punctuated the sombre clouds for a few fleeting minutes.

"I was very sad when I heard your father had not returned from market," Yankele said, turning his head towards me. "That's why I haven't been telling you any of my jokes." I smiled at the earnest, elongated face staring down at me.

"Don't worry, Yankele," I responded. "That's absolutely fine … I really appreciate your concern."

Then he told me a story that he failed to realise would make my blood run cold. "Joshua, did you ever hear of the body they found on the track between our village and the town about ten years ago?" I shook my head, mouth agape. "Well, I suppose they've kept the horrible tale from the children. Anyway, old Zvi, the village tailor, went missing one market day. He'd gone to town to buy some cloth for the rabbi's new suit. A few days later, they found what was left of a human body in the woods. It was so cut up, by what some said were claw marks, that the remains couldn't be identified. It was probably Zvi, but no one was sure. They never even found his wagon or his horse."

As Yankele's wagon rolled into the outskirts of the town later in the day, I was still trembling to think of the dreadful incident he had described to me. But at least I was heartened moderately by the fact that, during our journey, we had found nothing gruesome nor noticed any indications of wreckage or other untoward evidence connected to father's disappearance. We soon arrived at an imposing redbrick house where Yankele brought the horse and carriage to a grinding halt, handed me an envelope containing the rabbi's letter, addressed to Mr Solomon, and wished me good luck. I jumped down from the wagon and grabbed my small, ramshackle suitcase from the back of the cart. As my trustworthy companion of several hours waved me goodbye, I approached the fine wooden door and used the highly polished, brass knocker. A young woman, dressed as a housemaid, appeared and asked to know my business. I handed her the letter, which I explained had been written by Rabbi Zalman to Mr Solomon by way of my introduction. She politely requested me to remain in the wood-panelled hall as she closed the street door and vanished in search of her master.

Mr Solomon, who was a robust man of medium height with a kindly, weathered face and a neat grey beard, met me in his book-lined study. He had evidently read his rabbinical friend's missive, which lay open on his desk, and was very sympathetic towards me. He pumped my hand and declared his delight at having me in his home. But, at the same time, he expressed his profound regret that my visit had come about in such fraught circumstances.

"Tonight, Joshua, you'll rest after your long and tiring journey, but not before you've had dinner with my family. Early tomorrow morning, we'll begin our search about the town for your father and make enquiries. If we're unable to discover his whereabouts, you and I will proceed to the police station and the town hall. We'll report your father's disappearance and provide any necessary information. The maid will show you to your room now, where you can relax until she fetches you for dinner."

I thanked Mr Solomon for agreeing to shelter me and help find my father. Then I followed the young woman upstairs to the first floor.

At the dinner table that evening, I was at first somewhat embarrassed by the fact that my clothes were not quite up to the same standard as the Solomon family. The head of the prosperous household had changed into a very well cut, dark blue suit; and his wife and three daughters were dressed very elegantly in lovely dresses. I was still wearing my everyday clothes. There was so much silver cutlery in front of me that I was hard pressed to know which knives, forks or spoons to use for each succeeding course of quite the most delicious food. But everyone was wonderfully tolerant and comprehending. Mr and Mrs Solomon and their three teenage daughters – Deborah, Sarah and Miriam – were so very charming, and so completely understanding of my situation, that any initial self-conscious discomfort I may have felt had quickly evaporated. I soon found myself very much at ease in their company. Mrs Solomon thanked me profusely for the lovely cheese I had brought with me.

I hoped that, although my sartorial appearance may have been somewhat modest, my conversation was fairly intelligent. I owed this to my fervour in devouring any book that I could lay my hands on; and the lengthy discussions about them I had frequently enjoyed with my father. I had the feeling that Mr Solomon was quite impressed with the grasp of history and current affairs displayed by one as young as myself. And I noticed that it was not the master of the house alone who seemed to have been taken with me. Miriam, who was the youngest daughter and about my age, persisted in throwing demure little glances in my direction. She was pretty in a subtle kind of way; and the apparently special attention she was according me certainly helped lift, at least for a short while, the worry and sadness of the undertaking that had brought me to her father's house.

I slept only fitfully that night; but, as I tossed and turned in the strange bed, I could not stop thinking about Miriam and the sweet smile on her delicate face. These frivolous thoughts, which almost monopolised my wakeful hours, made me feel rather guilty. I should have been concentrating my mind on producing ideas to find my father. The next morning, shortly after breakfast, Mr Solomon and I left the house in our endeavour to locate him. I was hopeful and optimistic, as Rabbi Zalman had advised me to be. Mr Solomon had also banished any notion of pessimism from his attitude, striding purposefully towards the town's market square with me close at his side.

Of course, Thursday's traders from the region's dispersed villages were no longer in the town. But we spoke to the local tradesmen who had set up stalls in the cobbled square on that day. Although they knew my father well as one of the popular regulars, and remembered him stalling away on his wagon at the end of Thursday's market, they had no knowledge of his present situation if he was not back at home. Everyone tried to be as helpful as possible but, as we continued through the morning talking to the merchants and shopkeepers in the central district, I grew more disconsolate at their negative responses. Mr Solomon sought to allay my dejection by noting that, for some reason, my father might have become disorientated. And that he may have wandered off with his wagon in some direction unknown to him. My guide and companion suggested that we return to his home for lunch. But I was not very hungry, so Mr Solomon benevolently agreed to forego his midday meal and, instead, to attend the police station and the town hall.

At the headquarters of the local police regiment, and with Mr Solomon's assistance, I completed a long form to report a missing person. This had to be done before we were permitted to see an officer. When Mr Solomon and I were finally summoned into a uniformed sergeant's room, we were compelled to stand throughout the interview. In the outer reception area, we had been treated with blatant contempt by the surly and officious station staff. Without doubt, they were all anti-Semites and could not have cared less about the mysterious disappearance of my father. The hard-faced sergeant, who doubtless also hated Jews, sat behind a desk cursorily flicking through the document I had completed.

Then he screamed at me: "There's nothing we can do for you here, Jew boy … we haven't got the resources. Maybe your stupid old man is wallowing in a muddy ditch somewhere, as drunk as a sailor on shore leave…"

After that outburst, he exploded into booming laughter.

I was stunned by the officer's vituperative reaction to my serious predicament. Mr Solomon stepped forward, and was obviously about to protest about our vile treatment, when the sergeant held up a threatening hand.

"Get out of here you loathsome, moaning Jews. Get out now, or else …"

As we hurriedly left the despicable Jew-baiter's office, I thought I heard the sound of paper being ripped apart. In the street, tears welled up in my eyes. Mr Solomon put a reassuring hand on my shoulder.

"I don't think we'll go to the town hall, Joshua," he said. "I don't believe there's any chance of help for us there either. Come, we'll return home. I know some horsemen who will search the surrounding area of countryside for me. I'll see their leader this afternoon and ask him to report back to me by tomorrow morning, before Yankele collects you."

Back at the house, Mrs Solomon and her daughters looked after me with much appreciated kindness and empathy after hearing of my dreadful experience at the police station. Miriam's eyes were full of compassion as she offered me a hot drink and said how sorry she was. We spoke for a while, just the two of us, seated at the table while her mother and sisters sat elsewhere in the spacious room working on some handicraft. Mr Solomon had gone out again to arrange for the horsemen to look for my father.

"I really enjoyed the conversation at dinner last night," Miriam said brightly. "You're quite clever for your age, aren't you?"

I half-smiled at her. "I've a feeling that I'm not as clever as you are, though."

The young girl lowered lively green eyes to her slim hands. "Maybe we'll find out some day," she responded enigmatically, staring directly at me. "Will you always want to live and work in your village, Joshua?" she enquired, with a precocious sparkle in her expressive eyes.

"I don't really know," I answered, honestly. "I'd like to go out into the world and learn more. But this is a terrible thing that's happened to my family, and I'm not certain how it will end."

Miriam could see that I was very downcast and desisted at once from any further talk about the future.

"I'll get you another tea," she said, lightly touching my arm as she took my empty cup.

Next morning the leader of the men, who had been out all night hunting for any clues to my father's location, reported to Mr Solomon. He called me into his study after the man had left the house.

"I'm so sorry to tell you Joshua that my searchers have been unable to locate your father. They've ridden a goodly distance from the town, and they've spoken to a number of farmers and other people residing within the area. Regrettably, they've learned nothing that might be of any value in tracing him. It grieves me to say that there seems little more that we can usefully do for now. We can only hope and pray that your father will return home at some time."

I said my farewells to the family, and a special goodbye to Miriam. When Yankele came to pick me up just before midday, I was ready with my little old case. As the horse pulled our wagon away from the Solomon residence, I turned to wave at Miriam who was standing by the front door. She touched the palm of her right hand with her lips and blew the kiss towards me, then stepped back into the house.

It would not be productive to relate the story of my homecoming with the sorrowfully negative news I had to bear. Suffice to say that my mother and siblings were distraught. The rabbi and his rebbetzen, and indeed the entire community, rallied round to offer support and comfort to us in any way they could. I have to tell you that my father never did return home; and we discovered neither what had overcome him, nor his ultimate fate. Through force of will, my mother eventually pulled herself out of her depressive state. It took several years but, in the end, she remarried. My stepfather was much older than my mother, but he was very kind and affectionate towards her and the children. My older sisters married and left the village for the cities of Vilna and Minsk. My brothers grew to adulthood and followed them into the world beyond our village.

I returned to the Solomon household on a number of occasions. Mr Solomon harboured much confidence in my intellectual ability, and was kind enough to ensure that I received a good secular and Jewish education, including a year's study at the yeshivah. When the time came, he arranged for me to travel to the United States to study law at one of the top universities. After qualifying, I returned to that small market town where the Solomon family still lived. There I was married to Miriam, to whom I had become betrothed before departing for America. Rabbi Zalman conducted the wedding service with tears of joy in his eyes. Afterwards, Miriam and I sailed to New York where I carried on my law practice, I'm glad to say, highly successfully for many years. Our first child was a boy. We named him Aryeh … after my father.

Out of the greyness had finally come the light.

The Decision

MIDDAY AND I was sitting beside the lake at Bletchley Park struggling to complete the day's Su Doku logic puzzle in The Times. A series of loud splashes distracted me from the frustrating but addictive brainteaser. I looked up from the newspaper. One of the Park's two white swans was flapping huge wings before ploughing a frothy furrow across its home lagoon. A balmy, early spring sun dappled the water at Britain's Second World War code-breaking centre, formerly known as "Station X", some 45 miles north of London. Beyond the large, circular pond and its surrounding, daffodil-sprinkled greensward loomed the oddly eclectic architecture of "the mansion". Together with its extensive, adjoining estate, the manor house had once been owned by Sir Harry Leon, a Jewish stockbroker, a Liberal member of parliament in the Gladstone era and a friend of the Rothschilds banking family.

I grabbed a bite of homemade egg, lettuce and tomato baguette from my open canvas shoulder bag sitting beside me on the wooden bench. I glanced uncertainly at the morning paper resting on my lap. The Su Doku nine-by-nine grid of eighty-one squares, comprising blanks and printed digits from one to nine, stared back at me like a wily poker player hiding a winning hand. The daily conundrum, classified according to the number of given numerals, was graded "fiendish" for that day. Too true! I had managed to insert just a few of the missing figures. Although reasonably numerate and logical, I needed to mentally justify my meagre performance. I took another chunk out of my salad sandwich.

As my eyes flashed around the grid seeking clues, it struck me that the cerebral exercise involved a logical interplay of assumptions, deductions and extrapolations. What my brain was striving to accomplish, albeit in a primitive way, was very much akin to the wartime decrypting apparatus employed at Bletchley. The so-called bombes, which made use of early computer technology, helped inventor and maths genius Alan Turing and his team to decipher enemy naval, army and air force codes.

That morning, in the Block B museum, I had viewed German Enigma coding machines, captured from U-boats, trawlers and weather ships. It is said that the vital intelligence, known as Ultra and resulting from the code-breakers' painstaking efforts, probably shortened the war and saved countless lives. I was intrigued to learn that Polish mathematicians had broken earlier versions of Enigma. They had passed their know-how to the British before Hitler invaded their homeland in 1939 and set about the wholesale destruction of Poland's Jewry. Beneath a group of shade-giving trees in the Bletchley grounds, I had stood beside a monument acknowledging the Poles' invaluable work.

I placed my newspaper on the bench and gazed across the lake towards Hut 8. There, in that elongated wooden shed, the eccentric Turing (he often cycled through the countryside wearing a gasmask) and his fellow cryptographers poured over thousands of enemy messages picked up by listening stations sprinkled across Britain. Their studious work, through highs and lows, produced the kind of information that helped the Royal

Air Force to decimate the Luftwaffe during the Battle of Britain; and enabled the Admiralty to reroute Atlantic convoys to evade U-boat wolf packs. And, all the time, the German High Command, who believed their Enigma codes to be unfathomable, was totally ignorant about the existence of top-secret Station X.

The afternoon sun was becoming surprisingly warm for late March. I had spent the morning walking my way around the various huts and museum buildings where many hundreds of people had operated during the war. I was starting to grow sleepy when a voice close by brought me back to full consciousness.

"Have you finished with this?" the voice asked, rather insistently I thought.

I detected an East European accent as I turned to face the speaker, now sitting next to me on the bench. His age was difficult to gauge. The oval face lent an overall impression of boyishness, despite the high cheekbones. But the stoop of his shoulders, the straggly whiff of white hair on a mottled pate, the deeply lined forehead and ragged neck suggested a man well into his eighties. Above all, I noticed the blue eyes behind rimless spectacles, absurdly glowing yet seeming to harbour deep emotions, which I could then interpret only as profound pain and sadness.

"Sorry?" I responded, taking in the old man's check shirt, which peeped from behind a nondescript woollen cardigan. Both garments were almost concealed by, for him, an oversized dark blue anorak that had witnessed better days.

"Have you finished with this?" he repeated, very offhandedly.

He was pointing to my abandoned copy of The Times, open at the Su Doku page.

"Well?" he added, quite rudely in my view.

"Y-yes, of course," I replied, taken aback by the man's intensely abrasive manner.

Without more, he seized the newspaper, extracted a biro from an inside pocket and began examining closely the puzzle grid. Within seconds, I was amazed to observe him stabbing numbers into the blank spaces. In no more than a minute, and with a deep sigh, he had finished.

The old man returned the newspaper to the bench and grinned disconcertingly at me.

"Please do forgive me," he said, his eyes earnest but twinkling. "I was extremely boorish and discourteous to you."

Before I could insist that his apology was unnecessary, he continued: "I've become very foolish with my advancing years. But every time I visit Bletchley Park, I'm overcome, disturbed you might say."

I had taken no real offence at his earlier brusqueness, making some allowances for his age. I did not require any explanation. But before I was able to express some of these sentiments, the man added with a winning smile:

"In any case, whenever I see a Su Doku grid, I can't be responsible for my actions."

At that, I smiled too, knowing precisely what he meant. Apparently, he had been unable to buy The Times that morning. He confessed to being like a coiled spring when he had spotted a copy lying on the bench. Now, he said, he felt only satisfied relief. We laughed together at our mutual addiction and exchanged first names.

I discovered that Emil was Hungarian in origin. He had immigrated to Britain after the failed revolution against the Soviets in his homeland in 1956. A few years later, he had become a naturalised Brit. He seemed quite happy to talk to me; though, from his general demeanour, I still harboured the feeling that here was a man with an unhappy past. I expressed my admiration at the incredible speed with which he had mastered the logic puzzle. Political correctness inhibited me from adding any reference to his advanced age. The old man's face brightened.

"I was a student of mathematics at the university in Budapest in the 1930s," he informed me. "I was fanatical about the subject. By the way, do you know what the words Su Doku mean?"

I hesitated, struggling with my recollection.

"They're Japanese, as you're no doubt aware," Emil advanced. "A rough translation gives us 'number place', which I suppose is quite appropriate for our present location, eh?"

I nodded.

I recalled noticing that Hut 4, which had been responsible for breaking German naval codes, now provided rather prosaic licensed refreshments. Emil intrigued me, so I invited him to join me for a drink. He seemed surprised at my offer but readily agreed. We moved off towards the hut, which stands close by the mansion. The Hungarian was shorter than me, and walked with a slight limp. The single storey structure we were heading for is of brick construction and reasonably spacious. Divided into two rooms, one houses a canteen, the other a bar. Both sections were fairly quiet. We decided on a pint of beer each and, nursing our jars, found a couple of comfortable faux leather armchairs at a low table next to a window. Through it I could see the one-fifth-scale model of a U-boat, which had been specially crafted for the Enigma movie.

Emil withdrew a briar pipe from his pocket.

"Do you mind?" he asked, waving the obviously treasured article in the air.

I shook my head. My companion filled his pipe with tobacco from an ancient tin and lit up with a match. I took a pull from my drink and wiped the frothy head from my upper lip.

"This is my first visit to Bletchley," I said. "But, Emil, didn't you mention that you've been here previously?"

The old man despatched a spiral of smoke towards the wood-beamed ceiling. I could smell a bittersweet aroma in the leaf.

"You know what," he remarked. "This place was covered by the Official Secrets Act until 1995. Fifty years after the end of the war! Amazing, eh?"

I nodded, not mentioning that I had learned that incredible fact in the Block B museum.

"I've been coming here about three times a year," Emil added. "Ever since the Park was opened to the public."

He could probably perceive from my expression that I was curious to know the reason behind his regular visits. The unmistakable glint in his eyes confirmed my impression.

"I come here as often as I can because of a dreadful decision I was forced to make more than sixty years ago," Emil said, taking a long draw on his pipe.

At that moment, it seemed as if the room contained only the old man and me. The bartender and the few other drinkers had ceased to exist. My newfound Hungarian friend rested the pipe in an ashtray and picked up his lager. He quaffed some of the golden liquid and replaced the glass on the table. Emil retrieved his briar, sucked in a mouthful of smoke and leaned towards me, conspiratorially.

"You're Jewish, aren't you?" he whispered.

I was mildly astonished by the question. I am not often recognised as being Jewish.

"How did you know?" I enquired.

Emil grinned and indicated the ring on my right index finger.

I nodded, smiling.

"Easy, eh?" he chuckled.

I glanced at the quite wide, gold band, which had been fashioned in Jerusalem and engraved with my Jewish name in Hebrew.

"You're very observant," I noted.

Emil's features adopted an oddly whimsical look.

"Yes and no," he replied, enigmatically. "Yes, I do

concentrate on the detail. That's my mathematical training. But no, I'm not observant … as a Jew, that is. Yes, I'm also of the Jewish race, and you may well have suspected that. Though I'm afraid that I lost my faith a long time ago. And yes, of that I am afraid …"

Suddenly, I experienced a deep-down sadness for Emil. I wanted to reach out and comfort him in some ill-defined way. Why? I didn't really know. I think he sensed my melancholy discomfort.

"Maybe I should go now," he said, flatly. "I don't want to burden you with the troubled memories of an old man."

He made to rise but I stopped him with a hand on his arm.

"You really don't have to leavc," I said. "I assure you it's absolutely unnecessary. Finish your pipe … and your drink. Please. I'm quite okay. Really."

Emil leaned back in the armchair.

"I would like to tell you something," he said. "Something that, as a Jew, you may find very disturbing. But, believe me, I couldn't help it. I couldn't help it!"

Moisture appeared at the corners of his drooping eyes. It was not difficult for me to see that whatever he desired, or even needed, to relate was something that had been slicing deeply into his Jewish soul over many years.

"When Germany invaded Poland in September 1939, I was twenty-two years old," Emil began. "I'd just graduated from university in Budapest with a first class honours degree in mathematics. I lived with my parents and two younger sisters in a large villa on the edge of the city. My father owned an important wireless and telecommunications equipment factory in the Hungarian capital. I started working for him as an engineer in the design section. In 1942, I was promoted to head that department when the incumbent was unfortunately killed in a road accident. We knew of the terrible persecution of our fellow Jews in the neighbouring, Nazi-occupied countries. Our nation had become allied to the Reich. But German propaganda declared that this was to help thwart the Soviet communist threat. By and large, although there were serious problems, Hungary's Jewish population hadn't received brutal treatment from the fascist authorities."

Emil moistened his throat with an intake of beer and continued.

"I was married early in 1943. And, at the beginning of 1944, my adorable wife presented me with beautiful twin daughters. I was so happy, and despite the deteriorating situation of the Jews in my own land. But worse was to come. By February of that year, with victorious Russian forces advancing from the east, Hitler suspected that our government was preparing to make peace overtures with the Allies. To stiffen our leaders' resolve, and to ensure that Hungarian Jewry didn't escape the Final Solution, he ordered German troops to invade and occupy his recalcitrant ally."

Much of what Emil was telling me I had read in books about the war and the Nazi Holocaust of European Jewry. But I was deeply moved to hear of the plight of the Hungarian Jews from someone who had personally been caught up in that maelstrom of hate and violence. I was apprehensive about hearing what he might mention of his family. Yet, admittedly, I was curious about the "dreadful decision" he had apparently needed to make.

"The murderous SS followed the German army," he went on. "Adolf Eichmann, heading a special task force of two hundred personnel, set up office in the Budapest Hotel Majestic. From there, he created the centralised Jewish Council to ensure community compliance with his orders. Jews were rounded up from the countryside and concentrated in the capital's ghetto. In the city, most Jews lost their jobs and livelihoods. In a way, I was one of the lucky ones. Although our factory was expropriated, it continued producing essential wireless and telephone components for the German forces. I was permitted to retain my specialist post, but my father wasn't allowed to work. Our homes were confiscated and we were bundled into two small rooms in a dilapidated tenement block in the old Jewish quarter. There were eight of us: my father, mother and two sisters, my wife, our two daughters and myself. Our privations were horrendous. You probably couldn't even imagine them. But at least we were all alive and together."

Emil explained how the deportation transports began rolling out of Budapest in April 1944.

"We were informed by the authorities, and we naively believed them, that the Jewish population was being transferred to work camps out in the countryside. But I suppose we simply believed what we wanted to believe. We just sublimated the terrifying rumours of mass killings of Jews in Poland and elsewhere."

Emil expelled some smoke, a grey column of mist drifting upwards.

"Four trains, each pulling goods wagons and packed with a cargo of three thousand Jews, departed daily from the city's main railway stations throughout that summer. After the war, it gradually became known that over 400,000 Hungarian Jews were gassed at Auschwitz-Birkenau, the vast majority immediately after arrival. But during those despairing few months of 1944, we knew only of our fears."

My mouth was as dry as haystack straw. I grabbed my drink and swallowed about half a pint. Emil sipped from his glass, and returned the pipe to its home between two rows of unusually white, very even and unmistakably false teeth. At one point in his sombre narrative, he had wiped his eyes and forehead with a handkerchief. I hoped that the retelling of his story would not totally unhinge him.

"Please don't go on if this is distressing you," I urged.

He waved me away.

"I want you to know," he insisted. "I want you to understand what happened. It will explain my regular visits to this place."

Tears welled up in his eyes, and I urged him to call a halt to this outpouring of painful memories. Stubbornly, he emphasised equally vehemently that he wished to continue. I was unable to stop him; and I could not consider leaving him in the circumstances.

"I happened to possess information which would be of supreme value to the Germans," he went on. "I was frantic to find a bargaining counter for my family. And I knew that I possessed one. It was a secret that my father had conveyed to me in absolute confidence. But, I questioned myself while listening at night to the fearful whimpering of my family, what is a secret compared to the survival of my loved ones? I needed to save them. I could think of nothing else. Certainly, the Nazis traded Jews for gold and diamonds. Doubtless, they would be prepared to negotiate for an invaluable secret."

I was stunned when Emil identified the highly confidential knowledge that he had faithfully concealed for many years.

"My father was Hungarian, but my mother was Polish," he told me. "Before the war, they'd often visited Warsaw and Krakow to see her relatives. I don't know the full details but my father, a mathematician himself, somehow discovered from contacts in Poland that the supposedly unbreakable German Enigma codes had been unravelled by Polish cryptographers before the war. He was also aware that the Poles, through French intermediaries, had transmitted the vital decoding information to the British government. I was one hundred percent sure that the Allies had been making good wartime use of that data to break German military ciphers. As I listened to the heartbreaking sobs of my mother, my wife and my sisters, and the constant wheezing of my father's lungs, I resolved to barter for their lives with our Nazi enemies.

"It was difficult, but I managed to secure an appointment to see Eichmann at his HQ. He was very busy. Yes, indeed he was … extremely busy arranging the industrial slaughter of hundreds of thousands of my Jewish compatriots. On the telephone, his aide asked me, naturally, why I needed to see such an important man so urgently. I knew that my family was due to report at the railway depot the following morning. I lied that my request concerned a crucial matter at the factory. Eichmann agreed to see me. I dashed to the Hotel Majestic and was shown by his assistant to an anteroom."

My heart was beating much faster than normal, as I listened intently to every one of Emil's words.

"During the almost unbearable hour that I waited to see the Nazi monster, I fought with my conscience. Was it my conscience? I really don't know. But there were two distinct voices inside my head engaged in a titanic battle with each other. One was urging, 'Save your family, your beloved parents, siblings, wife and daughters. They are all you now possess in the world. Give Eichmann the secret information'. But the other voice was countering, 'Think of the thousands of lives that are being saved by the ability of the Allies to break the German codes. This secret knowledge will shorten the war, and perhaps safeguard many thousands of Jewish lives. Protect the information at all costs'. The dilemma was shattering me. I was about to be received by Eichmann. What should I tell him? What shouldn't I say to him?"

Emil stared at me, his glazed eyes locked onto mine.

"What would you have done?" he asked.

I pondered for a moment or two, as Emil drew on his pipe. Finally, and weakly, I responded.

"I'm sorry, Emil. I don't know. I really don't know. I just can't begin to imagine how terrible the decision must've been for you."

He nodded grimly, pursed his lips and, like one of those

plastic dogs at the rear window of a motorcar, continued nodding for some while. I did not dare visualise the terrifying mental image behind his fixed gaze. Eventually, he began speaking again.

"Well, I needed to come to some conclusion."

He recalled how he was led in to Eichmann's spacious and stylishly furnished office.

"The crisply uniformed obersturmbannführer sat behind a huge desk, which was littered with mounds of official-looking documents, files, lists of names and trays of papers. A large, military portrait of Hitler hung on the wall behind him. The other mass murderer in front of me beckoned with a peremptory curling of his forefinger, but didn't invite me to sit down in the chair opposite him. How stupid of me to have even expected a seat. I fought hard to conceal my hatred for this evil fiend.

"'What do you want?' Eichmann screamed at me. 'You have one minute, no more!'

I'd made my decision before I entered his office.

'I humbly request that my family be removed from the list for the transport tomorrow,' I said, politely.

The meticulous, Holocaust organiser shuffled through some papers in an open buff folder on his desk. Then he glared at me with cold, steely eyes, like a killer shark targeting its prey.

'You've got a nerve, you Jewish swine,' he shrieked. 'Wasting my time. Request denied.'

Before he could summon his aide, I implored him, 'Then please add my name to the list.'

Eichmann glanced quickly at the folder again.

'You work for the Reich. Request denied. Now get out of my sight!'

A torrent of foul, anti-Semitic abuse pursued me to the door. I rushed home in a panic, my heart thumping against my rib cage. What had I done? What hadn't I done? What had I done? I kept repeating the same questions out loud. In the street, I stopped suddenly and turned, taking a few steps. Maybe he would see me again. I will tell him my secret this time. I collapsed sobbing into the filth-strewn gutter, utterly exhausted and helpless. I knew that there was nothing more I could do. It was hopeless."

Emil wiped his eyes again.

"Four days later," he murmured, so softly I could barely hear the words, "my family consisted of a pile of grey, smouldering ash in an Auschwitz crematorium."

I was rendered speechless.

"Now you may understand a little about why I come to Bletchley Park so often," he said, a bit louder this time. "It disturbs me to be here because of my memories, which will haunt me until the day I die. But I also find some comfort here, too. Being at Station X helps me to come to terms with my sacrifice, my loss. I look around at the huts and buildings where brilliant crypto-analysts unlocked the Enigma codes. Thanks to those courageous Polish mathematicians. And I think of the thousands of lives that were saved by the secret work which, the authorities say, shortened the war by two years."

Emil rose awkwardly from his armchair, and I got up from mine.

"I really have to go now," he said, with a restrained smile. "Thank you so much for the drink ... and for listening to an irritating old man."

We shook hands warmly.

"God bless you, Emil," I said.

"Maybe, maybe not," he said, shrugging his shoulders.

He moved away, his limp seemingly accentuated, and stopped by the door. He opened it, turned and raised his hand in a gentle wave. His mouth opened slightly. He appeared to say something to me, but I could not catch his words. Then he was gone.

The memory Haggadah

A FEW years back, I happened to be in Jerusalem on business. It was just before the festival of Pesach, the Passover celebration of the Children of Israel's biblical Exodus from Egypt. The client I had come to see very kindly invited me to be a guest in his father's house for the Seder night, the family gathering where the story of the Exodus is retold. When the day came, I walked to the father's house from the son's nearby apartment, accompanied by his wife and their three children.

It was one of those gorgeous Israeli evenings, warm, precious and fragrant with the aroma of spices. On our short journey, I learned that my Seder host and his wife had three sons and two daughters. I also discovered that, as their domestic tradition apparently demanded, the five children had preceded their families to assist with "the complex preparations". I realised just how complex when I arrived at the parents' spacious, detached villa at the edge of the city. Here I found that, aside from the five children, there were also twelve grandchildren to cater for, including two babies.

Despite my embarrassed reluctance, I was compelled by the adults to occupy the chair at the immediate right hand of the white-haired head of the family. It would have been ungracious of me to continue overlong with my gentle protestations; and, finally, I accepted the place of honour. I felt deeply touched, and especially privileged, as I witnessed the entire mishpocheh happily taking their seats around the long table, the babies asleep in their mother's arms and the older boys and girls mildly teasing their younger siblings. I was struck particularly by the smooth, olive complexions of the children; they were all true sabras born in the state of Israel. Apart from the statistics of his huge family, I had learned that my host was a Holocaust survivor. He had reached the Holy Land in 1946, aged sixteen, as an illegal immigrant on a leaking rust-bucket of a steamer that had managed to evade the British blockade.

I glanced around at the assembly in the spacious, elegantly furnished dining room. It was clear to me that the teenager, literally from hell, had subsequently led a successful, contented and prosperous life. I have to say that this filled me with gladness; though I shuddered inwardly at the horrors he had doubtless witnessed as a child. As a host, he was very pleasant and welcoming to me, as were his charming wife and the rest of his lovely family. Although I knew that he had lived in Israel for more than half a century, longer than the history of the State itself, I detected in his voice the lingering trace of an East European accent. I thought it was probably Polish. My own ancestors had come to England from the town of Łódz in the late nineteenth century.

There was a good deal of banter and babble around the table, which was covered with the requisite white cloth, lit candles, silver goblets for the requisite four cups of wine, a capacious plate for various ritual objects, matzot (otherwise known as unleavened bread, which the Israelites baked on their hasty exit from Egypt) and the Exodus story-telling books known as Haggadahs. But the hubbub gradually diminished and finally subsided as the host began to recite the Seder service from his Haggadah.

It was not immediately apparent to me who would be the youngest child capable of reciting from the Haggadah the Mah Nishtanah, the four traditional questions related to the Exodus. When the time came, Moshe, who was only three years old, falteringly but successfully carried the slim but large and unwieldy, children's edition to his grandfather's side, placed the prolifically illustrated book on the table, opened it and began asking the time-honoured questions. His angelic face shone in the glow of the candlelight, as he stood, almost comically, to attention, and started to read the Hebrew clearly and confidently. The entire company, but especially his parents and grandparents, displayed love and pride in the small boy's prowess.

It was while the child slowly, but assuredly, said his piece that, for the first time, I took notice of his grandfather's Haggadah. It was quite unlike any that I had seen before, whether at a Seder service, in a Judaica shop or even within a Jewish museum. The book appeared to be bound in unexceptional leather covers and looked quite worn, almost decrepit. The pages seemed to be made, though not entirely symmetrically, of waxen manuscript. They were of unequal size, of uneven dimensions and roughly frayed or torn at the edges. The Hebrew words, though neatly presented, were of a varying script and density suggestive of a handwritten rather than a printed work. I noticed that its owner held the book not only with fingers gnarled by rheumatism but also with a kind of profound reverence. Naturally, I was both intrigued and mystified.

As the little boy completed his recitation and ran back, beaming, to the chair beside his father, I felt a hand patting my arm. I looked up from my book to see my host smiling knowingly at me. Then he whispered something.

"I could tell you're interested in my old Haggadah. I've got to tell you, it's my most treasured possession. After the meal, I'll answer the questions I see in your eyes. Right now, I have to answer my grandson Moshe's four questions."

During the service, as wine for the adults and grape juice for the kids were poured into silver bechers or paper cups and imbibed, and as the age-old story was retold about the enslavement of the Jews by the Egyptians, the twelve plagues and the Exodus of the Israelites pursued by Pharaoh's chariot army, I was filled with a nagging anticipation. I could hardly wait for the traditional Seder night "Meal" and what might prove to be another fascinating story.

As we all consumed Hillel's famous "sandwich" of matzah and bitter herbs, I knew we were fast approaching the dinner interval.

As the women cleared the table and fetched platters piled high with enough food for a regiment or two, and their men-folk tried valiantly to maintain order amongst the children, my host took me quietly to one side. He was clutching his unusual Haggadah.

"Take it in your hands," he urged, offering the book to me.

Diffidently, I did so, clasping the seemingly frail, slim volume, but not too tightly.

"What do you feel?" my host asked, quickly, strangely, his deep blue eyes dancing into mine. "Close your eyes. It may help."

I felt odd and self-conscious in the unfamiliar surroundings. But I also sensed an obligation to obey his instruction. I shut my eyes, feeling only the fragile book in my grasp and an anxiety not to harm it in any way.

"What do you feel now?" he asked.

I sensed a lessening of activity in the room. People were getting ready to eat and I did not want to prolong my uneasy experience. I replied quietly to my host's question.

"I don't think I can feel anything … other, that is, than the book in my hands. I'm sorry if there was something else you expected of me."

I opened my eyes. The grandfather gazed at me for what

seemed a long time, but was probably no more than a few moments. He sighed deeply, then grinned warmly and beckoned me to sit down.

"No, my dear friend, I'm the one who needs to apologise. I'm a complete idiot. Look, everyone's nodding in agreement. Please forgive me. After we've eaten, I'll tell you my story … and what I feel when I hold this extraordinary book in my hands."

It was no less than a magnificent repast. My host's wife and the daughters who assisted her are wonderful chefs. I was overwhelmed by the family's generosity and kindness to me. I was not at all surprised to learn, though I almost needed to drag the information from her, that my modest hostess had studied cordon bleu cuisine in France. I gathered from one of the sons that, once the dishes were cleared away and before the continuation of the service, it was customary for my host to speak of Passovers in der Heim, the old country. But that Pesach, because of my interest in his Haggadah, he would tell of a not so happy time when he ceased to be a boy and became a man beyond his years.

Meanwhile, the babies had been put to bed, and the younger children struggled to keep awake, doubtless with a profitable search for the afikoman, the hidden half of matzah, in mind. The main room lights had been lowered by dimmer switches to help in their efforts. As the flickering candles radiated orange-yellow beams across the reconstituted Seder table, the old man leaned against his cushion and began his story.

"My parents, siblings and such of my wider family still alive were driven from the ghetto by the SS and transported to Auschwitz. You understand I need say no more about their fate. That one, evil name tells you everything. To this time, I can't remember how I managed to escape the soldiers' sweep of the putrid tenements. All I can recollect is the slamming of doors, the heartrending cries, the splintering of wood, the crashing of glass on cobbles, the gunshots, blood flowing in the streets, the continuous barking of fierce dogs and the brutal, guttural screams of their handlers, 'Juden, raus! Raus, raus … raus! Jews, get out! Out, out, out!' The shrieks of murderous hate still fill my head. Somehow, I survived the mad hell of that day and night. I was confused, terrified and crushingly devastated by my loss.

"My evasion of capture, however, was short-lived. A week later, I was discovered in my bolthole by mopping-up SS troops. I can't explain to you the black depth of my fear. Remember, I was barely into my teens. But one thing was in my favour. I looked older than my years. Perhaps it was the ghetto's ghastly privations that had aged me beyond my time. In any case, I was reasonably tall and, despite the circumstances, passably fit. With other boys rounded up in this final trawl before the old Jewish quarter was demolished, I was despatched by truck to a slave labour camp some distance away.

"The conditions were harsh, to say the very least. The work was back breaking, the food, when there was any, miserable, the guards and overseers unpredictably vicious. It was a daily struggle to keep body and soul together, particularly during the freezing winter months. Death was always hovering one short breath away. But my will was strong, and I was determined to survive. Over two years or so, I was moved from one work camp to another until, early in 1945, I was slaving at a vast complex close to the Czech border. There had been rumours that the Russians were advancing rapidly from the east. I was almost certain we could hear the distant rumble of their artillery. We could also detect a growing edginess amongst our guards. One day, the entire laager was hurriedly dismantled; and a long, ragged column of inmates, mostly Jews, was forced to march westwards.

"There were more than two thousand of us. The weather was atrocious, freezing sleet alternating with blinding snowstorms. We were all in rags, and very few of us possessed serviceable footwear. We knew that, by the end of the trek, barely half of us would have survived winter's onslaught, and the roadside shootings of the weak and the dying. Many just abandoned all hope, fell to their knees and were quickly despatched with a bullet through the head. It may seem callous, but those of us determined to go on living dragged the tattered remnants of clothes and boots from the bodies of the dead. And we ransacked their pockets for the hoarded, rock-hard crusts of bread they would never need. In the wake of our column lay strewn a pathetic trail of what looked like contorted rag dolls."

I glanced surreptitiously at the family seated around the table. The children were listening in rapt silence to their grandfather. I wondered what disturbing thoughts were invading their tender, innocent minds. Like me, they were hanging on every word of this tragic story. The host continued.

"After some days, we reached what appeared to be rail-yards. An old locomotive steamed out of a siding pulling a long line of cattle trucks. On the roof of every other wagon stood a soldier with a rifle. We were loaded quickly into the wooden boxcars, which carried an unbearable stench, like overflowing sewers. Despite the biting cold outside, it soon became stiflingly hot in the overcrowded space. Exhausted men groaned and collapsed, crying for water. I squeezed into a corner but couldn't make enough room to sit down. There was a crashing jolt and the train began to move. One small, high, barred opening served as our window on the passing wintry landscape.

"It was soon revealed that the planks forming the floor of the wagon were rotten. When we found that they could easily be pulled up, thoughts turned rapidly to escape. Most were fearful that the guards would shoot them during any attempt to flee. Despite my terror, I volunteered to be the guinea pig. I realised it would be my only chance for survival. The noisy rattle of the ancient trucks on the single track masked the wrenching up of the decayed floorboards. When the hole was big enough, I was lowered head first with my legs held firmly, until I could grip bars on the underside and wedge my feet between them.

'Good luck, lad,' my fellow Jews whispered through the gap above me, as I clung on firmly like a circus artiste on a trapeze.

"Peering round fearfully, I could make out snow-covered fields on either side of the line. Beyond the white pastures were low, wooded hills. I'd been advised to wait until the forested slopes were closer to the railway before seizing my opportunity. Otherwise, the snow would slow me down and I'd offer an easy target for the train's sentries. I'd also been told that I needed to hold on until we slowed down on a turning incline.

"There were so many things to think about, so many dangers. When the time came, I'd drop to the track, remain very still until the train had completely passed overhead and then roll down the embankment. I was to run as fast as I could, in a zigzag pattern, across the fields to the relative safety of the forest. Hopefully, the guards wouldn't be alerted. Luckily, all the necessary ingredients for my one shot came together about thirty minutes after I'd descended through the rotten floor. I couldn't have held on for much longer in any event; my hands were frozen and my legs stiff from their tortuous position. The locomotive gradually reduced speed and I fell to the hard ground between the sleepers. My heart was hammering as I moved my lower limbs cautiously to restore circulation. When the last wagon passed over me, I cartwheeled down the banking slope, picked myself up and started my hazardous run across the field. Fortunately, the snow wasn't so thick here and I made good progress towards the tree line, about one hundred metres away. No shouts or shots pursued me and I began to hope that I'd achieved complete surprise.

"My thoughts were premature. I heard shouts behind me. Looking back, I could see puffs of smoke from the guns of the roof guards. Then I heard the sighing whine of bullets, and spotted little spouts of snow flying up around me. I continued to meander as I'd been told. The trees were now just a few metres from me when I felt a hard blow to my right thigh. I sensed no pain and my momentum powered me on towards the forest. I collapsed just inside the shelter of the trees. I could still hear the sharp cracks of rifle fire as I dragged myself further into the thick cover of the wood.

"A bullet had passed through my leg. Blood was oozing from my trousers. With all my remaining strength, I hauled myself deeper into the undergrowth beneath the tall, shadowy trees. I listened intently, breathing wildly. The firing had now stopped. Were they coming after me? Yes? No. I heard a shrill steam whistle in the distance and I realised to my utter relief that the train was moving away. The soldiers wouldn't be searching for me. I'd been very lucky. Or had I? I needed urgently to apply a tourniquet or I'd bleed to death. I propped myself against a sturdy trunk, tore off my rope belt and tied it tightly around my thigh. I sensed myself blacking out with the almost unbearable pain after the initially deadening shock. It felt like I was dying.

"When I came to, I thought I had died ... and maybe gone to heaven. I was stretched out on a comparatively clean mattress in a small tent, and being tended by a very pretty young girl in what looked like a makeshift battledress. On fully regaining my senses, I was informed that I'd been unconscious for three days; and that, at one stage, I'd been perilously close to death. Oddly enough, and despite some lingering pain in my leg, I was absolutely famished and rapidly demolished whatever food was given to me.

"A Jewish partisan group in the area, alerted by the sound of shooting, had discovered me in the forest. This armed band of young men and women, based in the wooded Czech hills, had nursed me back to life. Luckily, a doctor amongst them had managed to save my leg, but only just. As my health recovered over the weeks, I became anxious to join the guerrilla troop. I was so grateful to every one of its members. But it wasn't gratitude that impelled me to take up arms alongside my Jewish comrades. It was rather my strong desire to seize this chance to fight the evil enemies of my people.

"It so happened that the festival of Pesach was approaching. Of course, it wasn't possible to obtain all the necessary prerequisites to celebrate the Seder, and our forefathers' escape from oppression. But we were resolute. On the night in question, we sat together in the wild, forested hills, forty of us, illuminated by candlelight. It was the most bizarre, yet most moving and poignant, service I've ever experienced, before or since. I sobbed continually, thinking of my family; and was constantly comforted by my new friends and fellow warriors, whose losses were no less painful than my own.

"The one religious Jew amongst us read from our only Haggadah. It's the very same one I am using tonight. It was made and written secretly in one of the Nazi concentration camps, nobody knew which one, and smuggled out during a death march westwards. The Jewish partisans had come across it, with a scrawled note of explanation folded inside, on a decaying body by the roadside. After the unusual Seder in our hilly encampment, I asked to examine the improvised book. I was told that it had been the painstaking work of more than one hand. And a few minor errors in the text confirmed that it had probably been reproduced entirely from memory. It was truly a miraculous achievement in the dreadful circumstances of its creation."

My host stopped speaking. I'd been astounded to hear the story of what he called "the memory Haggadah", which now rested on the still pristine white tablecloth. I was about to say something when he continued his narrative.

"A few days later, our group was attacked by German mountain troops. As we fled the ambush, most of my comrades were cut down by machine gun fire. Few escaped the assault but I was fortunate to be amongst them. We ran and ran for what seemed like hours, until we finally collapsed, totally exhausted. There were just five survivors of the raid, including the orthodox Jew who'd conducted the Seder service. He'd sustained a serious wound and it was a miracle that he'd survived to reach our temporary refuge.

"Fortunately, the doctor was also with us. As he examined the injury, it was clear to me that the medic considered it to be fatal. His brave patient insisted on being told the worst, so that he could recite the appropriate prayers. The dying young man beckoned me to his side and, with some difficulty, withdrew from his pocket a small bundle wrapped in a tattered piece of nondescript material. It was this very Haggadah. He gestured me to come even closer and whispered something that I couldn't really hear. He was now very weak. I felt so sad and helpless. I put my ear near to his mouth. His last, rasping words to me were, 'Use it in good health …' Then he died."

I could see tears collecting in the old man's eyes. His wife came round the table and placed an arm on her husband's shoulders, stooping to tenderly kiss his cheek. I leaned forward and held one of his hands. My action surprised me but I wanted to reach out and touch his painful memories.

"Forgive me," he said, turning to me and wiping his eyes. "Sometimes, nowadays, my emotions get the better of me."

I nodded, with all the sympathy I could muster, and gently drummed on his fingers.

"But now we must look to the children," our host said, quickly recovering his composure and smiling broadly. "There's something to be found … and we all know what that is, don't we?"

The younger children shouted with joy, and jumped up and down with excitement. Doubtless they all held the expectation of some very nice gifts.

As the kids hunted for the afikoman, my host took hold of my arm.

"You know," he said, his eyes now sparkling, "when I was in Italy after the war, waiting to be smuggled into the Promised Land, I often held this unique Haggadah in my hands. The courage and suffering of its creators gave me the strength to be patient, to hope. I cannot tell you how often I would repeat, and repeat, the book's final words … 'Next year in Jerusalem'. My hopes and prayers have been fulfilled, as you can see, while those of millions of others have sadly come to naught. Why? Of course, it's a question I frequently ask myself. Why? Why me? Only the Almighty knows the answer to that one."

The old man glanced around at his grandchildren as they laughed and giggled happily, and enjoyed their gleeful search for the hidden segment of matzah. He picked up his precious Haggadah from the table and clasped it lovingly in his arms.

"Do you know," he murmured, "I can feel its creators' neshomahs. I can feel their Jewish souls. They are with us here, tonight. They will always be with us …"

Mordechai's diary

EARLY IN 2003, during excavations in central Warsaw for a new commercial building, workmen discovered a battered, old tin box buried in the sub-surface rubble. In the development's site office, the badly warped lid was prised off the container, which was about the size of a breakfast cereal packet. Inside was found a stained and crumpled, schoolchild's exercise book. The pages appeared to be filled with a small but neat pencil manuscript. There was nothing else in the box except for dust.

One of the construction engineers, knowing something about paper restoration, took the book home. After several hours of painstaking work, he managed to clean and repair the tainted and partially tattered pages. As a result of his careful and sensitive work with this fragile document, practically all the writing became reasonably legible or, in a few instances, readily surmised. What the engineer was then amazed to read were six-decade old entries in the makeshift diary of a Jewish boy, aged twelve, who lived in the Warsaw Ghetto during the Nazis' wartime occupation.

The young diarist's name was Mordechai; unfortunately, his

surname was unreadable. From his vivid descriptions and mature comments, he seems to have been a very observant youngster, intelligent beyond his years and all too tragically aware of the vortex of persecution, destruction and death in which he was inexorably trapped. The following text is an account of what may well have been the final days and hours of his short life, as translated from the entries in the diary, his own simple but poignant and final legacy to the world.

"*2nd February 1943*

I'm very annoyed today. Yesterday, I lost all the exercise books containing my diary entries since my parents and three sisters were taken to the Umschlagplatz, the deportation assembly area, last summer. For resettlement in the east, the authorities said. But I can remember that my very first entry was all about my narrow escape from the deportations last July. I managed to get back to the overcrowded and rat-infested tenement where our family had survived (barely) since 1941.

Last night, I was forced to run from our hiding place a few blocks from here. In my desperation to evade the screaming, jackbooted troops, who were closing in on us ghetto kids, I grabbed my bag of simple possessions but forgot to take my writing books. That's why I'm so angry with myself. I'll have to start again now, with the only exercise book I've got left. By the way, my name's Mordechai … and I'm twelve years and eight months old. I'm sorry about this tiny writing but I'm trying to save paper.

Three of us skeletal waifs have found shelter here. How can I describe our new sanctuary? Well, it's like a dark and freezing cave. We think it may be part of a cellar that has been largely crushed by the partial collapse of the building above us. We hope it doesn't topple down on us, because then this place will be our tomb. We managed to scramble inside through a small gap in the brickwork. It was just big enough for us to squeeze through our starving bodies, the taut skin of which looks (and feels) like yellow parchment. But I suppose it prevents our protruding bones from bursting out. I think we're safe here for the time being. But we may soon need to search for another bolthole, just in case.

There are only three of us left in our gang now. Yerzy is eleven and Mira is ten. We've been through a lot together. None of us knows where our parents and family have been taken. We've got no real homes. We've witnessed the horrible massacres in the ghetto, and heard terrible stories about mass gassings in concentration camps. So we don't hold out much hope of ever seeing our loved ones alive again. We're probably orphans now.

I'm still thinking about our little friend Janusz. Sadly, we lost him yesterday evening. He was only nine but he was an excellent runner for a long time. Unfortunately, he had a swollen and badly infected foot, and his breathing wasn't too good either. We street kids all have bad feet, with cuts, bruises and sores. And they're as filthy as a chimney sweep's face. It all comes from running around without any shoes or socks. I think poor Janusz was quite ill really, though he was very brave and never complained. But he couldn't run fast enough any more. He wasn't that far behind us when the soldiers caught up with him in the alleyway. We could hear his terrible screams as they mercilessly bayoneted him to death.

I'm writing this diary by the tiny light of a small, flickering candle. Yerzy and Mira are sleeping curled up together in the corner. We found an old coal sack down here. It's black as night, heavy and pungent but they're using it as a blanket. The poor kids are cold and exhausted. So am I. And there's a foul stench coming from somewhere. It's really dreadful, but I know the stink very well. Probably there's a rotting corpse nearby, buried in the rubble. I don't think that I can write any more tonight. My eyes are very tired and I'm feeling so sleepy.

5th February

The last few days have been very hectic and dangerous for the three of us. I've not had a chance to write anything until now. Yerzy, Mira and I went to see the man we call Mr Big. We don't know his real name but he's one of the black marketeers in the ghetto. We wanted to continue as smugglers for his highly profitable business. It's the only way we know to survive round here. For quite a while, we've been ignoring the night curfews and going through narrow breaks in the ghetto wall. We bring back mostly vegetables from Mr Big's contacts on the Aryan side.

I told the boss that we'd needed to lie low for a few days. He was sorry to hear about Janusz, but said that he wasn't the first Jewish child to be killed by the Nazis, and wouldn't be the last. Tell us something we don't know, I'd thought to myself. Three weeks back, we lost our good friend Artur on a smuggling run. He was the same age as me. I was with him the night he was murdered. We'd just collected several kilos of potatoes, carrots and turnips. They were stashed inside the specially fitted carriers we wear under our long coats. Loaded up like that we ragamuffin kids look just like heavily pregnant little women. It would be quite comical, really, if it wasn't so serious. Of course, the extra weight slows us down.

Anyway, the two of us had managed to get back inside the ghetto wall by outwitting the German sentries. Unluckily, in the gloom, Artur trod on a dying cat. The poor pussy let out an ear-shattering shriek. We heard running footfalls on the cobbles and then saw the flashing light of a torch. Suddenly, one of the white-coated and black-capped, Jewish policemen appeared. Clearly, he'd been alerted by the feline's piercing howl.

Some of the ghetto police are sympathetic towards us and turn a blind eye to our contraband operations. Though, needless to say, a few might be taking bribes from Mr Big and his like. Others are unnecessarily nasty, sadistic and brutal, only too anxious to please their SS controllers. Unfortunately, the policeman we know as Janka spotted us making off fast along one of our rat runs. He's one of his Nazi master's most ardent boot-lickers, and as fat as the pig he is. Janka shouted an order to halt; and when we didn't, he lumbered after us.

Gradually, we were outrunning our pursuer but, on taking a corner too sharply, Artur lost his balance. Handicapped by his cargo he fell heavily, spilling his load of vegetables across the street. I stopped in my tracks and ran back to help him. "I think I've broken my ankle!" he cried out in pain. We could hear Janka approaching. He was hollering, "Stop, stop!" Artur urged me to leave him and save myself. I thought about staying to tackle Janka. But he's a colossal oaf of a man, well nourished with Nazi food handouts. And he wields a heavy wooden truncheon. I didn't think I stood a chance so, reluctantly, I left my pal to talk his way out of trouble. It works sometimes.

As I ran away, I heard Artur scream when the bully hit the helpless lad with his lead-weighted stick. Then the sound of a sharp whistle came to me through the shadowy night. It was Janka calling for assistance. The next day, we learned on the grapevine that two SS guards quickly arrived on the scene with a pair of huge, slathering Alsation hounds. The soldiers set the vicious animals on poor Artur, until they'd mauled and bitten him to death. I can't think of a more horrific way for someone to die. But I'm sure the Nazis could.

8th February

Jerzy, Mira and I watched the other day as a girl we know from another smuggling group was taken out of the ghetto for burial. Anna wasn't killed. She'd merely died of starvation, like loads of other kids I knew from school and cheder. So there's nothing remarkable here, then. What remained of Anna's small and emaciated body was piled on the back of a wooden cart, alongside a heap of other dead street urchins. Sometimes, I think that they're the lucky ones. At least, these boys and girls are now free from the agony and suffering of the ghetto. But then I begin to feel strongly that I must try to survive this hell on Earth. So that I can tell the world how we lived and died in this dreadful place.

Like a pair of old farm horses, two men pulled the wagon through the ghetto gates into the Aryan part of Warsaw. I don't even think they always bury the dead Jewish bodies.

Sometimes, they lie around for many days, putrefying in the sewage-running gutters. I've heard that Russian POWs are forced to build mountains of these rotting corpses on the edges of the city. Then the putrid mixture of flesh and bone is doused with petrol and set ablaze. They say that the black columns of smoke can be seen from a great distance.

I've also heard that, from time to time, huge pits are dug in the woods by slave labour. The cadavers are thrown into them, covered with quick lime and buried with the excavated earth. I think the ghetto and the city authorities are very worried that some awful disease, like plague or cholera, might break out and infect the general population.

Mind you, the inmates of the ghetto have been much reduced over the last year, what with the transports to the east, the random pogroms and the thousands of deaths from sickness and starvation. Mr Big keeps complaining about the decline in the number of his customers and the fierce competition from rivals. I don't know what he has got to moan about. He and his large family are nourished like fat cats enjoying a daily saucer of thick cream.

And his eager clients haven't generally come from the starving ghetto peasants. But from those wealthy residents who've managed to bring in money, gold and silver, diamond jewellery and valuable paintings under the noses of the Germans. Most of the rich have so far managed to bribe their way off the deportation lists. Or they've bought the work documents that enable them to claim they're labouring in the few scattered factories and workshops the Nazis still permit in the ghetto. But they're deluding themselves if they believe that the soldiers and police won't come for them after the miserable poor and sick have been liquidated.

12th February

Jerzy and I have made two smuggling trips through our gaps in the wall during the last couple of days. But Mira hasn't been at all well. I think she has a high temperature and her face is horribly puffed up. She says she feels quite weak. It's no wonder, really. Look at the conditions in which we have to exist. We don't know exactly what's wrong with her. It's very worrying.

I'm very fond of Mira. I've got no family of my own now and she's like a sister to me. Mr Big promised to send us a doctor for her, but we haven't seen anyone yet. Anyway, medicine is a rare commodity in the ghetto and requires a lot of money, which we don't have of course. Meanwhile, Mira is lying in our very unhealthy cellar refuge. And for long periods, she's all on her own. At least we can make her some warming turnip soup from our smuggling cut.

14th February

Something is brewing in the ghetto, and I don't mean hot drinks or even illicit vodka. There's talk and rumour of some kind of armed resistance to the Nazis. I know there are many young men and women who refuse to be deported. They don't comply with orders to report to the Umschlagplatz and become fugitives. They would sooner die fighting than surrender to the Germans. They're hiding in tenements, basements and bunkers all over the ghetto. I've heard that their commander's name is Anielewicz, and that he's only in his twenties. I'm proud to state that I share my first name with him. I think the SS and the Jewish police know about some of the people involved, and even their whereabouts.

Someone told me that the headquarters of the Jewish resistance is situated between Mila Street and Niska Street. But I believe the military people are too scared to go in and get them. Why? It's because the Jews have revolvers, rifles and even a few submachine guns. Mr Big said that the weapons have been smuggled into the ghetto from the Polish Underground and the Jewish partisans in the forests. Isn't it wonderful to know that the cowardly Nazis are afraid of the Jews when we have the power to strike back hard? Mr Big suspects that the Germans are awaiting orders from Berlin, and troop reinforcements, before assaulting the hideouts of the Jewish resistance. He says it's only a matter of time before the enemy attack.

16th February

Mira died yesterday afternoon. Jerzy and I couldn't stop crying for a long time. But we didn't want her ravaged little body to be thrown onto the cart for burning or mass burial. In the middle of the night, we carried her to a small, overgrown garden just a few blocks away. We organised a shovel and took turns digging a hole in the hard ground. It was really tiring work; and, by the time we'd finished, it was nearly dawn and we were worn out. We lowered Mira carefully and gently into the grave and covered her once pretty face with an old piece of cloth I'd found nearby.

As we shovelled the earth, Jerzy wanted me to say a Hebrew prayer for Mira's dear soul. But I told him that I wasn't sure whether I believed in God any more. Jerzy is younger than me but maybe he has got more sense. He's normally quite passive but he was quite angry at my response. "You should be ashamed of yourself!" he shouted at me, waving his arms in the air. "All this isn't God's fault. It's the fault of evil men." He was right, of course. I just wasn't thinking straight. I shouldn't blame the Almighty for the terrible wrongs committed by mere mortals. Mankind has been given the free will to do good or bad things.

Sadly, we're now under the power of wicked men. So I said the Kaddish memorial prayer for Mira, even though there wasn't a minyan, I'm not a real relative and I haven't been barmitzvah yet.

17th February

An elderly Jewish doctor came to our refuge in the collapsed cellar this morning. He was carrying a small black case. He said that Mr Big had sent him to examine Mira. We told him he was too late, and to push off. He expressed his sincere regrets and condolences and left hurriedly.

Not long afterwards, Jerzy and I heard a lot of crashing about above us. We didn't think there were any more residents left in the building. The tenement was in a very dangerous and uninhabitable condition. It could've caved in at any moment, like others have done in the ghetto. Suddenly, you might hear a strange, metallic sound, like steel girders grinding against brickwork. That's the time to get out quickly, and to run as far away as possible. Then there's a hellishly explosive, whooshing noise as the weakened floors concertina downwards like a collapsing house of cards. Sharp-edged debris flies all over the place, like shrapnel. And a great billowing black cloud of choking dust, like a rushing wall of water, floods into the surrounding streets.

But we realised that the commotion we could hear wasn't the sound of the building about to fall on top of us. People were screaming. We peered through the diminutive hole that provides our entry. Three young men, two young women and a boy about eight or nine years old were being driven into the street by a dozen SS troops. Jerzy and I were scared stiff and wondered whether we might be discovered too. Our hearts were pounding like piston engines. Maybe these people made up one of the cells of the Jewish resistance movement in the ghetto. The lad could've been one of their runners, helping to carry messages to and from Anielewicz's HQ in Mila Street.

We could see the SS officer in charge. He was brandishing a Lüger pistol and shouting commands. His black-helmeted men, who were carrying rifles or Schmeiser automatics, herded the terrified group of captives, their arms raised high, across the road. We had a clear view of what happened next. The five young adults and the little lad were roughly lined up against the building opposite us. They were forced to face the wall. One of the men was hit on the shoulder with a rifle butt and slumped to the ground. He was dragged up by a pair of SS men and slammed upright against the brickwork.

The soldiers slowly backed away, their weapons pointed towards the row of trembling prisoners. In a flash, the boy made a dash for freedom. He ran along the street as fast as his skinny legs could carry him. But he couldn't outrun a bullet. The officer raised his handgun, aimed and fired. The lad was struck in the back mid-stride and launched into the air like a startled bird. He fell to the ground and lay still. The soldiers burst into ugly laughter at the victim's death antics. The officer swaggered to the boy, kicked his lifeless body and put another bullet into his head. Returning to the firing squad, he shrieked an order. The patrol opened fire and the bullet-riddled bodies of the Jewish youngsters performed a gruesome dance before hitting the pavement.

Jerzy and I slid away from our concealed viewpoint, stared horrified at one another for a moment or two then buried our heads in our hands. But we didn't weep. That would have meant noise, and our survival instincts had kicked in. We didn't want to make even the slightest sound to give ourselves away. It's terrible, really. Just think about it. Not being able to cry in order to save your life. I've even heard heartrending stories of babies who've been smothered to death by their desperate mothers. The mums were forced to prevent the little one from crying out and giving away a hiding place under a bed, behind a cupboard or up in a loft. What a nightmare world we're living in!

19th February

Today, on one of his scavenging expeditions around the ghetto, Jerzy found an old tin box. He's given it to me to keep my diary in. This is really very good of him. In an emergency, or even when I'm out foraging or smuggling, it'll be possible to hide such a container. I've already prepared a deep niche in a corner of the cellar and a pile of earth, stones and rubble. If we need to evacuate this place in a hurry, I can quickly bury my exercise book with these scribbles. Maybe someday they'll be found; and a future generation will come to know what we suffered here, in the Jewish ghetto of Warsaw.

Jerzy and I are going on another smuggling expedition tonight. We're collecting a load of turnips. I'm getting really fed up with turnip soup. I'll soon begin to look like a turnip, if I don't already. But, you know what, it's like caviar to me (not that I've ever tasted caviar). Look, I suppose even rich people can get fed up with caviar! Anyway, I mustn't complain. There are sick children lying out in the streets who haven't even got the strength to beg. The poor little souls are slowly and agonisingly starving to death.

Mr Big told us that Anielewicz wants to see us. He thinks we may be able to help him, as there aren't many half-alive, able-bodied kids left in the ghetto. It's probably to run messages between the resistance cells in the scattered hideouts. We're going to see the great man tomorrow morning. Jerzy and I can't wait. It means Anielewicz has heard about us, about our exploits and evasions of the Germans and ghetto police. It also means that we can help our fellow Jews resist the Nazis. My first name sake can place his trust in us. Perhaps Jerzy and I will become famous freedom fighters. Wonderful!

20th February

Jerzy and I went to meet Anielewicz in his Mila Street bunker early this morning. On the way, we noticed Janka, the murderous ghetto policeman. I think he spotted us too, but he couldn't really do anything about it. We weren't doing anything wrong, just walking in the street. Mind you, that hasn't stopped the mindless brute from beating kids up. This time, he just glared and shook a big fat fist at us.

There's so much security from the young guards. It was ages before we reached the resistance leader's inner sanctuary. But I suppose that's to be expected. Anielewicz is a marvellous person. You can easily see why he's so well respected by his many followers and comrades. He's got a bit of a beard, so he looks rather older than he is. He praised our brave smuggling operations, though he decried the necessary evil of the black marketeers. I think that most of the resistance people are socialists.

There were quite a few people in the bunker, which has many rooms. Passing one of them, we saw lots of wooden crates stacked against the wall. It looked like they contained guns of various calibres, and a great deal of ammunition. A woman frowned at us and quickly closed the door. In another room off the long corridor there was a printing machine being operated by a couple of young, bearded men. We think they've been turning out the underground newssheets we've seen around the ghetto.

Anyone caught distributing them, or posting them on the walls, is shot on the spot. There've been several such summary executions, one of which I witnessed firsthand. The girl couldn't have been more than sixteen. She begged pitifully for her life but the SS guards pulled her screaming into a tenement courtyard and shot her twice in the head. When the soldiers had gone, some of us were curious to have a look at the body. The girl's shattered skull was resting in a widening pool of blood and brain tissue. It was really horrible, but not particularly unusual.

There was an exciting buzz of activity at the HQ, at least it was exciting for Jerzy and me. We wished that we were older and could actually work there. We said as much to Anielewicz.

He grinned, patted our heads and said we would be more useful to him on the streets. He wants us to run messages around the ghetto; but first, he said, there was an important smuggling job coming up tonight. He warned us that it would be extremely hazardous, and asked whether we were still willing to do it. We jumped at the opportunity. After all, I explained to our courageous leader, danger is like a part of our bodies. It's with us all the time. And, as if to prove my point, after we'd left the bunker we spotted Janka and another ghetto policeman observing us from a few blocks away.

21st February

Last night, Jerzy and I carried out the perilous mission that Anielewicz briefed us about late yesterday evening. We felt like secret agents, and very grown up to be entrusted with such an important task. But it really was dangerous. We had to go over to a safe house on the Aryan side, used now and again by Jewish partisans. This time our trip wasn't to collect a load of vegetables. What we had to bring back to the ghetto were ten army revolvers.

It must've been just after midnight when we scrambled through the hidden break in the wall and disappeared into the dark streets of the city. It was raining hard and we were getting drenched. The apartment we were heading for is in the district of Povonski, not far from Danzig railway station in the northern part of Warsaw. We had a couple of close shaves dodging the Germans' night curfew patrols. But finally we arrived, soaked to the skin, at our destination.

Jerzy and I were shivering cold and wet. The two men in the flat took pity on us and made some hot drinks. Both of them were wearing balaclavas to hide their faces, so that we wouldn't be able to identify them. It was really scary for us; but perhaps they were even more nervous than we were. Anyhow, they handed over five pistols to each of us. We stowed them in special leather containers we'd been fitted with in the Mila bunker. One of Anielewicz' colleagues had made sure they were fixed securely around our bodies, and that they fitted comfortably. After all, we were both mostly skin and bone.

The weight of the guns slowed us down after we'd left the apartment. But gradually, and very warily, we made our way back to the ghetto. Two German sentries were chatting and smoking cigarettes close to our usual crossing point. It was still very dark, though dawn wasn't far off, so we discussed whether we should take a chance. In the end, we decided it would be too risky. If we were caught, the discovery of guns would be considerably worse for us than carrots and turnips. We waited patiently until the soldiers realised they were neglecting their duties and moved off in opposite directions.

When we reported back with the weapons, Anielewicz was delighted with the efficient and sensibly cautious way we had successfully carried out our first job for him. One of the young women made a hot and satisfying meal for us. The food may even have included some protein; though in that case, it was probably horsemeat. What would my old rabbi have said, may the Almighty rest his dear soul?

On leaving the bunker, we found the sky dour, grey and intimidating. It was also drizzling in that niggling way rain has of annoying you. So Jerzy and I hurriedly returned to our bolthole in the cellar. I'm exhausted but my belly is quite full for a change. We're grateful to Anielewicz. Feeding us is probably the only way he can show his appreciation for the risks we've taken. I'm sure he doesn't see it as a bribe. We don't. On the way back, we saw Janka talking to an SS guard, and he saw us.

22nd February

We both slept most of yesterday. Our nocturnal errand for Anielewicz must've taken a lot out of us. I don't just mean the physical exertion but also the anguish and fear, even more so than when we're smuggling vegetables for Mr Big. This morning, my faithful companion and I rummaged around the ghetto. Then we went to see the boss again.

He informed us there would be another run tonight, and that we should return later.

We're starting to have that hollow, empty stomach feeling again. The food at Mila Street is now a distant (though very pleasant) memory. Maybe we'll soon see again the inside of the bunker. Perhaps we'll be allowed to fight when the time comes. I think those brave young Jewish men and women in the ghetto will teach the cowardly Nazis a lesson they won't forget in a hurry."

That was the final entry in Mordechai's neatly written diary. It is impossible to know precisely what happened to him. But we have every reason to assume that 22nd February 1943 was the zealous young diarist's last day on Earth. His fate at the hands of the Nazis is unknown to us, as is the terror of his final moments. The tragedy of his death was the tragedy of six million Jews, including one and a half million children, during the black era of genocide that we know as the Holocaust.

On 19th April 1943, the Warsaw Ghetto uprising began. The Jewish resistance held off the massively superior, German assault for an incredible three weeks. Standing alone, desperately outnumbered and outgunned by tanks and artillery, these courageous young men and women gave the shocked assault troops, led by SS-Brig.Fhr Jürgen Stroop, a seriously bloody nose.

The outcome, however, was sadly inevitable. Anielewicz and over one hundred of his brave young comrades died fighting to their last breath in the Mila Street bunker. Many thousands of Jews were killed during the savage onslaught. The survivors were either executed on the spot or transported to the death camp at Treblinka. Only the glowing flames of the burning ghetto remained as a beacon to the heroic Jewish stand against Nazi tyranny.

Below the Borscht Belt

FATE CAN sometimes deal a sorrowful hand. Look, I am just a mere human being. I cannot be expected to fathom the reasons for life's little mysteries. But there it is. The dealer shuffles the pack and every player in the game has to pick up the cards.

★ ★ ★

Some forty or so years back I spent a working summer vacation in North America. It's a long time ago, middle of the Swinging Sixties, the era of the Beatles, the Rolling Stones, Freddie and the Dreamers and Helen Shapiro! A year earlier I had graduated from London University with a law degree. Having completed my professional exams, I was waiting to start my practical training with a law firm.

Before that, a long, hot, paying holiday stretched out alluringly ahead of me. Finally, I was at liberty, free of the study regime, released from the fretful shackles of midnight oil. I was like a newborn butterfly emerging from its constricting cocoon, eager to taste some freedom by soaring skywards to the sun. It was a real chance to unwind, to do something completely different. So what was that crazy something completely different? Well, it was eight weeks waiting at table at one of the strictly kosher hotels in the then fashionable, and now legendary, Borscht Belt, that expanding waistline of Jewish resorts in the Catskill Mountains, west of New York.

A law degree, even a good one, does not necessarily qualify you to lay and serve properly a table for ten to twelve people. Nonetheless, at Meir's, the highly efficient management expected absolute precision. Not a shiny knife, fork or spoon was to be out of place.

"If I see just one piece of cutlery off beam, you'll be washing up for the next two months!" warned an all-knowing, all-seeing Mr Goldman, known as Mr G, the superficially militaristic but basically fair and benevolent maître d'. After a morning's instruction alongside my other male colleagues, mostly Jewish students from America's Ivy League colleges, I was let loose on my first victims … sorry, guests.

Many came straight in to lunch from their various activities, including swimming in the pool, boating on the lake and horse riding or hiking in the surrounding hills. Well, I suppose in reality that accounted for about five percent of the clients! The remainder entered the spacious and elegantly chandeliered dining room from other pursuits, largely sunbathing, sleeping or schmoozing on the comfy steamer chairs in the extensive, beautifully landscaped gardens or around the pool area.

Each of the waiters had the elaborate needs of two tables, some twenty diners, to satisfy impeccably. I guess I was lucky compared to some of the other guys, who had a real handful of, let us just say, buoyant Brooklyn youngsters to handle. At first, my tables comprised mostly more mature guests, a top Manhattan lawyer, two accountants and a psychiatrist, with a smattering of delightful bubbehs and zaydehs and a couple of well-behaved teenagers. Mr G had explained that, if we looked after our tables "nicely", we could expect some truly excellent tips. Modesty aside, I think everyone on my tables liked me and considered that I served them well … "for a novice".

"You're really sweet, honey," Mrs Rosenberg, who was a lively eighty-one years young, a widow and long-stay guest, whispered to me as I served her chicken soup with lokshen and kreplach on my second night at work. "And a lawyer, noch …" ("Well not quite yet, Mrs Rosenberg.") "If I were a few years younger, sweetheart …" she added, winking naughtily and pinching my cheek so that I almost spilled the hot soup over her shlaffing brother. Mr Dorffman, one of the accountants, could not sit close to the table because his gargantuan belly, bloated with a lifetime's intake of mile-high pastrami sandwiches and thousands of root beers, heavily intervened. His wife kept exhorting him, with surreptitious nudges at a well-cushioned ribcage, to wipe his greasy chins, all three or four of them. And Mrs de Sousser, the attorney's blindingly bejewelled spouse, offered to find her blushing young waiter, "a good shidduch, no problem".

A few weeks later, two guests arrived that especially intrigued me. Mr Rozansky sat stooped in his wheelchair at one of my tables. He must have suffered from what we now know as Alzheimer's, but was then a degenerative enigma to the medical profession. His thin strands of white hair straggled around features that at one time, I felt certain, had been handsome and distinguished. His body, now wracked by the cruel ravages of his condition, was doubtless a sad shadow of what Mr Rozansky had once been. By his side sat a young woman, his granddaughter, who was probably a couple of years younger than me. Her name was Sophie. She was slim and attractive, with a wan, heart-shaped face, long dark hair and matching lashes shading innocent, azure eyes. I put her pale complexion down to the stress of a constant and unwavering care and attention that she lavished on her elderly charge. But when she smiled shyly at me, I sensed a profound melancholy in her. Often, I would observe Sophie from the kitchen's batwing doors as, with loving tenderness, she helped her father to eat.

⋆ ⋆ ⋆

At night, in my tiny attic room in the functional staff accommodation, I lay awake in bed and thought about Sophie and her grandfather. I really admired the remarkably attentive way in which she looked after the old man, unstintingly, without any indication of sacrifice, always beside him, tending to his needs, talking to him and holding his hands beneath the cool, tall trees in the hotel's immaculately manicured grounds. I really wanted to learn more about her. During my first few days in the job, the hotel's management had discovered that I could string a few written sentences together reasonably grammatically. So I was put in charge of compiling and distributing the daily activities schedule for the guests.

Each day's social events always included a one-hour cabaret after dinner. Almost invariably, there was a male crooner, a trio of sequined female singers, a heimische comedian and a magician, acrobat or juggler of some sort. Performers changed every fortnight, unless they "died" prematurely on the stage of the hotel's banqueting suite.

Following the show, the serried rows of chairs would be rearranged around tables by the wall. And a resident dance band heralded the evening's principal and highly popular entertainment. Then everyone eagerly awaited 10 o'clock, when huge platters of sandwiches, gateaux and pastries were brought in, together with hot and cold beverages. Older guests, more taken with playing cards in the games room or schmoozing in the spacious lounges, stampeded into the ballroom at the first tempting whiff of lox, gateaux, cream pastries and coffee. Never had I seen such nocturnally athletic octogenarians.

Part of the young waiters' duties was to attend these jolly festivities – hair smartly brushed and combed, and wearing mandatory white shirt and dark slacks – and to invite single ladies, of whatever age, ability and appearance, to trip the light fantastic. I knew that Sophie and her grandfather ventured routinely into the ballroom after dinner. The old man seemed to enjoy the music whilst scrutinising dancers swirling around the floor. It was the only time I detected any hint of emotion on his otherwise rigid features. Sophie, pallid as ever, appeared to delight in his obvious gratification as she sat loyally and quietly by his side. I stood on the sidelines with my fellow student "gigolos", watching her with a certain feeling that I had never experienced before.

I saw her fumble in a bijou, silver-coloured handbag and withdraw a small tin box. Opening it, she plucked out what looked like a tiny white pill and swallowed it. It was quite warm in the room, and the air conditioning could barely cope. I was concerned that she might have a headache. I threaded my way to her through the tangled knots of swaying dancers.

"Are you okay, Miss Jacobs?" I enquired, a little diffidently.

Sophie looked up at me, surprised at my sudden appearance, and I noticed a tear pearl on her cheek.

"I-I'm fine," she responded, unconvincingly, dabbing her face with a lacy handkerchief.

"Are you sure?" I pressed gently.

"Yes, I'm fine, really … and it's all right for you to call me Sophie, you know," she said, confidently recovering her composure.

"In that case, would you like to dance … Sophie?"

Glancing at her grandfather, and assured that he appeared comfortable and content, she nodded, allowing me to take her hand.

We rocked to a Beatles' number in that modern manner of touch-me-not dancing. She moved with a good rhythm, her slender frame, in its short black cocktail dress, tilting to and fro in tune with the music; though I suspected she did not have the opportunity to dance very often. It was difficult for us to converse in competition with a noisy band, so I just kept grinning at Sophie, probably quite inanely. She smiled back, but there seemed to be more than a little effort involved. Perhaps she was bored with me already. Maybe she did not like me. Was I nuts or something? She did not know anything about me. Apart, that is, from my job serving her with chopped liver, roast chicken, salt beef and latkes or warm apple strudel and parve ice cream. Though I was fully aware that she did not eat very much of anything.

We apparently dashing, young dance-partners were expected to circulate amongst all the unattached women, without favouritism. But Mr G was not in evidence so, when the band took a well-earned break, I took Sophie's arm.

"It's becoming so heady in here. Would you like to go into the garden for a while?"

She quickly withdrew her wrist from my gentle grasp.

"Thanks for the dance," she said, starting to walk away. "But I've got to get back to my Pops. He's not particularly good today."

I did not want her to leave.

"I know," I responded, as sympathetically as I could. "But he seems to be reasonably okay at the moment. Maybe Mrs Rosenberg can keep an eye on him for ten minutes. Please, Sophie, I'd like to talk with you for a while."

She glanced at her grandfather, who seemed to be sleeping peacefully. Sitting next to him was my eighty-one-year-old admirer. Sophie turned back to me.

"Wait," she said. "I'll have a word with her."

A short while later I could see the old lady nodding. Sophie was pointing at me. Mrs Rosenberg threw me an air kiss and, when the young girl's back was turned, followed it with a naughty wink.

Sophie and I emerged into the luxuriant garden and strolled across the lawn towards a bench seat at the lakeside. A full moon illuminated the fragrant night, its large silver disc reflected in the luminescent water. Cicadas chattered in the bougainvillaea; and wafting to us on the soft, lulling breeze were the renewed but muted sounds of the sixties. We sat in silence for a time, absorbing the sublime beauty of the late evening yet struggling maybe to read each other's thoughts. When Sophie spoke at last she did not look directly at me. She peered intently at the lake as if the glimmering water might reveal some of life's hidden answers. The young girl told me her story briefly and without emotion, and it almost made me want to cry.

"My parents were killed in a car crash during my first year at college," she began. "They were Holocaust survivors, the only survivors with my maternal grandfather of their families in Poland. They came to America after the war … my mother was pregnant with me at the time. I was the only child. We lived, the four of us, in a large apartment in Manhattan. My father and Pops were in business together for many years. We had lots of very good friends but to the best of our knowledge, no other living relatives. When my parents died, I needed to give up my studies to look after my grandfather. No, that's not right … I wanted very much to care for Pops. He was, is, a lovely, kind and gentle man. I couldn't bear to see him in a home."

I let Sophie relate her story without interruption. She spoke calmly and evenly, but I sensed in her an undercurrent of loss, pain and sadness. I could barely think how to reply.

"I'm so sorry, so very sorry," I mumbled self-consciously when she had stopped speaking. "It seems so inadequate to say just that, but …"

Sophie put her hand on my arm.

"Don't say any more, please … there's no need," she said.

For all sorts of confused reasons whirling around my head

that night, I wanted to enfold her in my arms and kiss her lips with all the tender warmth I could muster. But I did not attempt to embrace her because not only did I feel inhibited but also, deep within me, I felt that a piece of the jigsaw was missing.

I was about to add something, I cannot recall what, when Sophie looked hurriedly at her wristwatch and apologised for having to leave me. She walked quickly up the grassy slope to the bright lights of the hotel. I followed her at a discreet distance, knowing for sure she did not want me to catch up. When finally I reached the lobby area, I saw Sophie waiting with her grandfather for the elevator. I hung back and, just before the lift doors closed on them, I spotted Sophie pushing another pill into her mouth.

Compiling the social listings did not relieve me of waiting at table. In a way, I was becoming ambivalent about this. I knew that I wanted to see Sophie as often as possible, even if we did not speak to each other. On the other hand, and this might seem strange, I wondered whether my proximity while serving could be of concern to her. I suppose I was just perplexed. I cannot explain why, but I asked Mr G if I could exchange tables with one of the other waiters. Almost instantly I regretted my request and was relieved when he refused it. For the next few days, but without much heart, I served my guests at breakfast, lunch and dinner, drew up the activities timetables and acted out my gigolo role at night. Not once did Sophie acknowledge my existence. I was desolate.

The eagle-eyed Mr G had little difficulty noticing my evident lack of enthusiasm. After lunch one day, he took me aside.

"Look, I don't know what's going on inside that clever little head of yours. And you probably have no wish to tell me. But you're to buck up your ideas, okay? Your guests just adore the English accent. You're a conscientious worker, and I've no problems there. But you need to smile more, like when you started here. If you're miserable, the clients are miserable. That's not good business. I'm sure you understand what I'm saying. We're here to give the paying customers what they want. Smiley faces. That's what they want. And that's just what they're gonna get! I'll be watching you …"

I had been duly reprimanded and warned to pull my socks up. I slunk away with my tail between my legs. That night, as I showered, groomed myself and dressed to wait at dinner, I vowed to forget about Sophie and concentrate on the job for which I was getting paid. She did not seem very interested in me, anyway. My friend and colleague Saul, a Harvard law student, had a shrewd idea about what might be getting to me. As we strolled together from the staff quarters to the hotel dining room, he laid an arm across my shoulders.

"Take my advice," he said earnestly. "You don't want to get romantically involved with a guest, however attractive she is."

I stopped and stared at him.

"But …" I began. Saul did not allow me to finish.

"No 'buts'! Listen to me. Just don't do it. I speak from painful experience. I tried it on last year at another hotel, in Miami. She was quite a stunner. But what did I get out of it? I'll tell you. A severe talking to from irate parents, a lost job and a geltless vacation!"

I could hear what Saul was saying but I was not really listening. That night, I bombarded my two tables with smiles, big smiles, wide smiles, beaming smiles. Mrs Rosenberg was so happy she even pinched my toches, the wicked old woman. But Sophie did not even acknowledge my presence. Why should she? She would not even look at me when reading out her selections from the menu. Undeterred, I continued flooding my table with endless smiles, just like Mr G wanted. I was earning my pay and keep. But, somehow, I knew my pretence could not be maintained.

In the ballroom that evening, I spotted Sophie wearing a short red dress. She was sitting in her usual place talking quietly to her grandfather. I knew what I wanted to do, but doubted my courage. As the band started playing a slow number, with its shapely female singer vocalising the love ballad, I hesitantly crossed the floor and asked Sophie to dance. To my surprise, she agreed at once.

"As time goes by …" she said, with an odd kind of unsettling laugh as we stepped onto the dance floor. I held her as close as I dared. I did not want to frighten her away again.

"What do you mean?" I asked.

"Nothing really," she replied, gazing at the svelte chanteuse. "I was just thinking about the song she's singing. But never mind."

I looked at Sophie quizzically.

"But what's so amusing?"

She chuckled and shook her head, fanning her hair around slender shoulders. Before I could say any more, the music ended. She turned to go back to her seat. I went to take her arm but she moved away.

"I wanted you to have one more dance with me," she said, enigmatically.

"Why only one?" I responded whimsically, as other dancers rapidly vacated the floor.

Of course, it was almost feeding frenzy time. Sophie's bright blue eyes seemed to glaze over as she stared at me.

"Please don't ask me to dance again, please …"

I felt a firm hand suddenly grip my shoulder. I swivelled round to find myself confronting a red-faced Mr G.

"Come to my office!" he fumed, but in a controlled kind of way. "And make that right now!"

I packed and left Meir's early the next day. There was a sort of vacuum in my stomach as I boarded the Greyhound bus back to New York. And it was nothing to do with a missed breakfast.

As we sped along the state highway, I gazed darkly through the rain-spattered window. Memories were already starting to take shape.

* * *

Some seven years later, I bumped into Saul at an international lawyers' conference in London. I barely recognised him. He'd lost a considerable amount of hair but, by way of compensation, had gained quite a substantial girth. We arranged to meet one evening, for a quiet drink and a slice of nostalgia, in the bar of the Park Lane Inter-Continental Hotel, where Saul was staying. After some light-hearted ribbing and reminiscing about our shenanigans in the Borscht Belt, I said:

"Remember that pretty girl at Meir's?"

Saul was pensive for a few moments.

"You know the one …" I went on. "Sophie … the girl with the ailing grandfather in the wheelchair. I really had this thing about her."

Saul picked up his chunky crystal glass and drained the remaining malt whisky in one gulp.

"Yes, I do," he replied, thoughtfully.

"And?" I enquired, expectantly.

Still gripping his empty glass, Saul sank further into the deep leather armchair.

"I'm afraid Sophie died," he murmured, lowering his eyes. "I'm sorry."

I was stunned. How could this be?

"When? Why? How?" I blurted in quick succession, whilst my memory scrolled on fast rewind to the nineteen sixties.

"It happened almost seven years ago," Saul said quietly. "Mr G told me when I turned up for work the summer after you left, somewhat prematurely as I recall."

Questions tumbled from my mouth again.

"But how? Why? Was it an accident?"

Seeing that I was clearly shaken by the news, my old Catskills' pal sat up, leaned forward and buried my hands in his chunky grasp.

"No, it wasn't an accident. Actually, she was dying when you met her at Meir's. You may have spotted her popping pills ..."

I nodded slowly, still unable to comprehend fully. As Saul aptly ordered some more stiff drinks from a passing waiter, I pondered the tragic irony of misconstrued headaches, anxieties about caring for a sick old man and the adverse effects of stuffy ballrooms.

"Sadly, Sophie had been diagnosed with a rare and incurable condition," Saul went on.

"Apparently, the fatal diagnosis was made just a few weeks before she took her seat at your table."

Many more questions formed up in my head. Only one emerged.

"But why did she come to the hotel?"

Saul shook his head and rubbed his eyes. I thought he was going to start sobbing.

"She was a very courageous young lady," he said. "And she didn't want to deny her beloved Pops his annual vacation. In his deteriorating world, she knew how much he had looked forward to the holiday."

I wanted to scream out loud, but merely made a simple enquiry.

"When exactly did she die, Saul?"

"She'd been given around six months by her medical advisers. Sophie passed away in December sixty-five."

After a pause, and as the double whiskies arrived, I asked Saul whether he knew anything of the grandfather's fate.

"Yeah, I do. I learned later that the old man had lingered on for some two years or so after Sophie died. Pops passed away peacefully in a home for the aged and infirm in New York."

* * *

All this happened a long time ago now and oceans of water have passed beneath the proverbial bridge. But whenever someone mentions the Catskills, though they seldom do nowadays, I think of a pretty and plucky young girl and the losing hand of cards she was dealt by fate. Whatever deep emotions she had engendered in me those many years past have been gradually diluting to a fond memory … as time goes by.

Skin deep

WE SUCCEEDED in landing on a heath in North West London on a dry and moonless night. There were three of us in the crew. Happily, we all survived the rare, technical failure that had forced us down. We buried the ship, which, fortunately, was totally intact. My two colleagues and I agreed to return to the landing spot when we had managed to configure a vital replacement part to get us home.

I should tell you that we possess the morphing ability to adopt the mindset, verbal communication and outward appearance of any living creature. So it was fairly straightforward to transform ourselves into human beings. Actually, the three of us quite admired the handsome, male, twenty-something, physical entities into which we had transmogrified. Before leaving our ship, we had quickly manufactured, and put on, the clothes our onboard computers had advised as suitable for our Earth age, time and location. Afterwards, we made our way down from the dark common, finally ending up in a place called Hendon.

We were lucky enough to find accommodation almost immediately, the three of us sharing a converted, first floor flat in a large detached house. My two colleagues easily found work in a local supermarket. I acquired a job in a local kosher delicatessen. Most of my time was taken up shlepping (good Yiddish, eh?) heavy boxes to the storeroom, making sure the shelves in the shop were fully stacked and helping customers to carry purchases to their vehicles.

One morning, when I was bending down to put Mrs Goldstein's bags into the boot of her Chelsea tractor, she squeezed my bottom.

"You've got a lovely toches, Michael," she said.

Then she smiled in an odd kind of way and stuffed a five-pound note into my hand. The next day, as I stooped to place a cardboard box full of goods into a customer's Volvo, I said: "Do you think I've got a lovely toches, Mrs Cohen?"

All she gave me was a look that could've killed, before she adjusted her sheitl, leapt into the driver's seat and slammed the car door. I really didn't understand why she'd refrained from squeezing my bottom.

During my lunch breaks, I was allowed to eat some food from the deli counter. When I got back to my friends at night, I told them they had to try some gefilte fish with chrayn.

It tasted really fantastic. I loved the schmaltz and pickled herrings, and the smoked salmon and cream cheese on bagels. One evening, I bought some fried fish balls and chopped herring, a rye bread, a jar of heimische cucumbers and a large wedge of apple strudel, and took the lot back to the flat. My mates were ecstatic, demolishing the kosher goodies in very short order. Then and there, we decided that we just had to become Jewish. We borrowed some books from the local public lending library and read them from cover to cover. Then we looked closely at each other's lower bodies, winked and finally assented in unison.

Believe me, circumcision is no big deal for an adult with a morphing skill. Anyway, I think I look Jewish. You know, I have this appearance of a nice, clean-cut Jewish boy. And my boss Stan never even suspected to the contrary. I always cycled to work sporting a bright yellow baseball cap; and I wore it all day. He must have thought that I was a real frummer (hey, I'm getting to speak this Yiddish like a true chassid). Our landlord was Jewish, as normally were his tenants, so we already had mezuzahs on our doorposts. We weren't earning very much, so that was quite useful.

One day Stan asked what a good-looking, intelligent Jewish lad like me was doing humping in a deli. I told him that I was in my gap year before going up to Leeds to study law (I'd heard a kvelling customer drool this about her son). Stan wanted to know why I wasn't going to Thailand. I thought he meant Tie Land, a designer men's boutique in Golders Green selling shirts and neckwear. (That's before I knew Thailand was a country in the Far East, you understand.) So I said that I never liked wearing ties. My boss stared at me like I was some kind of shlemiel and shook his head. I bet he soon reappraised his view that I was an intelligent young man. I hoped this rethink would put him off considering me as a potential shidduch for his daughter. (Actually, Susan was a really pretty girl, studying for her A-levels at the time.)

Later, when I was better informed about "gap" years, I mentioned to Stan that I couldn't afford to take a year off before university to travel the world; what with fees, board and lodging, student loans and suchlike. I needed to make a few quid before starting my law studies. He was a kind and sympathetic bloke, my boss. When he heard my story, he gave me a raise. At some point, he enquired what synagogue my family belonged to. With one of my skilfully produced, sad looks, I replied that I was an orphan with no known relatives here. After he'd upped my wages again, I spent some time thinking about what might prompt further increases. I believe he was beginning to twig that I wasn't such a shlemiel after all. In all fairness, though, I felt that he really liked me a lot.

As Passover approached, we became frantically busy in the shop. In fact, it was chaotic … a real gevalt! Everything had to be changed around, cleaned and prepared for the incoming Pesach products. Customers had started asking about them several weeks beforehand. Would we stock milk? What would be our prices for matzah? I'd read thoroughly about the subject and endeavoured to instil some enthusiasm into my roommates about the forthcoming festival. They took some convincing about cleaning and clearing the flat of chametz and changing the crockery and cutlery. But then, of course, they spent most of their time with Gentiles.

"You're forgetting who you are," I admonished them.

"Are you crazy?" they screamed at me, with cynical grins. "We're flipping aliens, don't you know!"

"Where are you going first Seder night, Michael?" Stan asked as we were closing up one evening just before Pesach.

I'd intended to persuade my fellow spacemen to have a service in the flat. I'd even visited the Judaica emporium in Brent Street and bought three Haggadahs, the book that tells the story of the Israelites' Exodus from Egypt. But on rapid reflection, I satisfied myself that my colleagues wouldn't be at all keen. Whilst the guys enjoyed salt beef and latkes, and all the traditional kosher fare, they weren't so enthusiastic about the religious aspects of being Jewish. I think they were being pulled by influences at the supermarket.

Anyhow, I told Stan that I had no plans, as yet.

"You must come to us," he insisted at once. "And I won't take no for an answer. Is that clear, Michael?"

What could I do, but accept his kind offer.

"Just one thing," he added, gazing disapprovingly at my bright, sporty headgear. "I don't care if it's soldered to you skull, but please come to my home with a proper kippah instead of that monstrosity! I really can do without someone looking like a canary at my Seder table. And come to think of it, maybe you should also pay a visit to Tie Land."

The chutzpah of the man, I thought. For crying out aloud, Stan was already talking to me like a potential father-in-law! If only he knew, I sighed.

I'd not appreciated that Susan was Stan and Hillary's only child. It was abundantly clear that they loved her dearly and were so very proud of her. There were eight of us around the table on that first Seder night at their detached Hendon home, including four grandparents. There was Stan's Mum and Dad, Alice and Harvey; and the maternal bubbeh and zaydeh were Doreen and Morris. They were lovely, heimische people, very feisty for their ages and still doing knees-ups, they informed me proudly, at their various evergreen clubs and day centres. And they were all marvellously friendly towards me, the stranger in their midst.

As her Dad began reciting the first part of the Haggadah, I noticed Susan stealing little approving glances in my direction. I pretended not to see, burying my head in the book. But without being too immodest, I did look quite smart in my new, dark blue suit, crisp white shirt, red and blue striped, silk tie and black skullcap. Even Stan barely recognised the shlepper when he opened the street door to me. Once, I spotted Hillary smiling inanely at her daughter as Susan stole a quick peep at the well-turned-out young man across the table. What had I let myself in for?

As customary, being the youngest present, Susan recited the Mah Nishtanah, four questions relating to the Exodus. She actually sang the Hebrew words; and everyone around the table, including me, was very moved by her soft, sweet voice. When she'd finished, Susan looked up and peeked shyly at me. Occasionally, we'd enjoyed brief conversations in the deli and I'd sensed a gentle, warm personality. Now I lobbed my best manly smile at her, and nodded my admiration for her performance. She smiled back and lowered her eyes. For the first time, I saw how truly beautiful she was. I had to confess to myself that I'd suddenly experienced a very strange feeling.

During the meal, which was absolutely scrumptious, I was bombarded with queries from the curious grandparents. I thought that on Seder night there were only supposed to be four questions; and they'd been asked already. The grandparents must've been told about my parental loss. So they struggled to steer fairly sensitively around the subject in case they might upset me.

"Have you always lived in this area, Michael?" Morris enquired politely.

This was a tricky one. I knew it could crop up, so I'd prepared a vaguely dismissive response.

"No," I replied. "I spent quite a few years in various institutions along the south coast. Everyone was very kind, of course, but I'd rather not talk about those times. I hope you'll understand."

My fellow guests nodded with suitable compassion, tucking into their chicken dinners.

Harvey withdrew a well-sucked wishbone from his mouth and coughed.

"Where did your family come from originally?" he asked.

His wife Alice, eyes glaring, gave him a conspicuous nudge.

"Michael won't mind me asking, will you Michael?" Morris went on, apologetically, doubtless fearful of further spousal retribution.

"No, I don't mind you asking," I said. "In fact, they came from the same starting place your ancestors came from."

They took the bait.

"You mean Russia and Poland," Stan piped up, and everyone mouthed agreement.

In fact, I was thinking of stardust.

At the end of the evening (it was actually 12:30 in the morning), we said our goodbyes and I offered my sincere thanks for the kind and generous invite. Everyone shook my hand warmly, except Susan. At the front door, she put her hand on my arm and gave me a quick peck on the cheek. I was almost struck dumb. All I could blurt was:

"T-Thanks, Susan"; and then I scuttled off into the night.

I was working at the shop on the first day Chol Hamoed, the period between the first and last two days of Passover. It was amazingly busy. Stan had reduced prices to attract custom away from some of our trade rivals in the area. All I could hear from customers were the competitive statistics of their Seders.

"We had ten people around our table."

"Oh, we had fifteen round ours!"

"Really, my next door neighbour had twenty, yes twenty, guests."

"Well, my cousin in America had thirty last year!"

Then …

"We didn't finish 'til one o'clock in the morning."

"You don't say. We were up until two-thirty!"

"That's nothing. The rabbi's Seder went on another two hours, yet!"

As my ears filled with all this well-intentioned, Passover one-upmanship, one thought occurred to me. It's great to be Jewish! If only I knew more about it.

Back at the flat, problems had been developing. We were still working feverishly to fashion the requisite part to get our ship mobile again. But, that aside, my two colleagues had suddenly changed their attitude towards me, and towards their Jewish identity. In fact, one of their workmates at the supermarket was a member of an extreme rightwing, political party. He was unaware that his fellow shelf-stackers were "Jewish", and they didn't tell him. It came as a bombshell when, after work one night, my roommates advised me that they'd reversed their circumcisions. I confronted them.

"How can you believe the drivel these ignorant, bigoted, racist morons spout?" I lashed out.

They just ignored my outburst. I really didn't know how things were going to work out with them.

Susan assisted in the deli during Passover. So we got to talk a little more about our lives, and our hopes and plans for the future. I felt a terrible fraud having to lie to her about my terrestrial ambitions. And I really didn't want her to think of me in that special kind of way that I feared she was starting to think. She was proposing to embark on medical studies at university after her A-level results, which I knew would be brilliant. I believed she was anxious for me to ask her out on a date. So I needed to use some nimble, verbal footwork, if that doesn't sound too weird, to avoid the issue.

By now, we were putting the finishing touches to our concealed ship. It had been very difficult for us to locate and buy suitable components in London. We estimated a further week or so before completion of the work. It would be a dreadful wrench to leave Stan and all the other people I'd met during my time on Earth, especially Susan. But I was also missing my own family and friends back home.

Ten days later, in the middle of the night, I suddenly awoke in a cold, clammy sweat. I got up to make myself a hot drink, only to discover that my fellow crewmen had vanished. Frantic, I hastened to expose our hiding place for the vital part that we'd been meticulously manufacturing. It was gone, too. I dressed quickly, grabbed my bike and cycled swiftly to Hampstead Heath. I was too late. The ship had been re-launched. They'd left without me. I gazed up at the billions of stars glimmering in the clear night sky. I stared up at the astronomically distant specks of light until sunrise veiled them from my moist eyes.

On returning to the empty flat, I realised that I'd got an immediate and rational decision to make. If I could admit it to myself, I knew that I felt something akin to human love for Susan. I believed she also carried some deep feelings for me. But I'd watched a film on TV one evening, a movie called Fiddler on the Roof. In one scene, the character Tevye, a shtetl milkman, spoke the words, A bird may love a fish, but where would they make a home? I knew it was hopeless. I packed a suitcase and left the flat. I left Hendon, London and England.

Today I'm writing this from a long way away. Well, not so far away as my home planet, anyway. Actually, I'm learning at a yeshivah in Jerusalem. No one in Hendon knows that I'm in Israel. I wondered about sending a letter to Susan but decided against that. It would've been very unfair to her. I've been studying here for two years now. The Rosh Yeshivah, the head of this advanced Jewish studies academy, and my fellow yeshivah bochas have been very good to me. They don't ask questions about my past.

Every night, I study in my small room with my books. From time to time, I glance up through the tiny skylight to the twinkling stars. After a few moments, my thoughts return to the pages before me on my desk. I'm content … really. I've been accepted here for what I am or, rather, for what I've become.

Past, present and future

IN JUNE 1942, a great air and sea battle was fought near the Midway Islands in the central Pacific, about 1,800 kilometres north west of Hawaii. American navy planes, launched from US carriers, sunk four Japanese flat tops, the pride of the Imperial Fleet. It was payback time for the surprise attack on Pearl Harbor in December 1941. The naval combat, which became known as the Battle of Midway, was a turning point in the United States' war against Japan. That conflict ended finally with the dropping of atomic bombs on Hiroshima and Nagasaki in August 1945.

Midway was decided more than sixty years ago. There is no reason why I should ever have given it any special attention, beyond the general interest I have as a reader of books about the Second World War. But since a conversation I had with an elderly American Jew a few years ago, the battle often comes to mind.

I met Paul quite by chance in Tokyo. We happened to be staying at the same hotel in the glitzy, skyscraper district of Shinjuku. Late one evening, I was enjoying a quiet, post-prandial drink in one of the swanky bars on the hotel's forty-fifth floor. The views were staggering. I was mesmerised by the shimmering night vistas of the exciting Japanese capital revealed by the commanding, panoramic windows.

"Great view, isn't it?" remarked an unmistakably North American voice.

I looked up to see a tall, silver-haired man, probably in his mid-seventies.

"Mind if I join you?" he requested, jauntily. "My darling wife's just gone to bed … I think we did a bit too much touring for her today."

I smiled, nodded assent, mentioned that my spouse too had turned in early and indicated the vacant leather armchair on the other side of a low, smoked glass table.

We introduced ourselves and Paul placed his dry martini opposite my almost drained, old-fashioned tumbler of Suntory whisky.

"What are you drinking?" he asked.

I told him and, despite my gentle protests, he ordered another for me from the striking, split-skirted, cocktail waitress.

"This Japanese whisky is actually very good," I said. "Compares favourably with our Scottish equivalents."

The eye candy returned, substituted new for old and backed away with a demure bow. I noticed a small, gold Magen David, a Star of David, on Paul's jacket lapel and asked whether he was Jewish.

After clinking glasses in an implicit toast to our shared religion, and maybe also to mild hedonism, we glanced sideways to admire the city's rivers of glimmering neon far below.

Paul mentioned that he was a retired engineer. I gathered that, although he had spent much time over the years visiting Japan on business assignments, this was the first occasion his wife Shirley had accompanied him. In return, I said that I was a retired architect enjoying a first vacation in the land of the rising sun. It seemed inevitable that our conversation would turn eventually to the Second World War and the clash of two mighty nations in the Pacific. Having some interest in the history of that conflict, which ended in nemesis for Japan, I was intrigued to learn that my new companion had served with the US forces on Midway atoll.

"Oh no, I wasn't there during the famous Pacific battle," he said with a chuckle. "I would've been only about fifteen at that time and still at school."

He told me that he had worked for a year or so on Midway in the late 1940s, during the US occupation of Japan, before being posted to Korea. He had set up his own engineering company after leaving the Forces in the late 1950s.

"I helped maintain the airfields on the atoll," Paul said, in response to my question about his work on Midway. "But, when I wasn't on duty, I'd spend a lot of time just wandering around the perimeter of the tiny island or rowing out to its even more miniscule coral neighbours. Or I guess I'd be hanging loose, fishing, sunbathing, meditating and suchlike."

Paul took a sip of his drink and continued.

"You know, in the middle of a vast ocean, with just the sky, the waves and maybe a few seabirds for company, you sort of discover, or perhaps have revealed to you, things about yourself and about life in general. The kind of things you may never have thought about before. I guess it must've been a bit like that for our forefathers in the desert of Sinai, kind of strange and mystical."

I nodded while Paul picked up his drink.

Before he put the glass to his lips, he said:

"You know at that time I could actually see into the future."

I had been talking to Paul for a while, and I felt that I was getting to know him reasonably well. I was taken with his honesty, frankness and sincerity of expression. To say the least, I was amazed by what he had just observed in a characteristically level tone and down-to-earth manner. I noticed the hint of a sparkle in his eyes. I imagined that he was measuring the effect his last few words were having on me. I gulped a mouthful of whisky and leaned forward, my body language working overtime.

"You could actually see into the future?" I repeated, almost robotically, and doubtless with puzzlement and scepticism masking my face. "How do you mean, Paul?"

My newfound friend stared at me.

"Yep, I could see into the future," he confirmed with a swing of his silver-haired head.

Before I could press him further, he held up his hands. It looked as if he was surrendering in some way, or maybe just preventing me from making a fool of myself.

"I really could see into the future," he went on. "But not necessarily in the way you may be thinking about."

Paul grinned artfully.

"You see, to the west of the Midway Islands is an imaginary boundary," he explained. "I'm sure you know about the International Date Line."

I nodded, thoughtfully.

"It's a modification of the 180th meridian that marks the difference in time between east and west. The date is put forward a day when you cross the line going west, and back a day when you travel east. Look, I'm sorry if I gave you the mischievous impression that I was some kind of screwball seer with a crystal globe."

I looked at Paul and threw a smile that must have appeared coy.

"But it's true," he said, his eyes glinting. "As I gazed westwards from my vantage point on Midway, I was looking from today into tomorrow. Of course, you appreciate now that I'm speaking only in a fictitious sense … I was merely gazing into the endless sky and sea. But, technically, I'm unassailable."

Paul and I found that we shared a similar sense of humour

and enjoyed a good laugh together. We really warmed to each other, and our conversation continued unabated into the early hours. We ordered further rounds of drinks, and not only because we wanted to be pampered by the lissom Japanese waitresses.

Being informed by the past is good, wholesome and necessary. Sometimes, we need to consolidate and take stock of our lives and contemplate the future possibilities. It is easy to think about, or even to dwell upon, what has happened to us at earlier times in a negative way. Often it is more difficult for us to look ahead and to perceive something that may prove meaningful. On Midway, Paul had looked out into the "future" and had seen no more than an endless sky and an empty ocean. He was soon to tell me about the saddest time of his life, which prompted him to rethink his attitude towards what had been and what was to come.

Paul had met Shirley while he was stationed in Korea. As our drinks were replenished high above glittering Tokyo, I detected an increasingly emotional quality in Paul's voice.

"She was a young Jewish girl working as a nurse in the M.A.S.H. set-up," he said.

I gestured to indicate my knowledge of the acronym from watching the hilarious American TV series.

"We fell in love at the proverbial first sight. She was the dearest, most wonderful person I had ever met. That still stands, by the way. We married on our return to the States and were stationed at any army base on the West Coast."

Paul went on to tell me that they had had a child, a son, Ray.

"Unfortunately," he added, his eyes glassing slightly, "there were complications at the birth. As a result, the doctors advised that Shirley couldn't bear any more children. Although we weren't particularly religious, Shirley and I thanked the Almighty for our boy. We loved him more than life itself and Ray grew into a fine son."

Taking a handkerchief from his pocket, Paul wiped away the tears, apologising all the while for becoming maudlin. I reassured him as best I could, and he seemed to relax a little. I learned that, from a child, Ray had always wanted to become a navy pilot.

"I don't suppose you'll find that too surprising considering his formative years spent on military facilities," Paul observed. "Ray was a born flier and took to the heavens as an air cadet like a bird to the skies. In 1972, he was posted to the US fleet off Vietnam."

I had an uneasy feeling in my guts that I knew what Paul was about to tell me.

"In his last letter home from San Diego, Ray wrote about how much he loved us and missed us. And he thanked us for all the love and care we'd given him. He also said he was glad we hadn't smothered him, as an only child, with our love and affection. But had helped him to grow into an independent and confident human being."

Paul explained how Ray's aircraft had been hit on just his third sortie, that the plane had exploded in mid-air and that his boy would have died instantly.

We sat in silence for a while. Paul leaned back in the armchair, toying with his glass, his eyes closed. I stared down through the high wall of glass at the twinkling lights of the metropolis.

"I'm sorry for making you feel sad," Paul said. "Especially as you're on vacation. Please forgive me."

I waved my hands, a tad self-conscious at my inability to find some appropriate words of comfort and sympathy for my mid-night companion.

"Of course," he continued, "Shirley and I were devastated. We grieved for months, for years. The mind pain that wouldn't leave us affected our physical health. The medics finally insisted that we should take a long break. Even though I felt we couldn't really escape our anguish and the constant ache in our hearts, I left the business in the capable hands of my managers and rented a house on Hawaii."

Paul described how they had spent three months on that beautiful Pacific island.

"It gave us time to be together constantly," he said, softly. "We talked about Ray, his life and what he had meant to us, I suppose in an effort to keep him alive. But we gradually came to realise that dwelling on the tragedy is not what our boy would've wanted us to do. Our love for each other had been enriched by our son's love for us. That was a part of his legacy; so Shirley and I came to accept that we had the rest of our lives in front of us. I have to say that we'd become slightly more religious, though largely in a traditional sense. We hardly ever attended services in the synagogue. But we'd gone to see the rabbi when we first joined the community. Rabbi Feldman is a marvellous man. He perceived, rightly, that words of sympathy were less what we needed than confirmation that it was okay for Shirley and me to think about our future life together."

I more or less understood what I was being told. The minister appeared to have said no more than that Paul and his wife had a right to be happy, despite their terrible loss. And that this would not in any way detract from their love, and wonderful memories, of Ray, which would be cherished forever.

"I'll always remember what our rabbi told us," Paul mused. "He said, 'Being full of anticipation is what makes us happy … it gives us the ability to be glad. The trick is to look forward, not back.' We put great store by those very wise words."

Grim-faced, Paul told me that his son's remains were never recovered but that, every year, he and his wife visit the Vietnam War Memorial in Washington DC, where Ray's name is etched alongside those of thousands of his comrades who made the ultimate sacrifice.

Paul said: "We're certain that our boy would want us to be

glad, just like the rabbi told us. Glad in living constructive lives, trying to help others in our community who need assistance and looking forward to what remains of our time together."

* * *

Two days after I had met Paul, my wife and I flew home from the land of the rising sun. On the plane, I happened to read an article in the airline's glossy PR magazine about the great thinkers of the past. Among others, the author considered the existentialist Danish philosopher Søren Kierkegaard who once wrote, "Life can only be understood backwards, but it must be lived forwards."

Out of the depths

I WILL never forget that Pesach in Argentina. After many years in a wilderness without faith (for what I thought were good reasons), I found my salvation in a way that I could never have imagined. All this happened some years ago. I was visiting Buenos Aires on a combination vacation and business assignment (my Spanish is reasonably sound). This was my first time in the exciting tango capital of that huge South American country. It is a land of such endless grassy plains, cold parched deserts and desolate mountains, a terrain of such intense anonymity and emptiness that a man could, if he wished, easily lose himself, or maybe his soul, in its utter vastness.

The Big Apple was different. Although it is true that a man can also lose himself or his soul in such a great city, indeed in any unrestrained and magnetic metropolis, BA exuded vitality at its extreme, its people living life to the full twenty-four seven. I was intrigued to learn that the emotional tango itself is said to reflect the soul of the citizens, the porte nos. Perhaps in such a city a man could discover himself, or even reach inward to touch his very soul.

Outside of meetings, I immersed myself in this remarkably

cosmopolitan city's warm and friendly ambience, its tropical gardens, its sidewalk cafés, its smoky sensual dance clubs and the nightlife of the barrios, BA's distinctive cultural neighbourhoods. I was a single, youngish man without any familial responsibilities, in fact without any family at all. I was still struggling, more than twenty years after the end of the war, to come to terms with the murder of my grandparents, parents and siblings at the Nazi death camps in Poland. My mind painfully sought closure to the almost insurmountable guilt I harboured as a survivor of the Holocaust. "Say you're eighteen," a man in a soiled, striped tunic had whispered to me as I shuffled with hundreds of other exhausted and terrified Jews towards the selection ramp in Auschwitz-Birkenau. I was only fourteen years of age, but I was fairly tall and of reasonable build, despite years of malnutrition in the ghetto. I did what he said, and was chosen for work not immediate slaughter.

The strong religious belief in the Almighty that I had shared with my family perished with them in the gas chambers. How could the God of Israel allow this to happen? How could he who had saved the Israelites from oppression and slavery in Egypt, and led them to the Promised Land, stand back thousands of years later and permit the wholesale destruction of six million of Israel's children? Where was He when they prayed and wailed for deliverance and an Exodus from *their* suffering? I had lost my entire family and my faith; and I had not entered a synagogue for almost a quarter of a century.

During my stay in BA, I was aware that the festival of Passover was approaching. Despite my long, faithless years I could not eradicate knowledge of the earlier times of orthodox observance. In my travels around the city, which possessed a large and vibrant Jewish community, I had passed a number of kosher food stores, especially in the Villa Crespo district, selling matzot, the flat crisp unleavened bread, and other Pesach products. Many of the Jewish population had immigrated after the war, ironically alongside numerous Nazi war criminals escaping justice in Europe. I cannot explain why, but when I awoke in my hotel room on the Shabbos before the start of the coming Jewish festival, I fostered a compelling desire to attend a shul service.

My luxury hotel stood close by the famous Casa Rosada. From its balcony, Eva Perón had won the hearts and adulation of the descamisados, the "shirtless ones", massed in the broad Avenida de Mayo below. After the lavish buffet breakfast, which I later regretted taking too leisurely, I asked the concierge for directions to the nearest synagogue. Fortunately, there was (what he called) a "temple" not more than a few, palm-lined streets away. The old grid pattern of roads in the Centro made the building easy to find. As I turned the final corner, I donned a blue and white kippah that (inexplicably) I had purchased in the Jewish quarter the previous day. There before me rose up a grand, white-stoned, colonial-style edifice. Surrounded by a courtyard shaded with palm trees, the synagogue also boasted a perimeter of lofty, white-painted railings. High on the façade, above wide steps leading to a magnificent, pillared portico, a gold Star of David, emblem of Jews and Judaism, reflected the morning's brilliant sunshine from the centre of a circular, stained-glass window.

I spotted a man, short in height, wearing a light-coloured, linen suit and a panama hat, closing an iron-grilled gate in the railings. He took a key, held by a chain to his belt, the sign of an orthodox Jew wishing to uphold the prohibition against carrying items on the Sabbath, and appeared to be locking up. Surprised, I walked quickly towards him. He turned sharply as he sensed me approaching, a look of trepidation lurking in his small, searching eyes. As a Jew, I fully comprehended his security need to be aware of sudden movements in the immediate vicinity. After I had explained my purpose, the man's moon-shaped, swarthy face, impressed with a little black moustache, broke into a charming smile.

"I'm so sorry, my friend, but you are too late for the Shabbat service. We begin early here, because of the heat you understand, and usually finish at around eleven. I am the tail end Charlie, so to speak. I have the dubious honour, as the shammas of this temple, of securing it when everyone else has gone home."

I glanced at my wristwatch, and could scarcely believe it was ten minutes past eleven. "You have no need to apologise," I said. "I should've spent less time over coffee and newspapers at my hotel this morning."

We introduced ourselves more formally; and I discovered, in an amazingly few minutes, that Arthur Shumann was a retired engineer who, with his wife Freda, had fled to South America from Austria in 1937. They had two sons, both doctors, who lived with their families in the United States.

"Where are you having lunch today?" Seňor Shumann enquired suddenly.

His question took me unawares, and I started blurting embarrassing gibberish.

"You must eat with us, of course," he insisted, taking firm hold of my arm. "Come along now."

I felt like a culpable schoolboy being led by an irate teacher to the headmaster's study. So, rather submissively (and, truth to tell, quite happily), I accompanied the man along the tree-fringed boulevards beneath a blazing orb of intense radiance. Little did I know that this was the beginning of a short journey towards recovering my religious belief.

The spacious, air-conditioned apartment was on the second floor of a magnificent, art nouveau house, which stood opposite a luxuriant park. The dark, shaded interior of the palatial building afforded a welcome haven from the city's wearying humidity. Before inviting me inside his home, Arthur (as he insisted I address him) politely requested me to wait in the wide, coolly tiled corridor while he alerted his wife to the presence of a lunch guest. Freda (as, in turn, she urged me to call her) soon appeared, a petite, smiling lady in a floral-patterned dress. A blue silk snood covered her hair entirely. She greeted me on the threshold like a long-lost relative and drew me into a pleasant hallway. Arthur, who had replaced his panama with a black skullcap, led me into a large, elegant dining room where he proceeded to make Kiddush for his wife and me. It was, personally, a nostalgically emotional moment. Shafts of sunlight streamed into the room from a pair of French windows, on the other side of which a wrought iron balcony overlooked the park.

Arthur and I sat down at the long dining table, which was covered with an exquisitely embroidered tablecloth and already prepared for three people. Freda entered bearing tall glasses of welcomingly fresh lemonade, placed the tray on a sideboard and joined us at the table. The room was filled with antique furniture and gilt-framed landscapes hung from the walls. But my attention was caught instantly by a rather incongruous, and therefore particularly fascinating, pair of similarly framed, black and white portrait photographs suspended side by side above a graceful bureau. One of the pictures appeared to be of a middle-aged rabbi with a mottled beard, lofty black kippah and the hint of a tallit about his shoulders.

Startlingly, the other photo looked very much like others I had seen in books about the Second World War, especially those relating to submarines. It seemed to be the image of a young U-boat captain, sporting a grizzled beard, a high peaked cap bearing the wartime German navy's Kriegsmarine badge and displaying an Iron Cross medal at his throat. Hauntingly, I was attracted to the eyes; that is to say, the eyes of both the apparent rabbi and the naval officer. It is said that however much the human face changes with age, the eyes remain the same. I almost gulped with astonishment as it struck me, quite forcefully, that the two portraits were of one and the same individual. But how could that be? I pondered. My initial impression was probably wildly wide of the mark, the victim of a vivid imagination.

Arthur and Freda had clearly noted the peculiar expression I undoubtedly disclosed at that moment.

"I'm always telling him to take the naval one down," my hostess remarked, somewhat agitated, a look of mortification marring her still attractive features. "At best it's liable to create confusion and misconception. At worst, it can and has caused offence, especially to Jewish people, like you, who are not aware of all the circumstances."

From what Freda was saying, I had the inkling that my first thought was probably correct. I looked at Arthur, who was shaking his head.

"I cannot remove the naval one, you know that Freda," he responded with a deep sigh. "We've been through this so many times before. The two photographs would be meaningless separated."

Arthur turned to me, as if seeking support for his advocacy.

"Rabbi Karl Dieter is one of our dearest friends. It was, inspirationally, through him that I returned to Torah and Yiddishkeit."

I could barely understand what I was hearing. My profound curiosity must have been glaringly obvious to my hosts. Arthur took pity on me.

"Let's enjoy our lunch now, my friend," he said, smilingly. "If you wish, I'll be pleased to explain everything to you after we've eaten."

Freda was a marvellous cook. We ate an excellently prepared lunch, which was temptingly presented. I was genuinely profuse with my compliments for her hospitality and cuisine. But she insisted that I was far too generous for such a simple meal. She then apologised profusely for retiring to have her usual Shabbat afternoon siesta.

"I hope we meet again before you return home to England," she said finally, before leaving the room with the little wave of a delicate hand.

Her husband conducted me into a delightfully airy, adjoining space, which appeared to double as both a library and a sitting room. Here we settled into two comfortable, brown leather armchairs. A bottle of a malt whisky brand well known to me, and two old-fashioned tumblers, stood on the low, antique table between us.

"Would you like a drink while I tell you about my friend Karl?" Arthur asked, leaning forward to grasp the bottle.

I shook my head, thirsting more to hear the story.

"Do you mind if I have one?"

Again I shook my head, this time maybe a little too dogmatically. I regretted that my host might have sensed some rude impatience in my peremptory movement. But he merely grinned, quickly poured himself some of the honey-hued liquid and, gripping his heavy crystal glass, slowly sunk into his chair.

"I first met Karl about ten years back at a charity function here in Buenos Aires," Arthur began, swallowing a little of his whisky. "He was studying for his semichah, you know, to become a rabbi. Believe me, I was just as astonished as you are now to learn about this yeshivah bocha's background in the German navy during the war. Over lunch, you told me how your family perished at the hands of the Nazis. I think you were not so surprised to hear that most of mine had been similarly eliminated."

I nodded, and my host continued.

"At this moment, it may be very difficult for you to appreciate how I could befriend someone who had fought for Hitler's evil regime. And how I, as an irreligious Jew at that time, could have been influenced by such a person to rediscover my abandoned faith. But listen to the tale that Karl narrated at our second, pre-arranged meeting. He was sitting in the very same armchair you are occupying now."

I relaxed into its deep, luxury padding as Arthur went on.

"In late April 1945, Kapitan Karl Dieter was in command

of U-2576, on patrol under the Ionian Sea in the central Mediterranean. At twenty-six, he was one of the Kriegsmarine's youngest and most skilful submarine captains. There were not many left at that stage of the war. He had served in U-boats since the so-called Happy Time in 1942, when Grand Admiral Doenitz's wolf packs were decimating enemy shipping in the north Atlantic. But the advent of the convoy system, destroyer escorts, longer-range reconnaissance aircraft and other weapon and detecting improvements, eventually won the Battle of the Atlantic for the Allies. Karl knew that the war must end in defeat for Germany. American and British troops were deep inside his homeland; and Soviet armies were storming Berlin, where the Führer still raged in his Chancellery bunker. But when Karl had sailed from his base at Lorient, on the west coast of France, he was under clear orders to sink any enemy ships that he encountered on his assigned route.

"At midday on the 28th of April, when U-2576 was at periscope depth, the first watch officer sighted smoke on the horizon. Kapitan Dieter was completing the boat's log in his cramped cupboard of a cabin. Immediately, he ordered action stations and hastened to the control room. As captain, he acknowledged the sighting of an enemy steamer and registered its range, speed and bearing. As the distance shortened, Karl noted that the vessel's deck appeared to be packed solid with people. He deduced that a troopship had been intercepted, but requested a recognition check in the reference manuals. It was confirmed that, earlier in the conflict, the ship had been employed by the Italians to ferry soldiers to North Africa. Now that Italy had surrendered and joined the Allies, its merchant fleet was in enemy hands and thus liable to be sunk. Karl ordered a surface attack and the U-boat broke through the pounding waves beneath a leaden sky.

"A spread of two torpedoes was launched from the forward tubes. Karl stood on the bridge of the conning tower with his second in command, while two seamen in steel helmets manned the deck gun. Sea spray cascaded over the diesel submarine as its senior officers, in black waterproofs, observed the enemy ship through their heavy-duty, rubber-coated binoculars. Up through the open conning hatch came the shouted timings of the deadly silver fish, heading on course for contact with a steel-plated hull.

"Two explosions on the troop carrier, forward and amidships, sent towering plumes of flame and black smoke skywards. Karl heard boisterous cries emanating from within his boat, but felt strangely overcome with sadness, an emotion he had not experienced on his many, previously successful sorties. He raised his glasses to see the enemy ship lift itself out of the water, fold in the middle and break into two sections. The stern end sank first. A few seconds later, the bow slid quickly beneath the roiling ocean. The captain called for the U-boat to proceed to the spot where the transport had disappeared, though he did not expect to find any survivors. It would have been a cataclysmic end for those poor souls on board the doomed steamer.

"He was right. There were no survivors to be seen; though a large number of bodies floated like broken dolls amongst the debris of a drifting and spreading oil slick. As the U-boat glided slowly through the carnage, many of the dead appeared to be women. Karl sincerely regretted this, but he knew that army nurses and female, administrative staff were frequently transported alongside the soldiers. As he stared down from the high conning tower at the blackened corpses, he grew very disturbed. Amongst the burned and contorted bodies, he noticed that some were those of children."

Arthur stopped speaking, obviously affected by what he was now relating to me. He drained the whisky in his glass and poured another, even larger measure than earlier. He downed the spirit in one giant gulp, and filled up again. It seemed as if he wanted to drown himself in the golden liquid. I watched him with growing anxiety, but I was completely absorbed by the story. I could never have guessed where it was leading.

After a short, silent pause, Arthur took up where he had left off.

"With the U-boat's engines ordered to be stopped, Karl spotted a small, wooden chest bobbing in the debris strewn water. He commanded one of the gun crew on deck to fish the box out and take it below. The helmeted rating grabbed a long, metal boat hook attached to the side of the tower and pulled the object out of the sea. That evening, in the privacy of his compact quarters, the captain forced open the locked chest. Inside, protected from exposure to the water, was what Karl much later discovered to be a Sefer Torah, a hand-written scroll of the Five Books of Moses, the essence of the Jewish religion, sheathed within a red velvet mantle."

My face doubtless revealed my shocked reaction. Arthur beamed.

"Wait, my friend," he said, knowingly. "There is more. Much more."

This time he took only a sip of his whisky, as he resumed.

"Karl was quite puzzled by his find. And, because of the unusual presence of children on what was supposed to be a troopship, he began to question the true nature of the vessel he had torpedoed. In the next few days, he learned of Hitler's suicide; and that the war had ended with Germany's unconditional surrender.

"Ignoring the victors' demands that German naval units at sea should surrender at the nearest Allied or neutral port, Karl, with the agreement of his forty-nine crew members, scuttled the U-boat close to the Turkish coast on a moonless night. The seamen rowed ashore in the sub's inflatable dinghies and split up, each sailor facing his own personal destiny. Karl, a single man whose family had been killed in the incendiary bombing of

Hamburg, decided that there was little left for him in defeated Germany. He resolved to make for South America, though he hardly realised the problems he would face. With him on the cold, wave-battered shores of Anatolia that black, menacing night were his meagre belongings, hastily bundled into a seaman's sack. Amongst his few possessions was the Torah manuscript, which he had salvaged from the bloody waters of the Mediterranean.

"To cut the story shorter, as they say, Karl did eventually make it to South America, to Brazil in fact, via a crew job on a Panamanian-registered merchant ship out of Lisbon. It was the summer of 1946 when he eventually found himself in Buenos Aires. During the following months, having a talent for languages, he learned Spanish quickly. He found work with an import-export company, and rented a tiny apartment in the harbour area of the city. It was during this period that he discovered, to his utter surprise, that he possessed a Sefer Torah. But, to his deep dismay, he also learned the nature of the cargo that the steamer it had come from was actually carrying."

At this juncture, Arthur asked whether I would like a cold drink. I thanked him and he fetched me a fresh glass of lemonade from the kitchen. I certainly needed to be refreshed. After settling himself back in his armchair, my host gulped some more whisky (he could certainly take his liquor) and resumed his narrative.

"At his employer's office, Karl happened to alight on a copy of an official report of shipping sunk by German U-boats in the Mediterranean. He was devastated to read that the ship he had torpedoed was carrying eight hundred and fifty civilians. And he was even more stricken to note that all the passengers were Jewish refugees, including some rabbis, from Eastern Europe. The steamer he had destroyed had sailed from a port on the north west coast of Yugoslavia. Its destination was Palestine, in an illegal attempt to breach the British blockade of its mandated territory.

"Karl has urged me to believe that he and his family had never been anti-Semitic; and that they had never been aware of the Nazi's extermination camps. Knowing him now as I do, I accept what he says without question. He is a good man. His family, like many others, had felt helpless against National Socialism's increasingly oppressive rule. Karl had been called to fight for his country, and he could not refuse. He has told me repeatedly that he and his family had felt constant and deep shame, and guilt, for allowing the Nazis to attain and hold power. But it was not the feelings of shame and guilt that influenced the future course of his life here in Argentina.

"Karl became desperately depressed by what he had discovered. His work suffered and he lost his job. Surviving on the meagre income from casual employment, he was compelled to move to a very rundown part of the city. His only solace was to be found in devouring book after book. He was determined to teach himself to read, and understand, the Hebrew writing in his Sefer Torah. As I have mentioned, Karl is a natural linguist. Before very long, he had mastered the ancient language of the Jews.

"He had been brought up as a Lutheran but had never felt particularly religious. Over time, he read through the entire parchment scroll. Then he began borrowing books on the Jewish religion from the public lending library. He was still seriously downcast; but, as the months went by, he absorbed more and more about the history, heritage and faith of Judaism, and the culture and customs of the Jewish people. The affect seemed to him to be a marked lifting of his spirits. Gradually, he was coming to the realisation that he cradled within himself a profound belief in the Almighty, and a strong attraction to the tenets of the Jewish faith.

"By now, he had exhausted all the volumes on Judaism in the library and was considering the next step in his Jewish studies. With a distinct improvement in his health, Karl found a good permanent position and moved into a small apartment in a more salubrious neighbourhood. It was not long before he realised that he was residing in an area where there was a big Jewish community. He bought, and thoroughly enjoyed, practically all of the traditional kosher food products in the local Jewish stores. And he saved enough money to buy some weighty, and expensive, works on the Halachah, the Jewish laws, and rabbinic commentaries in a nearby Judaica shop. Some of the books contained large sections in Yiddish. But, as a German now expert in Hebrew, he had little trouble in translating the texts. After some months, he reached the most remarkable decision in his life. He wanted so much to become a Jew."

This was some story I was hearing. And even though the room was pleasantly cool, my mouth had grown increasingly arid with the relentless suspense. I leaned forward in my seat and quaffed some lemonade. Arthur waited patiently until I had again relaxed into the embrace of the comfortable armchair.

"The bearded, elderly proprietor of the Judaica shop, which Karl often visited to purchase books, became intrigued by the clean-shaven, fair-haired young man who was acquiring a collection of such learned religious tomes, but who did not wear any head-covering and was manifestly not Jewish. The owner considered that maybe he was buying the books for a Jew unable to do so himself, or even for a library somewhere. One afternoon, on Karl's day off work when he was reverently browsing the shelves of religious volumes and prayer books, the proprietor apologised for interrupting and began a conversation with his regular customer. They were still talking when the time came for the owner to close the store. He invited the German student of Judaism to have a coffee with him in his rooms above the premises. Three hours later, Karl walked home feeling happier than he had been in a long time. In his pocket, he held tight to a white paper bag on which the shopkeeper had written the name and telephone number of a local orthodox rabbi and inside which was neatly folded a brand new, black kippah.

"The very next evening, Karl eagerly telephoned the rabbi and an appointment was arranged. They met on several occasions at the minister's home. Each time the young man left the old rabbi after a long discussion, he felt hurt and depressed. The old man was strenuously seeking to convince the German that he did not really wish to convert, to become a Jew. That he was merely infatuated with his studies of the religion. And that he was striving to atone for the guilt he felt about his sinking of the refugee ship, and about the heinous crimes of the Third Reich. But Karl insisted on being allowed to visit the rabbi on a regular basis. He argued, pleaded, implored. On numerous occasions, the minister explained about the serious operation required for the Jewish conversion of a male. And that circumcision of someone of Karl's age could lead to physical, and possibly mental, complications. The young man was sufficiently intelligent to appreciate that the rabbi was continually testing and probing the sincerity of his desire to become an orthodox Jew, with all the restrictions and restraints that would involve. And he had already impressed the old man with the depth of his knowledge and practical comprehension of Jewish laws, customs and ritual.

"After two years of consistent attendance at the rabbi's home, Karl was permitted to begin the conversion process under the minister's close supervision. I cannot do justice to the way in which Karl expressed to me the joy he experienced at being allowed to embark on this journey. But he recognised, of course, that there was a long road for him to travel before he would be considered finally ready, if that point were ever reached. He was obliged to leave his apartment and to take up residence with an orthodox Jewish family well known to the rabbi. Karl's way of life changed dramatically, but he was more than willing to conform. He kept Shabbat and all the festivals, major and minor, as well as the Fast days. And he took great pride in learning to meticulous perfection all the necessary prayers and blessings, as well as the religious requirements in the home, the synagogue and the mikveh, the ritual bath. Throughout the three years he spent with his adoptive family, his probity was constantly tested, sometimes by extreme provocation. But the young man successfully passed every examination of his genuineness; and his modesty, warm empathetic character, Yiddishkeit and studiousness were much respected in the community.

"At long last, the rabbi informed Karl that he was now ready for the final stage before the Beth Din could declare his conversion. The young German was fully prepared for the requisite medical operation. Fortunately, everything went well; though it was some little while before he recovered completely. Karl told me that the first time he attended the synagogue after becoming a Jew, he broke down and sobbed unremittingly; and had to be comforted by his brethren. He had grown a beard again; and, as he recalled with a wry smile, it had become sopping wet with his tears.

"Karl continued to live with his adoptive family, where his affection for them, and especially for Sarah, one of the unmarried daughters, was clearly reciprocated. He was given employment by the head of the household who owned several jewellery shops in the city. In the evenings, he continued his Torah learning, which both his employer and rabbi heartily encouraged. There came a time, however, when Karl considered that he had taken his studies as far as he could by himself, and with the old rabbi, and wished to learn more at a yeshivah. His mentor was overjoyed; and Sarah's father was readily prepared to sponsor financially the young man's advanced religious education."

Arthur could see that I was absolutely riveted by Karl's story.

"A moment, please," he said, getting up and leaving the room.

My senses were still on overdrive when my host returned bearing two cups of black coffee and placed them on the table.

"Now where was I?" he beamed, retaking his seat.

"The yeshivah," I prompted eagerly.

"Ah, yes. Well, Karl moved to the most renowned yeshivah in Buenos Aires. After three years, he was sent to Israel where he was learning for another two years in Jerusalem. Afterwards, he returned to BA and began his final studies to take semichah. It was a year or two later that I first encountered him. Several months passed before he became a fully-fledged rabbi. Today, Karl is in his late forties and one of the most learned and respected rabbis in Argentina. Here, in the capital, he now presides over a community which has so much love and admiration for him that he is constantly embarrassed by its many kindnesses to him and his family."

"Did Karl ever marry?" I enquired, almost certain that I knew the answer.

Arthur took some hot coffee, his eyes sparkling.

"Oh, did I not mention it? How remiss of me. Yes, indeed he did. He wed the beautiful Sarah. They have three children, two boys and a girl. Look, they're coming here for tea tomorrow afternoon. If you are free, why don't you come along and meet them."

For a second or two, as we both stood up, a kind of wooziness overcame me. It is difficult to explain my emotions at that moment. Perhaps certain feelings were driven by the fact that I was being given an opportunity to meet Karl. Despite his subsequent dénouement, I could not dispel from my mind the knowledge that he had fought and killed for a regime that had murdered my family. Nevertheless, I was intrigued by the invitation and found myself, albeit with some doubt and apprehension, accepting my host's kind offer. After thanking him, and through him his wife, for a delicious lunch and an incredible story, I left to return to my hotel.

That night, I lay on the bed unable to fall asleep for thinking about Rabbi Karl Dieter, the former U-boat commander; and anxious about my possible reactions on meeting him. How could he come to terms with his past in such a way as to find a deep faith in the Almighty when I, an innocent victim, could not? What was the preternatural formula that enabled him but not me to overcome intellectually the absence of Divine intervention in our incongruously shared history? By the time I drifted into a troubled sleep of disturbing dreams, I had found no answers to these questions. I was soon to accept that there are no answers, only questions.

The following afternoon, not without feelings of unease and ambivalence, I returned to Arthur's apartment where I was introduced to Karl and his family. Suffice to say that I was completely captivated by the rabbi, his delightful rebbetzen and their three children. Everything that my Shabbos host had said about Karl was absolutely true. There were a few minutes when the rabbi and I were alone on the balcony overlooking the park. Shaded from the intensity of the sun by a colourfully striped awning, we each sat on a wrought iron, but deeply cushioned, chair and admired the wonderful, tropical flora in the gardens below.

We were silent momentarily after chatting aimlessly about something or other, when I blurted suddenly:

"Rabbi Dieter, where was the Almighty during the Holocaust?"

He looked at me, without blinking, without raising an eyebrow, without scratching his beard but with perhaps the warmest, sincerest smile I have ever been given.

His face was so serene, so sympathetic, so loving that I almost wept. His reply has lived with me ever since that still moment of time. His words lifted a veil that had prevented me from seeing the world, life and myself as clearly as I might have done. It was truly the catalyst for the recovery of my long-lost faith and even, maybe, my soul.

"No," the rabbi had responded softly, almost a whisper. "The question is not, 'Where was the Almighty?' The real question is, 'Where was Man?'"

The time of his life

IT'S A funny thing. Time, I mean. Now and again, it seems palpable. Like sand filtering away between your fingers. Every so often, it's just a sense of change, that oxymoronic and paradoxical cosmic constant. Like a breeze suddenly wafting from nowhere. The notion of time appears simple to us. Somewhere in the past, time may have had a beginning. Some place in the future maybe it will have an end. Perhaps it can exist only if there's a human mind to acknowledge it, like a scream in space. By looking around at the world, at our families, friends and colleagues, we sort of understand and accept, in our own primitive way, that time somehow passes.

Even assuming they think about it, youngsters may regard time with an enviable insouciance. The more mature have to recognise that time can make us sad. Of course, there's the shibboleth that, as you get older, time seems to accelerate. Religious festivals, and anniversaries of one kind or another, appear to arrive and depart with astounding rapidity. This sort of feeling may stem from a heightened awareness of mortality, possibly induced by cerebral chemistry. But we shouldn't allow this to encourage melancholy. For, in many ways, time can also be beautiful.

Take the old Royal Observatory in Greenwich Park as an example. Here you can marvel at John Harrison's amazing seagoing timepieces. Admire the remarkably aesthetic craftsmanship of his 18th century, marine chronometers. For the first time, their almost miraculous simplicity enabled a navigator to calculate, with great accuracy, his ship's position in terms of longitude. As I studied the finely balanced sea clocks, I thought of scientist-philosophers like Newton, Einstein and Hawking. They've done their level best to complicate time for us. Their theories speak of time-space continuums, a time-dependent universe, time warps and even time travel. As I pondered the mind-blowing concept of time and time travel, two thoughts impinged. One related to the Jewish Passover festival. The other concerned my friend Joe.

It occurred to me that the Haggadah, the book relating to the Exodus of the Israelites from ancient Egypt and read during the commemorative Seder service, is a kind of time machine. Think about it. As Jews sit around the Seder table in their homes, they're expected not merely to remember the suffering of their ancestors enslaved by the Pharaohs. But also they're bidden to put themselves in a position such that they're actually there, in the land of the pyramids, with the children of Israel. If this isn't time travelling back across more than three thousand years, then I don't know what is! My other thought was how the notion of time had, in an intriguing way, returned my friend Joe to his long-lost Jewish faith.

I suppose you could say that Joe is more a friend than an acquaintance. I meet him occasionally in the line of business. Maybe a couple of times a year we would lunch together at some London restaurant or other. Not that we wouldn't like to see each other more often. The fact is that Joe is a successful businessman living in the north of England, and I'm down in London. He's a widower without children and only infrequently makes trips south of Manchester. He's Jewish; but for as long as I've known him, only in a nominal sense.

During general conversations with him, I've gleaned that he'd been one of the first British soldiers to enter Bergen-Belsen, the Nazi concentration camp north of Hanover, in 1945. Often he has asked me (I'm glad to say, in a rhetorical way), "Why do bad things happen to good people?". He'd put the same question to me when we met at the end of September 2001. Doubtless, he'd then had in mind the 9/11 devastating, terrorist attacks on the twin towers of the World Trade Centre in New York and the Pentagon in Washington DC. I guess I almost understood why he'd decided to contract out of his religious faith and belief in the Almighty.

Early last year, he telephoned to say he was coming down to the capital on business. We hadn't seen each other for some months, so arranged to meet for lunch. But I was surprised when he insisted that we eat kosher. I was even more astonished when he arrived at the North West London restaurant wearing a black kippah. Aside from the normal pleasantries before the substantial starters were served, we barely spoke during the first course. Clearly there was something on Joe's mind. After the waiter had cleared away the empty plates, I poured two glasses of Merlot.

"What's with the chopped liver and the yarmulka?" I enquired, raising widened eyes to my friend's head covering, not intending to be as cynical as I probably sounded. "The last time we met, you still wanted nothing to do with religion."

Joe brought the tall-stemmed globe to his lips and almost smiled, somewhat coquettishly I thought for a tough-nut entrepreneur. He's several years older, and quite a few kilos heavier, than me. And the many stress lines that crisscross his face, like the "canals" of Mars, curve startlingly when he affects a grin. He tasted the drinkable ruby red wine, replaced the glass on an immaculately white tablecloth, flattened his thinning grey hair but said nothing. Now I know Joe to be a very confident character, but I figured he was somehow feeling a tad self-conscious and bashful at that moment.

"Come on, Joe," I began to tease. "When did you become Jewish again? And, more particularly, why now all of a sudden?"

I knew that he wouldn't take offence at my less than subtle baiting. We go back a long way, Joe and I. Before my lunch companion could react, the waiter was hovering and bearing our mains. My friend had selected traditional salt beef and latkes. I'd ordered the day's special, lamb casserole. As he began intensive surgery on his meal, cutting and forking a slice of new green cucumber from a side dish, he started speaking.

"Everything changed for me a couple of weeks ago."

I halted work on the tender wedge of meat on my plate and looked up, quizzically.

"A couple of weeks ago!" I repeated. "How do you mean, Joe?"

"I read a newspaper article," he responded unevenly whilst chomping his beef.

"It must've been a wonderful piece of writing," I commented, prodding my knife upwards in the direction of his skullcap. "Sorry, Joe … Please go on."

He swallowed a mouthful of his wine, and I refilled our glasses from the half empty bottle.

"It wasn't so much the writing as the content that got to me," he continued, as I became even more intrigued. "The feature was all about a new atomic clock, developed by American scientists. This clock is apparently the most accurate timepiece ever produced. It's precise to a single femtosecond."

At that moment I probably looked like a real putz. Joe grinned at me, his facial lines deepening like the geological formation of canyons.

"I take it you don't know what a femtosecond is?" he said.

"R-right first time, Joe," I replied, preoccupied with

dislodging an aggravating sliver of lamb from my front teeth with the tip of my tongue.

"Well, it's the smallest unit of time commonly used in science," my friend explained dutifully to a blank canvas. "This atomic timepiece ticks slightly more than a million billion, that's a quadrillion, times every second! Can you imagine it? Each tick lasts less than a femtosecond. That's a quadrillionth of a second! Can you believe it?"

I couldn't comprehend it let alone imagine or believe it. I shook my head, totally bemused by the astronomical statistics, and ecstatically removed the recalcitrant meat fragment from my mouth. My brain fought to engage third gear, and began an uphill struggle, boggling at the titanic figures. Joe is sufficiently savvy to recognise mental numbness when he sees it, and offered to help me out.

"Try to think of it this way," he said, sympathetically, deftly dissecting a potato pancake. "A femtosecond is to a second what a second is to thirty-two million years! Does that assist you?"

How could I be uncharitable?

"Y-yes, Joe, it does, I think … er, thanks a lot," I mumbled.

As I scooped up a mouthful of stewed lamb and vegetables, I took stock (no pun intended). Mathematics never was my forte. That's why I became a lawyer and not an accountant, though I suppose I'm fairly numerate. I did take Trust Accounts and bookkeeping in my professional finals. Actually, I believe I did appreciate what Joe was telling me. And I agreed with him. This atomic whatever was something else. But I couldn't fathom what it had to do with my friend suddenly sporting a kippah and relishing chopped liver and salt beef.

Did I tell you that Joe was also something of a mind reader?

"You're probably wondering what this clock contraption has got to do with me now wearing a kippah and eating kosher," he mused, mopping up the remnants of food on his plate.

I nodded.

"Well, take this on board, too, my dear friend," he went on. "I've now put up mezuzahs on the doorposts in my flat, I maintain a kosher home and I've joined, and regularly attend, my local synagogue. I really don't know what my late wife would've said!"

Never mind what his late wife would've said, I thought. I didn't know what to say.

"So tell me the connection, Joe," I invited after a short pause, during which the waiter collected our empty plates.

"The connection?"

"The relationship between that atomic clock and your renewal of faith," I expanded.

I wasn't amazed by what Joe then said, though at first I was surprised that he was saying it. His explanation actually humbled me.

"If puny mankind can create an instrument that can split time into such invisibly miniscule fragments," he observed, "then there's no doubt in my mind that the universe was created by the Almighty."

Look, there are people who try to find a way of rationalising their faith if it doesn't come easily to them. There's nothing wrong with that, so far as I can see. Sometimes we harbour doubts and questions, just like my friend. So far as concerns his dreadful experiences at the end of the war, Joe told me that he was now beginning to understand that mortal man maybe isn't equipped to comprehend the answers to the kind of profound questions that he'd been asking me, and others, for so many years.

I invited him to join us in London for our Passover Seder that year. Joe promised to try. As it happened, I was glad that he found the time.

The old man of Yad Vashem

THE FIRST time that I saw the old man at Yad Vashem was in 1975. But he did not speak to me until the final occasion that I approached him in 1981. It was only then that he told me his shattering secret. I have never forgotten him or his amazing story. I never will forget, nor could I. He comes to mind whenever I need to visit the Holocaust Memorial Museum in Jerusalem.

In the mid-1970s, I was working on my doctoral thesis. The subject encompassed the genocide of the Jewish people between the infamous Wannsee Conference in Berlin in January 1942, when the Nazi hierarchy launched their implementation of the Endlösung, the "Final Solution", and the end of the Second World War. Studies for my first degree and MA had spanned Jewish history from Biblical times to the creation of the State of Israel in 1948. There had been a huge range of possibilities for my PhD. But I was preoccupied with Hitler's destruction of European Jewry and its implications, both historical and theological. It came as no surprise to the university faculty that my postgraduate research would focus on that unique suffering of the Jews in our own era.

My first visit to Yad Vashem was in the spring of 1975. It was not my first time in Israel, and my spoken and written Ivrit is good; but on this occasion my objective was to work, not to holiday. I had prepared a month-long programme of research in the museum's extensive Holocaust archives. I was fortunate to acquire some reasonably priced accommodation in the hilly suburbs, and I travelled daily to the city centre on the Egged bus. Some days I spent in the library at the Hebrew University, though most of my working week was spent at the world-famous museum. I recall the weather being glorious, the days hot and sunny, the nights preciously cool. But I also remember the mood of the Israelis as being sombre and uncertain. On reflection, I attributed the brooding atmosphere in the capital to the bewilderment lingering after the Yom Kippur War of 1973.

When I first spotted the old man he was sitting on a wooden bench in front of the entrance to the museum's main building. It was just after ten in the morning, and the sun was rising warm. The coach loads of tourists had not yet arrived; I had noticed only a handful of visitors walking along the Avenue of the Righteous Gentiles, which honours those who saved Jewish lives during the Shoah. The relative emptiness and stillness of the grounds was one reason why my eyes had picked him out. Another was his shock of white hair on a head held face down and concealed in large hands. He sat bent forward as if deep in dreadful meditation; his sun-bronzed arms, emerging from a short-sleeved, white shirt, rested on dark trouser legs. It was not unusual to see elderly men and women, perhaps concentration camp survivors, profoundly moved by the Holocaust memorial.

I did not give the old man another thought that day. My mind was fully engaged by the cold, bureaucratic details, meticulously recorded, of massacres of Jews near Kiev by SS murder squads, eagerly aided by Ukrainian militiamen. At the end of my first day in the archives, I was already emotionally drained by the returns and reports provided by the Einsatzgruppen for their masters in Berlin. It was the actual handling of the original documentation that got to me finally. I arrived back at my small apartment late that night and went straight to bed without eating.

Next morning, the old man was sitting in exactly the same position as the previous day. Again I had a busy schedule, so I was unable to absorb much more of the sad and lonely figure before hurrying into the museum. The following day, I had an appointment at the university with a notable professor, a world authority on the Holocaust. Ostensibly, the interview was to comprise a two-hour discussion of my research portfolio. But we became so engrossed in our debate that it was continued over lunch in the refectory. In the afternoon, we joined a group of undergraduates in a further examination of study methods and techniques. That evening, however, I was delighted to be invited by one of the students to spend the weekend with his family in Tel Aviv.

On Monday morning, the old man was sitting statue-like on the bench as if he had not moved since I first saw him. I had to admit that I was becoming very curious. Before entering the building, I leaned against the wall and observed him closely. His features remained hidden in curved palms, elbows resting on his knees. The hair now looked more light grey than white and his clothes, though creased, appeared clean. This was no tramp seeking refuge in the gardens.

As I watched, he stirred suddenly. For the first time, I could see his face, which was dark and weathered, doubtless due to a constant past exposure to the sun. But it was his eyes that seriously impacted on me. They reflected an almost unbearable pain and anguish. I was now to become obsessively fascinated by this clearly distraught individual. When I retired that night, I decided to approach him the following day. Thus resolved, I was unbelievably disappointed that he was not to be seen in his seemingly normal place the next morning. My feeling was more than one of regret; it amounted to a real concern for his welfare. I strolled around the grounds for a while, hoping to catch a glimpse of the old man, but I could not find him.

During the morning, I spoke to one of the museum's archivists.

"Yes, we know of him," he said. "He's a regular visitor here."

We were having coffee in the canteen.

"Do you know who he is?" I asked.

"We do," my companion responded laconically.

"So you've spoken to him?" I queried with mounting interest.

The swift and equally succinct response baffled me.

"Never."

My next question was predictable.

"Then how do you know who he is?"

The youngish custodian, a slim, olive-complexioned sabra, sipped the hot black liquid in his sturdy paper cup.

"We," he began, "that is, staff at the museum, have seen him here over many years."

"Many years!" I exclaimed.

"Yes, indeed. Sometimes he comes almost every day for several weeks, then not at all for maybe a couple of months."

I could hardly contain my growing excitement.

"But who is he?" My voice sounded impatient. "And why does he come here so regularly?"

The archivist was generally a friendly guy and I had chatted to him previously. But now he stared at me like I was being acutely tiresome.

"I'm coming to your first question," he said brusquely. "I'm afraid we don't know the answer to your second one."

I cradled the cup in my hands. The warmth seemed strange in the air-conditioned room. I thought it was relatively okay for me to try again.

"Why have you never spoken to the old man?"

My tone sounded insistent and, instantly, I regretted it. My fellow coffee drinker grimaced as only an Israeli can.

"So many questions," he sighed, shaking his head. "Give me a chance, eh?"

At that moment, I probably looked like a schoolboy reprimanded in the headmaster's study.

"I'm sorry," I said, duly scolded and feeling suitably contrite. "Please, continue."

"For some time, of course, we weren't aware of the old man. The museum gets hundreds of thousands of visitors every year. You really don't notice one person in such crowds."

I nodded agreement and he went on.

"A few of my colleagues have the habit, like mad dogs and Englishmen, of going out in the midday sun. They enjoy sitting on the grass in our beautiful gardens, or even on the benches when not fully occupied, to eat their boxed lunches. One of the custodians sometimes sat next to our mutual friend. The old man was invariably in the position you've seen him adopt. Stooped forward, head buried in hands and sometimes to be heard weeping uncontrollably and begging forgiveness. For what or from whom nobody knows. From the way he carries on, you'd almost believe that he'd taken on himself full responsibility for the Holocaust."

I lifted my coffee cup and continued listening intently.

"From time to time, my colleague tried to talk to this sad old man. Couldn't get a peep out of him. No one can. I've witnessed tourists making an effort to comfort him, but without any success whatsoever."

I was puzzled.

"But you've said it's known who this man is," I pressed gently, raising my hands in mock surrender when I saw the caustic expression.

"We had noticed a number tattooed on the man's forearm, a concentration camp number. In a way, I suppose it was an invasion of his privacy. But someone at the museum memorised the numerals and checked them with our records …"

"Did you discover anything about him?" I interrupted, my restrained enthusiasm bubbling just below the surface.

"I'm coming to that just now."

Again, I felt like that schoolboy.

"The old man's name is Albert Dressmann. During the war he and his family were what they called 'U-boats'. These were German Jews living in Berlin and concealed by righteous Gentile neighbours or friends. It's understood that the family were betrayed to the Gestapo some time in 1944. Dressmann, his wife Miriam, and their three young children, one boy and two girls, were transported to Auschwitz-Birkenau. Miriam and the children were selected immediately on arrival for the gas chambers. Albert was sent to one of the sub-camps to be worked to death. Fortunately, or otherwise as he might think, the slave worker survived the horrors of his existence. After liberation by the Soviet army and some years in displaced persons' camps, he immigrated to Israel."

Having listened, almost without intervention, to the harrowing story of Albert Dressmann, I could now approach some understanding of his apparently odd behaviour. But as my companion rightly pointed out, the old man's continual visits to Yad Vashem had not been explained comprehensively. And certainly not by the mouth of this troubled man. As I journeyed home on the bus later that day, I considered the psychological options for his bizarre behaviour. I heated a pizza for supper and tried, without much success, to concentrate on a TV movie. Throughout the evening, I could not rid Dressmann's obvious despair from my mind. In the end, I dozed off on the sofa.

During my final weeks in Jerusalem, I did not see the old man again. The following year I obtained my doctorate and began lecturing at London University. The year after that, I enjoyed a long summer vacation in Israel. I took the opportunity, not only to look up friends but also to pursue some research for a book I was writing on some relatively untouched aspects of the Holocaust. Whilst most of my work was confined to the libraries of the Hebrew University, I spent a substantial amount of time at the Yad Vashem archives.

Since I was last in Israel's capital city, the old man had rarely strayed far from my thoughts. As I had strangely hoped, he was sitting on the same bench, his body moulded into the same position that I had first been disturbed to see it. If anything, the stoop now appeared even more pronounced, as though eventually the man would roll over and bury himself in the very earth. On each of my attendances at the museum, I would stop by his seat. Occasionally, I would sit beside him and endeavour to elicit a response to my greeting. But my words, however tender, sensitive and empathetic I could make them, fell heavily on stony ground. The following summer, still researching my book, I revisited Jerusalem. Again I tried, but yet again without success, to communicate with Albert Dressmann.

In the summer of 1981, I made a final trip to Israel to complete my research. Over the years, I had concluded that the reason for Dressmann's conduct was the deep and indefinable grief brought about by the tragic loss of his family, a fathomless and continuous sorrow, which few other human beings could come close to conceiving. On the penultimate day of my stay in Jerusalem, I was absolutely amazed when the old man finally reacted to me. I will never forget what he told me. At last, I possessed the reason for his continual appearances at the Holocaust museum. My shock and, yes, discomfiture, when he returned my gentle overtures were soon allayed by his heartfelt words of apology for the years of ignoring me and museum staff and others.

His eyes brimming with tears, he confided that he was not long for this world, but that he feared what would befall him in the world to come. I held his arthritic hands and urged that he, of all people, had nothing to fear on the Day of Judgement. He shook his head with a whimper and cried that he carried a terrible secret, a secret that had eaten into him like a cancer, a secret that he had never revealed to a living soul. Now he was nearing the end of his life, he said quietly, there was an urgent need in him to share that secret. And he wanted very much to share that secret with me. Then maybe, he added quite calmly, I would understand everything. This is the story that Albert Dressmann related to me in the gardens at Yad Vashem, with the words he actually used so far as I can recall them now.

"During the First World War, I was a soldier fighting for Germany. My family had lived in Berlin for over fifty years. It was 1916 and, against my parents' wishes, I enlisted in a local regiment of infantry. I'd only just turned eighteen, but I was eager to join my friends in the army. It was my patriotic duty to the Fatherland. Going into my father's furniture business would have to await the end of the conflict. Shortly after signing up, I was shipped to the Western Front. Within hours of my arrival in muddy Flanders, I was hurled into the horrors of trench warfare.

"In our sector of the line, we were opposed by the British. The artillery bombardments were hellish. Every centimetre of quagmire was fought over, often in desperate hand-to-hand combat. The firepower during a mass attack on the enemy's trench systems was murderous. I imagine they felt the same way about our machineguns as they sprayed the Tommies advancing across no-man's land. I could almost accept the notion of killing an Englishman when sniping with my rifle from three hundred metres. War is war. I was defending my homeland and my family; and, though I yearned for peace, battles had to be fought, and hopefully won. But I couldn't come to terms with bayoneting a screaming lad no older than myself, and possibly even younger, as we raided a trench at night to capture prisoners for interrogation.

"As dawn came up one morning, with the mist rising slowly from the debris of the previous day's fighting, I was despatched with a patrol to search for wounded comrades. On reaching a wooded area, we separated. Bunched up, we'd be easy meat for enemy sharpshooters camouflaged in the treetops. As I approached a clearing, I heard what sounded like somebody groaning. I crouched down instantly and instinctively, taking the cover of some undergrowth, and peered through the dissipating fog. At the opposite side of the glade, I made out a German soldier propped against a thick tree trunk. His rifle and helmet lay beside him. He was clutching his left thigh. His eyes were closed and he was moaning with pain. 'Help me, help me,' he cried. I was about to go to his aid when I detected a slight movement to my right. I pressed down against the forest floor, watched carefully and waited still and silent.

"It might've been nothing at all to concern me, an animal perhaps or a bird, though there was precious little wildlife in the battle zone. It could've been one of my squad, but you survived on the frontline by being constantly alert to danger signals. To my horror, into the clearing strode a huge British infantryman. He wore a low, rounded helmet and a greatcoat. He was carrying his rifle at port, with its long bayonet fixed. His dark, hooded eyes searched the surroundings slowly and deliberately, to ensure that only the wounded German soldier was in the vicinity. I held my breath and reached soundlessly for my rifle.

"The forest itself was as silent as a graveyard, that utter quiet accentuated by the whimpering of my comrade-in-arms and the soft, wary footfalls of the Englishman as he stealthily closed with his victim. My compatriot opened his eyes and gazed with stark terror as the enemy infantryman aimed the bayonet point at his heart. A shot rang out, and I realised it was the report from my own gun. In a flash, I'd grabbed for it in the mishmash of fallen twigs, branches and leaves, aimed and fired. The Tommy threw his weapon reflexively into the air, shrieked once and crashed to the forest floor, dying before he hit the ground with a thud.

"When I reached my German comrade his eyes were closed again and his face was deathly pale. His matted dark hair curved across his forehead, and there were spots of blood on his short, black moustache. I thought he was dead, so I tore the metal nametag from his neck and stuffed it inside one of my pockets. As I turned to go, having marked the place approximately on my map, I thought I heard the soldier breathing. He was still alive. I hoisted the man over my shoulder with some difficulty and, after a big effort, managed to carry him back to our lines. From the forward dressing station, he would be transported to our major hospital facilities at the rear. Later that day, I found my wounded compatriot's nametag in my pocket. I decided not to hand it in; it would soon be replaced if the man survived. Instead, I kept it as a souvenir of that day's frightening episode and the life I had saved. And I thought it would authenticate a good story if and when I returned home after the war."

Dressmann took out a handkerchief, wiped his eyes and mopped his sweat-strewn brow. I had been listening spellbound for several minutes, but I could not decipher the meaning or significance of his fascinating narrative. Had it not been for his purposeful clarity, I might have been forgiven for thinking that he was suffering from some kind of mental disorder. Then the old man started speaking again.

"When I got back home to Berlin after Germany's ignominious defeat, I put away the nametag in the drawer of my desk at the office. I often took it out and wondered what had happened to the wounded German soldier I had rescued that morning in the forest. I didn't have to wait too long to find out."

Dressmann withdrew an article from the back pocket of his trousers. He held the object tightly in a fisted hand as if to crush it to nothingness. Then he handed the item to me, as tears streamed down his anguished face and formed rivulets on his cheeks. Mystified, I accepted the thin, rectangular piece of metal from the outstretched and shaking hand. But my head began to spin as I noted, etched into the metal, a number and below the number a name. The name was Adolf Hitler …

The scarlet thread

THE SMALL wooden box that father kept in the wall safe behind mother's beautiful portrait painting had always fascinated me. From time to time, he would take the box, which looked very old, from the safe and sit in his favourite armchair. He would clasp the little container, no larger than a jeweller's presentation ring box, to his chest with one hand, close his eyes, scratch his salt and pepper beard then adjust his large, black skull cap. His lips would move as if he were praying. The worried expression on his face would frighten me as a small boy, but I loved him dearly. Father was all I possessed in the world after mother died tragically when I was six years old and totally confused by what had occurred.

Sometimes, before returning the box to the safe, father would open the hinged lid, peer inside, shake his head and sigh deeply, like all the troubles of Mankind rested on his broad shoulders. At other times, he would gaze at the contents and a wonderful look of hope would radiate from his countenance. If he spotted me spying on him from the doorway, father would quickly close the tiny coffer, as if it would be dangerous for me to catch a glimpse of what lay within. I never did see whatever was held so secretively inside the box. And father had never revealed it to me; that is, until one day last year, a day which happened to be my fourteenth birthday.

There had been trouble brewing in the town. There had often been trouble in the town of late, so far as we Jews are concerned. But incidents were becoming more serious, though the authorities were doing nothing about them. Father had not been at all well during the last few years, and the stress of these additional problems had not helped his condition. His doctor could not find a physical cause for father's debility but, even at my young and tender age, I believed it was due to a broken heart. Father often took to his bed now, staring through the large window at the wide expanse of sky and occasionally glancing at the old, electronic clock/calendar on the bedside table.

Sometimes, when our kindly Jewish doctor visited, we could take father downstairs. He was quite a big man and I could not manage him on my own. For some payment, an elderly woman neighbour would come in to look after his needs during the day when I was at school. She also prepared our evening meal. At night, I would sit at his bedside; he liked me to read to him from the Chumash, which contains the five Books of Moses. On the night of my birthday last year, I opened the leather-bound Pentateuch and began to read from Exodus: "And a new king arose who did not know Joseph …".

Father gazed at me with a heart-rending mixture of love and sadness in his watery eyes.

"Put the book down, my son," he said, wistfully. "I have something to give to you, and a story I must tell you, before I die."

I struggled to dispel the notion that father was dying, but he suddenly gripped my wrists in his large hands and with a strength that I thought had long vanished from them. Father looked at the clock/calendar face, then at mine.

"Very soon, they will come here and it will all be over for me," he said mysteriously, breathing heavily.

As he continued, I became very afraid.

"You must listen carefully to what I have to say and leave the house by the back door before dawn. You must run far away and never return to this place. Do you understand? Promise me, my son, that you will do this. Promise me!"

I was stunned by the words father was uttering with such vehemence. But the effort had clearly exceeded his apparent power. He loosened his grasp on my forearms and fell back, exhausted, onto the firm white pillows. After a short while, during which he fought to compose himself physically and emotionally, he raised himself up in the bed. He took my hands again, but this time more gently.

"Promise me, my son," he repeated, softly.

At that moment, I was unable to recognise fully the import of what he was trying to tell me. But I knew deep down that I would have to comply with his wishes.

"I promise, father, but …"

A quivering finger appeared in front of my nose.

"No 'buts'," came the stern voice from behind the wagging digit. "You must do precisely what I ask of you, without hesitation. Do you understand me, son?"

I nodded meekly.

"Y-yes, father … I think so."

My words seemed to relax him a little.

"Time is short," he went on, looking askance towards the black night beyond the window. "And I have much to explain."

I thought that I heard some pitiful screams coming from a distance. Maybe it was the sound of feral cats fighting in the dark, dank alleyways of the town. But it was a noise that somehow compelled a fear deep within my body. I shivered momentarily as father strained to retrieve something from the drawer of his bedside cupboard. I was amazed to see that it was the small wooden box from the wall safe in the sitting room. I had last seen it a few years back, but I had never had the opportunity to view inside it.

Despite the sombre and enigmatic exchange I had just engaged in with father, a stirring combination of curiosity and excitement grew inside me. I realised what was about to happen after all this time. Father raised the lid and turned the opened box in my direction so that I could perceive its content. I did not know exactly what I expected to see. A magnificent jewel, perhaps, that had belonged to my mother, or maybe some precious religious artefact. What I saw was simply a few coiled centimetres of scarlet thread resting on a tiny, black velvet cushion. I was surprised and not a little disappointed. But I did not display my feelings lest they should offend father.

After what seemed like ages, but was probably just a few moments, he spoke again.

"This short piece of thread," he began, not without a sense of pride in his tone, "has been in my family's possession for untold generations. It has been handed down, father to son, from time immemorial. But, regrettably, usually at times of great sorrow for our people."

I could hear and follow everything that father was saying. But my concentration was focused directly on the scarlet thread. This is just a piece of wool, I kept telling myself. What is so special about it? Why all the secrecy and mystery? But, somehow, as I continued to gaze at the content of the small box, the colour of the strand seemed to radiate an alluring glow. I sensed that it held an almost mystical quality that impelled attention. It was like a magnet attracting iron filings, which I had learned about in my science class at school.

"What is it, father? What is it for? What does it do?" I asked, eagerly. "And what do you mean by great sorrow for our people?"

He smiled weakly at me.

"Patience, my son," he said, glancing at the clock. "Time is indeed short, but there is still sufficient left for me to explain everything."

As he spoke, I was permitted to hold the box with its weird and wonderful content.

"I don't know all of the specific instances when the scarlet thread has been handed down. But they have been at times when the Jewish people have been subjected to severe persecution. My great-grandfather delivered it to his son during a terrible period of anti-Semitism in Eastern Europe. Militiamen burst into his home and murdered almost everyone. Only the eldest son escaped the massacre; he carried both himself and the thread to safety further east. Many years later, there were pogroms in Russia. This time, it was my own grandfather who was slaughtered without mercy alongside his family. But not before he had passed on the scarlet thread to one of his sons, who succeeded in evading the vicious mob of Jew-haters."

I was listening intently to every word father spoke, spellbound but troubled by the events he related. Perceiving in my eyes a certain sense of concern, he reached out and gently brushed my warm cheek with his cold fingers. Then he continued, taking a deep breath every few sentences.

"My father was only ten years of age when he received the fibre from my grandfather. Time passed peacefully. Our family lived well in Budapest for many years. Then war clouds gathered in 1939. Hungary sided with Germany and a pulse of fear spread through the Jewish community. Dreadful rumours reached us of the mass killing of Jews in death camps set up in Poland. When it seemed that Hungarian leaders were weakening in the face of Allied victories and the advancing Soviet armies, the Nazis occupied the country. My father quickly saw the writing on the wall. He managed to obtain some false papers; but, unfortunately, only for me. They helped me to survive with some sympathetic, and very brave, Gentile friends of the family until the end of the war. But before I was dragged weeping from my father's embrace, he entrusted me with the scarlet thread. My parents, sisters and baby brother were brutally rounded up with hundreds of thousands of other Hungarian Jews. They were transported in sealed cattle trucks and very soon perished in the gas chambers of Auschwitz. Eventually, after travelling the world, I settled here, never to return to my homeland."

I could see beads of tears forming at the corners of my father's eyes. I closed the box, placed it on the bedside cabinet and cuddled up to him. He was in his mid-eighties. He had married my mother, nearly twenty years his junior, late in life. He had loved her more than life itself; and I knew that he loved me, their only child, just as much. It pained me to see him distressed, especially as he was so very sick. Father was the only human being I now cared about, yet he was asking, no ordering, me to leave him. I was beginning to have some inkling of his motivation. But I could barely confront the reality of what it all meant. I picked up the box, opened it and lifted out the scarlet thread. Father reacted instantly.

"What are you doing?" he said, worry lines furrowing his brow.

The short length of thread dangled from between my thumb and forefinger.

"It doesn't appear to have brought our family much luck, father," I responded, with a cynicism I could not have intended at my young age. "You speak only of suffering and death. And now you want *me* to have it. In relay races at school we pass a baton from one runner to another. The baton you want to pass to me is red with blood. What's so marvellous about it?"

Father's eyes reddened and his features stiffened. I knew well the outward signs of his anger, and at once I regretted my uncharacteristic outburst. But our situation seemed far from normal. I quickly put away the thread in its little container and, remorsefully, touched my father's hand.

"I'm so sorry, father," I murmured, as if to speak louder would have denied the genuineness of my apology.

A dramatic transformation of expression swept aside my father's ire at my gratuitous behaviour.

"You have nothing to be sorry about, my son," he said, his eyes now pools of liquid benevolence. "Maybe I'm at fault. Perhaps I've not explained everything to you, as I should have done. You are quite right in a way. The thread emerges at times of great peril for the Jewish people. I've told you as much myself. But, if I might say so, you are missing a very important point. You are an intelligent and knowledgeable young man, and I'm so very proud of you. But you are still very young and innocent. I don't expect you to understand all things, not now anyway. But, in time, you will … indeed, you will. Suffice it for me to tell you that the scarlet thread, and there are many similar threads in other Jewish hands, is a symbol for our people."

Father's statement hardly satisfied my anxious desire to know more about the origins and purpose of the red-coloured symbol for our people. As sensitively as I could, I pressed father to tell me more.

"You have no need to persist," he reprimanded me, albeit with a weak smile. "I was about to inform you. As I mentioned, the scarlet thread is a symbol. It's a symbol of hope for the future. You well know that the Jewish people have suffered harassment and maltreatment for many hundreds of years. Over the centuries, evil, anti-Semitic tyrants and their raging mobs have decimated our family. But history has witnessed also the survival of the Jews, the survival of our family and the survival of our Torah, our faith and our culture, where many others have vanished from the face of the Earth. What we Jews have lacked in our ability to find peaceful, permanent homes, we have made up for in the continuity of our religion and heritage. Be assured, my son, the thread continues to exist and will continue to exist throughout time."

Father fell back onto the pillows and closed his eyes. It was obvious that he was very tired. But I was glad about what he had told me. I was able to grasp a little more of the thread's unique significance. There was one final question on my mind.

"Excuse me, father, but do you know where the thread comes from?"

He stirred and grimaced, clearly in some kind of pain. Then he opened his eyes, sighed to the innermost essence of his soul and gazed at me.

"In ancient Israel, there was a custom," he said, almost in a whisper so that I had to lean closer to him. "A scarlet thread was wrapped around the tomb of our Matriarch Rachel. As it says in the Book of Jeremiah, Rachel weeps for her children … . The tradition continued across the generations, down through the ages. I do not say that our piece of thread originates from Rachel's tomb in ancient times. I don't know. Perhaps it does. But whether it does or doesn't is not important. It's what the thread represents that matters. Do you agree, my son?"

Father gazed deep into my eyes as he put that question to me.

I nodded slowly and with all the humility I could muster for him. It was as if the light from a beacon had suddenly pierced the blackness.

"You must go now," he urged, glancing at the clock. "It's time."

It was as if a silent and mutual understanding existed between us that we would not shed a tear on our final parting. I stood up and turned to leave.

"Don't forget the scarlet thread," he reminded me.

I stepped back to collect the box from the bedside table. My movement was awkward and I sent the old clock/calendar flying to the floor. Fortunately, the plastic casing was quite sturdy and did not break. I stooped to pick it up and noticed that the last two digits of the current year were not showing. My ill-judged manoeuvring had broken part of the flashing display. The numerals were blinking the time, day and month of my fourteenth birthday but in the year 20 .....

But I love her, rabbi!

THE RABBI'S office, high above downtown Miami, Florida, USA …

"Your parents want me to speak to you about her, Simon."

"But I love her so much, rabbi!"

The rabbi curved a bulky arm around the youth's shoulders.

"Don't you think you're a bit young to fall in love? How old are you, Simon?"

"I think you know, rabbi. Fifteen. But she's the only one who understands me."

The rabbi scratched a black beard that dominated his face and chuckled, his bulky frame vibrating like a minor seismic tremor.

"I very much doubt if that's the case," he said with a broad grin. "Your parents care for you so much, Simon. You know they're really upset about all this."

Simon sat down in the minister's swivel chair.

"I know you're my friend, rabbi. Can't you speak to them?"

The rabbi rolled up his white shirtsleeves, placed two hands on his desk and hovered over the fair-haired teenager.

"I have spoken to your parents. That's why we're here this

morning, in my office. Look, Simon, I've known you since you were a baby. I blessed you at your bris. I officiated at your barmitzvah … it seems like yesterday. I've known your Mom and Dad a great deal longer. They're fine, traditional, Jewish folk, regulars at my synagogue over many years. They only want what's best for you … and so do I."

"And I've known Doris a long time, too, rabbi. I can talk to her like I can't talk to anyone else."

The rabbi sat down on the edge of his desk, whilst Simon gazed forlornly through the panoramic window at the cloudless blue sky.

"Look at me, Simon," the minister urged the young man. "Your parents think this is a dangerous liaison. I'm inclined to agree with them. They tell me how close you seem to be with this Doris. If you persist with the situation, they fear, as I do, that much sorrow may come out of it … for everyone involved."

Simon sighed, tear globules welling up in his bright blue eyes.

"But I really do love her."

"I know, I know, my son. But one thing must be clear. She cannot come to live with you."

The lad stood up and grasped the man's large hands.

"But now she's grown up, they want to send her away," the teenager blurted, his lower lip trembling. "They're sending her to a school in California."

The rabbi embraced the youth's hands in his pair of mighty fists and shook them.

"It's for the best," he said. "You'll get over her, believe me."

"I realise what everyone thinks," came the response, alongside a sceptical grin. "Just because Doris and I come from different environments, a different way of life, they think we would never make it together. So her parents didn't make it rich. So they only have a small pool. So what!"

The minister sat Simon back down in the chair.

"Excuse me for philosophising for a moment, my son. But life is very difficult at the best of times. You're an intelligent fellow. But when you get a bit older, you'll see that there's no sense in making things extra tough for yourself ..."

"You're just like my parents," the teenager interrupted. "I don't mean to be rude, rabbi, please forgive me. But I've read of many instances where such things happen ... and where both parties live together happily."

The minister sighed deeply, and tried again.

"Think of your dear parents, Simon. How would they cope if you brought Doris to live with you? Even assuming that she wants to come."

"She would want to come!"

"Okay, okay ... so she would want to come. But you've got to be realistic. How would you manage the responsibility? Remember, after all, you are only fifteen."

"I'll get a job, a real job, and move away from home," the youngster argued defiantly. "I could buy a house for us, with a small pool ... Doris and I could live swell together."

The rabbi patted Simon's knees.

"Please, Simon, be sensible. What kind of a job could you get at your age? Who would employ you at a salary that would allow you to get a loan to buy a house? No bank would give a fifteen-year-old a mortgage!"

The teenager grunted something unintelligible.

"Besides," the minister continued, "I'm told that you have excellent grades at school. And that you'll certainly go on to college, provided you work hard at your studies. You could make an accountant, like your Dad. Surely, you don't want to give up what will be a great future."

Simon grunted again.

"I don't want to be an accountant ... I just want to take care of Doris for the rest of her life."

The rabbi walked across his spacious office to a wall cupboard and opened its door.

"I think you're old enough for a small whiskey, eh Simon?"

The minister poured two measures into a pair of old fashioned glasses, handed one to his young visitor then intoned the appropriate blessing.

"L'Chaim!" he declared with brio.

"Yeah, cheers!" the youth responded half-heartedly.

The bearded religion teacher shook his head with resigned frustration.

"In the end," Simon remarked, "it's all because Jewish people in general, and my parents in particular, wouldn't want Doris in their homes or living with their sons. That's what this is all about, isn't it?"

His listener, who had heard many similarly problematic questions during long years of rabbinical duties, ran a hand through his luxuriant facial bush.

"Let's take a look at this as men," he went one. "You're a handsome, clever young man. You've got the whole of life's adventure ahead of you. I'm certain you feel something emotional for Doris. But consider carefully for just a moment. Could this feeling be no more than infatuation? Are you maybe smitten by her shapely body? Might you be mesmerised by the way she moves? Of course, I haven't seen Doris myself, but I'm sure she's very beautiful to you ..."

The teenager nodded slowly.

"But clearly, my son, I cannot favour or condone a relationship which, apart from anything else, may well end in sadness, if not disaster."

Simon shook his head and looked imploringly at the minister.

"I'm sorry but you don't understand. I want to be with Doris all the time."

The rabbi took a sip of the amber-coloured liquid in his chunky glass.

"You're risking so much," he said. "And your promising schoolwork will suffer as a result. Your dear parents tell me that you see Doris at least three or four times a week. Isn't that a bit expensive on your allowance?"

The teenager pushed back his long, shiny hair with a curving and practiced sweep of his right hand.

"I do lots of jobs for people … car washing, gardening, babysitting, shopping, that sort of thing. I make enough bucks. If Doris can work, so can I."

"When's Doris moving out to the west coast?" the rabbi enquired evenly.

"I'm not sure of the timing," came the reply from one wondering what was coming next.

The minister took the youth's empty glass and placed it on the desk beside his own.

"Promise me, Simon, that you'll at least consider what I've been saying to you."

There was a short pause.

"Okay, I promise."

The rabbi picked up his desk calendar and glanced at it.

"Purim begins tomorrow, Simon. As you know, we'll be remembering the attempt by the ancient Persians to kill off all their Jews, and commemorating the rescue of our ancestors by the brave Mordechai and his beautiful niece Esther. It really would be nice if you could tell your dear folks that you've got Doris out of your system. It would make them so happy."

The teenager was pensive for a while then stood up.

"But would it make me happy? I can't promise anything like that right now."

"That's fine by me, son. I just wanted you to think about all this. Okay?"

Simon nodded and, together, they walked towards the door

of the office on the twentieth floor of the Miami skyscraper.

"What work does Doris do?" the minister asked.

"I'll show you," the young man replied, leading the rabbi back across the room to the huge window.

"See down there?"

The minister's gaze followed the slim, pointing finger to the Miami Seaquarium hundreds of feet below. The rabbi then did something he had not done in one heck of a long time. He blushed.

"Don't tell me, Simon … Doris is a dolphin, right?"

"What else, rabbi?" the teenager said with a grin. "Happy Purim!"

Are we there yet, mummy?

"ARE WE there yet, mummy? It's been such a long journey. I'm so tired and thirsty."

"I think the train's just arriving at the station, darling."

"Can I have a drink soon, mummy? It's been so hot and crowded with people in here."

"I hope so, Miri my sweetheart. You're a very good little girl."

"Oops! I nearly fell over when the train just stopped. Will daddy be here?"

"I don't know, Miri. Hey, please stop pushing us from the back there! We'll all be getting out of this hell-hole in a few minutes."

"Where are we, mummy?"

"I'm not sure, darling. They said we were being taken to a work camp."

"What's a work camp?"

"It's a place where a lot of people work for other people."

"Are those other people Nazis, mummy? I don't like the Nazis."

"Yes, dear, I'm afraid they will be Nazis, Miri. But if we work hard for them, everything will be all right for us."

"Was daddy sent to work here?"

"I really don't know, but maybe he was. Then we'll see him soon, won't we?"

"Yes, mummy. I'm so looking forward to seeing daddy again. He missed my birthday."

"I know, Miri my precious. But that wasn't daddy's fault."

"Yes, mummy. I know … the naughty men took daddy away from us."

"I'm sure daddy would think you're a very brave girl for seven."

"Listen, mummy … I think the doors are being pushed open."

"Yes, I think you're right, darling."

"Ooh, fresh air! But there's so much noise here. So much shouting … and there are dogs barking. They frighten me, mummy. I want to go back home … to Budapest."

"Hush, sweetie. Mummy is holding you tight. Nothing will hurt you."

"Promise me, mummy."

"I promise."

"Maybe that old man in the striped pyjamas will help us get off the train. Why is he wearing his pyjamas in the daytime, mummy? Doesn't he look funny?"

"I'll call him over. Please don't push, you at the back of the wagon … there's a small child here."

"The man wearing pyjamas is coming over to us, mummy."

"Please would you be kind enough, sir, to help my daughter off the train."

"Thank you … thank you. Could you help my mummy down now, please?"

"Thank you, sir, you're very kind. Could you tell us where we are, please?"

"He's just walked away, mummy. He didn't answer you. I think that's very rude … even though he helped us from the train."

"Yes, dear."

"Wasn't it really horrible on that train? Those old people were groaning all the time and falling down. And I couldn't stand that horrible smell. I'm sorry I made my pants dirty. It was h-horrible, mummy …"

"There, there. Don't cry, my darling little baby. We're here now. Everything's going to be fine. I promised, didn't I Miri?"

"Yes, mummy. But there are so many people on this platform. The little babies don't stop crying. Will I get my drink soon, mummy?"

"I expect so. We've just got to be a little patient."

"But I'm so thirsty, mummy."

"I know, darling. So is mummy. But we'll soon be settled in. And then we'll have something to eat and drink."

"Yes, mummy. I can't wait …"

"You're such a good girl, Miri. Please don't cry any more. Mummy's got a little headache."

"Sorry, mummy. I'll try not to cry any more. But why is everyone queuing like this? I'm very tired. I wouldn't mind going to sleep soon … but only after I've had a drink."

"I don't know why we've been lined up, Miri. I can't see the head of the column. I expect they're trying to sort us out."

"What's that horrible black smoke over there, mummy? It goes right up to the sky."

"I don't know, darling. It's probably some kind of factory."

"What's a factory?"

"It's a place where people work and make things."

"Is daddy working there?"

"I don't know. Perhaps he is."

"Will we work there, mummy?"

"I suppose that I might … but you will have to go to school."

"I don't know where my school friends are. Will they come here, too?"

"I don't know. But you'll make new friends here."

"I suppose so. But I'll still miss my old friends."

"Wait, I think we're moving at last."

"What's happening, mummy?"

"They're putting people into two different groups."

"Why's that?"

"I don't know. We'll have to wait and see."

"Where's our suitcase?"

"Another man in striped pyjamas took it away with the other people's baggage."

"When will we get it back? My favourite little dolly is in there."

"The man said I'll be able to collect our case later today."

"Look, we're moving, mummy."

"Yes, it looks like the uniformed officers are asking people some questions. I suppose that's the reason for the hold-up."

"What questions, mummy?"

"I don't know, darling. I can't hear from so far away."

"What if I don't know the answers to the questions? Will I be punished?"

"They won't ask you any questions, Miri. But they may ask me some."

"What questions?"

"Oh, I don't know. Maybe they'll ask what kind of work I can do."

"What will you say, mummy?"

"I'll tell them I've been working in a factory."

"I don't remember you working in a factory."

"Yes, Miri … but you mustn't say anything. Do you understand me, sweetheart?"

"No, mummy, I don't. But I won't say anything, I promise."

"Good girl. You remember what grandma used to say about little children, don't you?"

"Yes, I do … she said that little children should be seen but not heard."

"That's right, darling."

"Where are grandma and grandpa now, mummy? Did the naughty men take them away, too?"

"Yes, they did, Miri. I don't know where they are now. Maybe they're here. Wouldn't that be good?"

"Oh yes, mummy. Then grandpa can tell me stories like he used to do … and grandma can brush my hair before I go to bed."

"Yes, darling. Keep thinking about nice things like that."

"We're nearly at the front of the queue, mummy."

"Yes, Miri. So remember what I said, won't you?"

"I will. Look, mummy. We're next."

"Yes, she's my daughter, sir. She's seven. Yes, she is very pretty …"

"Why have we been put with these people, mummy?"

"I suppose because this is the line for mummies with children or babies. Maybe we'll be taken to a separate camp from the men in that group over there."

"But there are men in this group as well."

"But they're old men, darling, who are probably unable to work hard."

"Why are there old women in our group? They don't have any children or babies?"

"Well, I think they're unable to work hard, too. Just like the old men. Perhaps things will be easier for them in our camp."

"Maybe the Nazis here are not so naughty, mummy."

"Yes, I'm sure you're right, Miri."

"Why didn't the man in uniform ask what work you did?"

"I don't know, darling. Maybe mothers with small children to look after don't have to work here."

"But what will you do when I go to school, mummy?"

"I'm sure we'll find out soon enough."

"Our line is moving, mummy. I hope we get a big drink soon. I'm so thirsty."

"I'll ask that soldier about drinks."

"He shouted at you, mummy. I don't like him … I-I-w-w-want to go home …"

"Please don't be upset, sweetheart. He just told me to carry on walking."

"Did he say anything about drinks?"

"Yes, he said we would all have something to eat and drink after our showers."

"Showers? Oh, must we have a shower, mummy? I prefer having a bath. Then I can play with my bath toys … only I don't have any here."

"I think we'll have to take a shower, Miri. We've been on that dreadful train a very long time. We're very dirty, aren't we darling?"

"Yes, mummy, I'm very, very dirty. And I'm really sorry about my pants. They feel really horrible against my skin."

"Hold my hand, Miri, so you won't get lost in this crowd."

"Look at that lady over there, mummy … can you see her, the one carrying the little baby and holding that boy's hand."

"Yes, I can see her."

"Why is she looking so sad?"

"I don't know, darling. Perhaps her husband was in the other group, the one with the men. And now they're separated."

"But why didn't she go with him? There were some young women with those men."

"You've got so many questions. Never mind, I suppose that I've got a lot of questions, too. Well, maybe those young women didn't have any husbands. And, of course, they wouldn't have any children, so they could work hard like the younger men."

"I suppose so. Oops!"

"Be careful how you walk, Miri. The pathway isn't very even in places."

"Where are we going now, mummy?"

"I expect we're heading for the place where we take our showers."

"Will we have to undress, mummy?"

"Don't be silly, darling. How can we have a proper shower if we don't take all our clothes off?"

"Will it be just the two of us in the shower?"

"I don't expect so, Miri. With all these hundreds of people, I think there's likely to be some kind of communal shower. Otherwise it would take ages to get us all clean."

"But I don't like undressing in front of other people, mummy."

"I'll see if we can do anything about that when we get to the showers."

"Thank you, mummy. But I want to have my shower very quickly so I can have my drink. I'm gasping."

"I know, my precious. It won't be long now."

"Why do the soldiers walking along with us have guns and dogs, mummy?"

"I think it's to make sure we don't run away. Though where anyone would run to in the middle of nowhere, I really don't know."

"Mummy, it looks like we're walking towards that grey building over there … the one next to the factory. I don't like all that black smoke. And doesn't it smell awful around here?"

"Yes, it does, doesn't it? Perhaps it's got something to do with what they make in the factory."

"What do you think they make, mummy?"

"I don't know, Miri. Maybe it's glue. When I was a little girl, we lived near a glue factory and it didn't smell very nice. Though it wasn't quite the same smell as this one."

"Look, mummy. The people at the front are going down those steps into the ground underneath the grey building."

"Yes, I can see that. I expect that's where the showers are."

"Can you hear that sound, mummy?"

"What sound, darling?"

"The singing. Listen, mummy. Some of the children are singing a song."

"Oh, yes. I can hear it now. Do you know that tune, Miri?"

"I don't think so. It's very nice, but doesn't it sound very sad?"

"Yes, doesn't it? Stay close to mummy, Miri. Hold my hand, we're going down the steps now."

"There's not much light down here."

"No, it's quite gloomy, darling. Hold my hand tight, we'll just follow the people in front so we won't get lost."

"I think we're going into that large room, mummy … where the people are starting to take their clothes off."

"In you go, sweetheart … into that corner, quickly. There's a hook on the wall for our things."

"It's really cold in here, mummy. Look, I'm shivering with cold without my clothes on. See, I've got those chicken pimples."

"They're called goose bumps, darling. Come close and hug me. I'll keep you nice and warm."

"Why are those horrible looking women in uniform shouting at us? We haven't done anything wrong."

"They're just telling us to remember the number on the wall beside our clothes hook. So we'll know where our things are when we come back in here. And they want us to hurry into the showers now. I expect they don't want us to catch our deaths of cold."

"Everyone's going through that doorway over there, mummy."

"Come on, Miri. Let's follow them inside. Quickly. The sooner we have our showers the better, eh?"

"It's a very big shower room, isn't it mummy?"

"Yes, darling. But there are a lot of people in here. Everyone seems to be huddling beneath those showerheads high up there in the ceiling. Come on, sweetheart. Let's try to find a space somewhere. And try not to drink the water when it comes out, Miri. I'm sure it won't be suitable for drinking."

"I'll try, mummy. But I am very thirsty. Oh, what was that loud bang, mummy?"

"I think they've just closed the door."

"It must've been a very heavy door to make such a big bang."

"I suppose so, Miri."

"Now the babies and children are crying, mummy … they were probably frightened by the door banging shut. It really frightened me. Oh, now some of the mummies are crying. Were they afraid of the door banging? Mummy, you're crying as well. Why are you crying, mummy? Were you frightened by the noisy door?"

"Y-yes, my darling, I was. Come, Miri, let's hug each other tightly. I love you so much."

"And I love you too, mummy …"

The fifth son

AS SOON as Sam declared that the first part of the Haggadah had been completed, and that it was time for the Pesach meal, his wife Sally rose from the Seder table followed closely by her younger sister, Susan.

"Can I help, too?" offered Anne, their mother, struggling to get up.

"No, Mum, it's okay," Sally said. "You've just had a hip replacement, remember? You rest yourself and keep the men in check."

Sam, his father-in-law Louis and Susan's husband Paul nodded in unison. Anne smiled sweetly and leaned back into the plump cushion with a sigh of relief.

Sally's a gutte neshomah, Anne thought to herself. Sam's a lucky man. And so is Paul, her mind-train continued, as the three men began uncorking bottles of Passover dinner wine from Israel amid jovial banter. It's just a real pity we've only got one grandchild after all these years. Adam. Anne smiled inwardly at the name of Sam and Sally's son, Adam, first and last. And where is he tonight? He's in a jungle somewhere, thousands of miles away. Taking a year out, he'd said. What did he call it? My head, these days … oh yes, a gap year. A mishegass. The only gap, Anne pondered, is in the boy's head, a loch in kop. She could see it in Sally's eyes, the tears sometimes, the anxiety for her son's safety. Sam says Adam will be all right, once he has got this freedom thing out of his system. Anne sighed deeply.

"You okay, Mum?" Sam enquired with a look of concern. "Not in any pain, are you?"

Before the speaker's mother-in-law could respond, Louis interjected:

"It's the matzos, son. They get behind our false teeth. Like little devils teasing our gums!"

Paul tugged at the corkscrew.

"Curse of the Pharaohs, those matzos. They play havoc with my digestive system! I lost three days in the cab last Pesach."

Anne shook her head at the false assumptions about her sigh.

In the kitchen, Sally and Susan were about to carry into the dining room a platter of hard-boiled eggs and a bowl of salt water. This was the traditional mourning fare in remembrance of the Holy Temple in Jerusalem.

"When did you last hear from Adam, Sal?"

Sally's younger sister by three years placed a large, wooden spoon on the egg platter.

"He sent us an e-mail from Bangkok about three weeks ago. Said he was well and heading upcountry with some Australian blokes he'd met at a hostel. I tell you, sis, he's been away for almost eight months. He's been to New Zealand, Australia and China. Now he's in Thailand. And I still can't stop worrying about him. You read such terrible stories, sis. And drugs seem to be the least of it."

Sally left unspoken the constant thought eating into her kishkes: If anything should happen to him … Susan tipped some salt into the plastic bowl of cold water she was holding and began swirling the mixture. But her hands began trembling and teardrops formed in her eyes. Quickly she stood the bowl on the polished wood, work surface and turned to face her sister.

"A-At least you've got a child to worry about," she whimpered.

Sally put down the platter of eggs and held her sobbing sister close to her body.

"Hush, love," she soothed softly, gently stroking Susan's back. "The others will hear you. We don't want to spoil their Seder night, do we now?"

Sally understood and empathised with her sister's almost continuous turmoil of pain and regret. In her shared blood, she could feel the hurt of Susan's albeit misplaced emotions of inadequacy since the doctors advised there could never be a baby. Counsellors, psychiatrists and Prozac had only partially helped to assuage the depressive condition. Sally felt for Paul, too. For some reason unknown to Sally, her sister and brother-in-law were unwilling to adopt a child. Sally held tightly to Susan's shivering hands.

"Come on, sis, dry those lovely blue eyes of yours. We've got work to do, and hungry mouths to feed."

After the eggs were served and consumed, the Passover meal began in earnest. As the family hungrily slurped Sally's homemade vegetable soup, Louis picked a piece of wayward carrot from his grey moustache.

"You know what, Sue, your Hebrew is still excellent," he said. "The way you rattled off the Mah Nishtanah … like nobody's business!"

Everyone round the table had noticed the younger sister's red eyes when she had returned to the dining room with the salt water. Those present knew better than to mention anything. But here was an opportunity to cheer her a little. They all nodded in agreement with Louis' praise.

"Well she did go to cheder every week for years," Anne said.

"Just like Sally … only it's the youngest at the table who must ask the questions."

Her husband threw her a sardonic look.

"Tell us something we don't know," he said.

Almost everyone conjured up a mind image of Adam reciting the Haggadah's four questions in previous years. He had been a boy chorister at the local synagogue. Such a sweet, soprano voice and so keen on attending the shul every Shabbos. Paul looked up from his bowl and broke the spell.

"Completely wasted my time at Hebrew classes," he confessed, remorsefully shaking his bald head. "Got the cane for messing about practically every night. I regret it now, of course. Perhaps if I went to shul as often as Sam here, things might be different."

Sam smiled, grabbed a bottle of wine and walked round the table filling glasses. Louis placed a gnarled hand on top of his glass.

"No more for me, son. I've got to pop a couple of pills soon. I'll stick to the grape juice."

Anne still held onto the mental picture of her one and only grandchild.

"What's happened with Adam?" she asked, glancing earnestly at his father.

The sisters nodded at each other and began clearing the soup dishes into the kitchen.

Sam played with the few wisps of hair gracing the top of his head, then rubbed his face as if washing it with soap and water.

"I was reading something this morning," he said, leaning forward in his chair. Its cushion fell to the carpeted floor but Sam did not pick it up. "It was in a leaflet about Passover. I was handed it yesterday outside the kosher deli near my office. Part of what I read relates to the various stages of the Seder service. It referred to the wise, the wicked, the simple and the innocent sons that figure in the Haggadah story. They're all equal in the

Almighty's eyes, the leaflet noted. But it also mentioned that we should remember another son, one who isn't experiencing the freedom of Pesach. He's the missing Jewish child, the so-called fifth son. Although he's not at the Seder table, spiritually he's our most important and treasured guest."

Sam could see from the facial expressions of his close relatives that he had aroused a distinct interest, even inquisitiveness, in what he was saying. Encouraged, he continued.

"Apparently, the fifth son is searching. No one's quite sure what he's searching for, but the Almighty knows. Our sages have said that we'll only reach this son's heart by embracing him with the joy of our Jewish heritage."

When the girls returned laden with trays of piping hot chicken and vegetables, they felt a strange and heavy silence in the room.

"What's wrong now?" Sally enquired suspiciously, as Sam and Paul made space on the table for the steaming dishes.

"Nothing at all," Louis replied instantly. "Your dear hubby has just given us some food for the soul … and now we're ready, more than ready, for some solid food for the body. But before we tuck into this delicious-looking feast – by the way, Sally, the soup was great – I think we should drink a toast to Adam. Wherever he is this evening."

Everyone raised wine glasses.

"To Adam!" Louis toasted. "May he be safe, healthy and happy in whatever far-flung spot he finds himself tonight. And hopefully he's thinking of us, too."

Everyone echoed: "To Adam!" then downed his or her respective beverage.

As she selected a top quarter from the chicken platter, Anne voiced a thought she had been cradling in her mind.

"I'm sorry, but I didn't really understand everything that Sam said just now. How can I embrace my grandson with the joy of our Jewish heritage if he isn't here?"

As Paul quietly brought Sally and Susan up to date with the leaflet, Sam addressed his mother-in-law.

"Look, Mum, I don't know what the author actually intended by those words. My interpretation is that, bearing in mind Adam's spiritual presence at our Seder tonight, we should all think good thoughts about him. Even though it seems our son's no longer interested in Judaism and Yiddishkeit. In other words, we ought to embrace him lovingly with our hearts and minds during this special service when the family are gathered together. And at a time when we're recalling the historic Exodus and the ancient Israelites' bid for freedom and redemption. With Adam very much in our minds, and to coin a phrase, maybe we should all say, Next year in England!"

His father-in-law patted Sam on the back.

"That was quite a speech, son … Shekoach!"

Anne shook her head, eyes glazing over, and forked some recalcitrant skin from the chicken breast on her plate. Sally picked up her glass of wine and aimlessly rolled the stem between her fingers.

"I suppose we're fortunate that Adam is away from home for a relatively short time," she said. "We expect him back in a month or so. But just think of those families where the children have gone to live permanently on the other side of the world. Australia or California, say. Or even made aliyah to Israel. I know of some cases. The parents and grandparents rarely see the children and, in some situations, the grandchildren."

Everyone nodded, except Susan who vacantly shifted the food around on her plate.

"What's Adam going to do when he gets home, Sally?" Anne asked before popping some chicken into her mouth.

"Your memory, Mum! I've told you umpteen times. He's got a part-time, summer job with a firm of chartered accountants in the City. Then he's off to Southampton University in October to study Economics and Maths."

While Sally and Susan disappeared into the kitchen to prepare the desserts, Paul topped up the wine glasses again. As he poured the Mount Hermon red into Sam's glass, he voiced a thought.

"Tell me, Sam, why do you think Adam's not interested in his religion any more? Look, I know nothing from nothing, and that's my own bloody fault. But Adam used to be so enthusiastic about his religious studies at school, about attending cheder and singing in the synagogue choir. I remember you telling me recently that one of his friends was going to learn at a yeshivah in Israel and hoping, one day, to take se-sem …"

Sam helped him out.

"To take semichah, to become a rabbi."

Paul nodded.

"Yeah, so what's happened with your son, Sam? Doesn't he believe any more?"

Sam rubbed his forehead, thoughtfully.

"I really don't sense that's the case, Paul," he said. "Deep down, I don't feel he has lost his faith. I talked about this with Adam before he left on his grand tour. He told me that he needs the time out to think about things, to think about everything … the meaning of life, if you like. Especially, Adam said, the meaning of his life. It's for him to make up his own mind, Paul. I know that Sally has been worried sick at times. I'm as concerned as she is, if only I'd admit it, about the kind of people he might be mixing with, the sort of things he might be getting up to. But you can't just say: Don't go, Adam, we're frightened for you. That's really not on."

After the sisters had cleared the remnants of fresh fruit, flans, puddings and ice creams, the Seder Plate was returned to the table. The afikoman, the hidden half of matzah, was revealed and grace after meals recited. Susan had been invited to hunt for the concealed piece of unleavened bread. Her quest took a mere few seconds. The matzah segment had been placed out of sight behind one of the silver-framed wedding photographs on the mahogany sideboard. Susan giggled with delight when Sam presented her with a large box of prettily wrapped, kosher for Pesach chocolates. Everyone sighed inwardly with relief, breaking into wide smiles and happy applause.

Soon came the time when eyes focused on the wine-filled, silver goblet standing in the middle of the table, the Cup of Elijah. As Sam began to recite the Shefoch Ha'matchah prayer, Sally rose from her chair and went out into the hall. She walked slowly towards the street door to welcome Elijah the prophet. Every year, she would follow this mystical and age-old custom. When she reached the door, Sally experienced a sudden and peculiar sensation, somewhere between her heart stopping and her brain blacking out. Believing she had been overcome momentarily by her wine intake that evening, Sally rested against the wall for a moment or two. Then she opened the door, gradually, curiously, expectantly.

On the doorstep rested a large and grubby backpack. Standing behind it was an equally large and grubby individual.

"A-am I-I too late, Mum?" the figure enquired, breathlessly.

Sally bit her lower lip and opened her arms.

"No, Adam, my darling son … you're not too late, you're not late at all."

Midnight son

SOME YEARS ago, I was travelling by train from Helsinki to Turku, and therefore from the new to the old capital of Finland. Finnish friends, who happened to be Jewish, had invited me to spend Passover with them. It was Erev Yomtov, the night before the beginning of the festival that commemorates the Exodus of the Children of Israel from the ancient Egypt of the Pharaohs. I had flown in that morning and was anxious to arrive at my destination before the Seder began that evening. The country was slowly emerging from the icy grip of a freezing and dark winter. But en route to the railway station by airport express bus I noticed how efficiently the roads had been ploughed clear of a recent heavy, April snowfall. Trains were running to schedule; but I decided to pay the supplement and journey the two hundred kilometres on the rapid Pendolino.

The sleek locomotive slid out of the main station precisely on cue. I settled back in my comfortable, reclining seat to enjoy the cocooned warmth of the open-plan carriage. Regularly spaced, wall-mounted monitors displayed the time, outside temperature, distance to destination and other information. There were a handful of passengers in the long, streamlined coach. One of them, a man, sat in the window seat opposite me. For a minute or two after sitting down, I had considered moving, for complete privacy, to one of the several other vacant, four-seat combinations. But I was too weary from my early morning flight, and dash to the rail terminus, to make the effort.

My eyelids felt droopy, like they were hung with hundreds of tiny weights. It would not be long before I drifted into welcome sleep. I had barely taken in the man across from me. Through my waning consciousness, I noticed that he was staring at me, though not in an unfriendly way.

"You're Jewish, aren't you?" he said suddenly.

In my semi-soporific state, I was startled, to say the least. Not so much by the almost accent-less English: I know that most Finns speak the language perfectly well. And not so much by the question being put to me: I was wearing a give-away, small black kippah that sat at the back of my head. It was more that my fellow passenger was breaching the normal Finnish reserve to say anything at all to a complete stranger.

I came fully awake, smiled at the man and tried quickly to absorb his appearance. Thinning hair topped an elongated, oddly swarthy face. I registered light blue eyes and a strong, jutting chin. It was difficult to judge exactly, but the man was probably in his early fifties, a few years younger than me.

"You've doubtless spotted my head-covering," I said.

"No," he responded, unexpectedly. "I saw your rings."

On entering the train, I had removed my overcoat, gloves and faux fur Russian headgear and stored them with my suitcase and flight bag in the overhead, airline-style locker. I have to admit to a penchant for gold rings. Usually, I sport four of my collection. Two of these I purchased in Israel, in Jerusalem and Netanya. One bears my Hebrew name in cut out lettering, the other has a raised Hebrew letter chai to represent life. I glanced down at my hands splayed on my lap; then I looked across at the middle-aged man and grinned.

"As it happens, I didn't see the skull cap on your head," he added.

"Are you Jewish, too?" I asked, rather diffidently.

"No, no," he replied, undoing the buttons of his dark blue jacket and fiddling with the knot of his plain red tie. "But … my father was."

I turned to look out of the window. We were passing thick forests of snow-blanketed fir trees. My action may have seemed discourteous to the man. But, somehow, I detected a slight nervousness on his part as he mentioned his father; and, for no clearly discernible reason, I felt uncomfortable. Perhaps it was the manner in which he had said the word father, almost apologetically; or the slight quivering of flesh at the corners of his mouth. My immediate impression was that he regretted having spoken to me at all.

After a short while, I turned away from the window with closed eyes and rested my head against the white seat covering. The train inclined gently and glided smoothly around a banked curve of track. But I shifted involuntarily in my seat. Strangely, I still felt a tad self-conscious; but the small movement impelled me to open my eyes. It was as if the man had been watching and waiting for me to look on the world again.

"I'm sorry," he said.

He refrained from explaining his apology; but, truth to say, there was an oddly unspoken yet total understanding in our exchange of glances.

"There's no need to apologise," I responded.

We smiled at each other and he held out his right hand.

"My name is Ralf," he said. "I'm a lawyer in Helsinki."

I introduced myself and we exchanged small talk for a while, conspicuously ignoring the conversation in which I, at least, wanted to engage.

Ralf intrigued me. I was eager to return to the topic of his father, though there seemed to be a mysterious sensitivity about that subject. I did not wish to be disrespectful, pushy or tactless in any way, so I decided on circumspection. I had visited Finland on several occasions, both for business and pleasure. I knew something of the small Jewish community in the country. More than once, I had been called to the reading of the Torah on the Sabbath in the Finnish capital's beautiful, domed synagogue.

"Do you know anything of the Jewish community in Helsinki, Ralf?" I enquired tentatively, using his first name as he had insisted.

He leaned forward in his seat.

"A little," he replied. "I know that there are about fifteen hundred Jews in the country, a thousand or so in Helsinki and a couple of hundred in the city of Turku. The remainder are scattered around the place."

My companion started toying with his tie again. I realised it was some kind of nervous movement.

"I don't know how much you know about the history of the Jews in Finland," he continued. "But many of them are the descendants of Jewish soldiers in the Russian armies of the old Tsars. As you may know, Finland was a Grand Duchy for over one hundred years before it gained independence in 1917."

I nodded and he went on.

"These Jewish soldiers, known as Cantonists, settled in this country after their lengthy military service here. Until independence, however, they were unable to acquire citizenship and suffered many other restrictions."

Clearly, Ralf knew more than a little about the Jewish community in Finland. I suspected the fact that his father was Jewish had some relevance to his knowledge. The resigned manner in which he leaned back in his seat and gazed pensively through the window suggested that he was reading my thoughts. I had the distinct impression he wanted to tell me something, perhaps about his father. Yet some inhibition appeared to be holding him back. I felt sorry for him, but I did not know why.

A refreshments trolley, pushed along the carriage aisle by a pretty young girl, provided a welcome distraction. I offered to buy Ralf a hot drink. He accepted and I paid for two piping coffees, handed over in crockery cups. I glanced surreptitiously at the window and saw Ralf's reflection. As he sipped the hot black liquid, his eyes studied me carefully, like he was measuring meticulously how I might react. Then he spoke again.

"Look," he began, "I know that, quite unintentionally, I've aroused your curiosity about my father."

I opened my mouth to speak, but he held up a hand to stop me.

"I don't often speak of what I'm about to tell you, especially not to Jewish people. But, somehow, I feel that I can talk to you about my father."

I assured him that it was unnecessary to tell me anything, but he insisted that he wanted to explain something to me. I thanked him for his trust and, encouraged by my words, he went on.

"I'm sure you're aware that, during the Second World War, Finland was an ally of Nazi Germany against the Soviet Union."

I nodded.

"But what you may not have considered is that a substantial number of Jewish men were serving in the Finnish army."

It was true that I had not known of this, but the tragic irony of their situation struck me at once. Ralf obviously noted the combination of disquiet and interest on my face.

"You may have guessed already that my father was one of those Jewish soldiers ..."

I shook my head.

"Well, he was. In fact he was an officer in the army. You cannot possibly imagine the terrible conflict in the minds of these serving Jews who were faithful, patriotic citizens of Finland. There was, indeed, a great threat to the country from communist Russia, which happened also to be an enemy of Germany. However, these men were not unaware of the dreadful persecution of their brethren in occupied Europe."

Ralf paused for a moment or two, as if to let me absorb fully what he was saying. He sighed and his shoulders appeared to sag.

"What could my father do? He had been called to serve and protect his country and family, his parents and his sisters. To its lasting credit, the Finnish government had repelled German requests to deliver up the nation's Jews. What would you have done in the circumstances my father found himself?"

I did not consider that an answer was expected. But, though I remained silent, my brain struggled to find one.

"My father was well educated. He was a teacher in a secondary school. He was, perhaps unfortunately, a talented linguist and a fluent German speaker. Because of his useful attributes, he found himself being posted to Berlin as Finnish military liaison officer with the German High Command."

I drank the remains of my now lukewarm coffee. The action served to calm my heartbeat, raised by the extraordinary development in Ralf's story.

"My father was unable to resist the transfer, and he was accepted warmly by his German military colleagues. Though they were unaware that he was Jewish."

At last, I felt able to say something.

"Ralf," I said, as sympathetically as I could, "I'm grateful to you for trusting me enough to tell me all this. Believe me, I can appreciate the sensitivity. Please don't take what I'm about to say as in any way offensive. During our conversation, I've had the impression that you're embarrassed by, or even ashamed of, your father. Please don't be ..."

Ralf frowned at me.

"Actually, you're quite wrong," he interrupted. "But please allow me to finish my story."

I nodded, with appropriate contrition for my bad value judgement. After a sip of his drink, Ralf continued.

"My father was stationed in the capital of the Nazi Reich for three years. Only an occasional leave home was permitted. During his time in Germany, he met and fell in love with a beautiful, Aryan woman. She was an army nurse, a few years older than her lover. My father's family were distraught when he broke the news to them during one brief furlough. But he continued the relationship. After the end of the war, he brought her home to Finland and married her in a civil ceremony. I was born a year later. My father's family refused to accept my mother or to see my father."

My travel companion swallowed what must have been cold coffee.

"I only ever saw my paternal grandparents a couple of times before they died some years ago. I never met my father's sisters. My parents settled in Turku but had no more children."

"Are your parents still alive?" I ventured.

Ralf quickly looked towards the window as the white forest flashed past. When he turned back to address me again, I could see that his eyes were clouding with emotion.

"My father died a few years back. My mother is resident in a nursing home in Turku. It's her birthday tomorrow. She will be eighty-five. I'm going to visit her, though regrettably the state of her mind is such that sometimes she fails to recognise me."

I shook my head and reached across to touch his arm. He withdrew a handkerchief from a jacket pocket and wiped his face.

"She was a wonderful mother to me, and a good wife to my father. It's hard for me to see her in this condition. She and her family had detested the Nazi regime. But they could do nothing, other than to respect and safeguard my father's secret during the war years in Berlin."

I felt only anguish at Ralf's amazing story, as we talked a little about his own life.

"You know," he said at one point, "my father used to call me his midnight son … S-O-N! You can hear it's a play on our country's daylong, summer light."

I smiled.

"I think my father was trying to tell me something. Something about hope in the midst of despair."

As he said this, I thought of the imminent Passover festival and the hope that the story of the Exodus inspires in the Jewish people every year. I mentioned this to Ralf and it seemed to spark a distant memory in him.

"Isn't that hope symbolised in the final words of the Haggadah?" he asked.

It was a rhetorical question because he quickly added another.

"Doesn't it say, Next year in Jerusalem?"

I nodded and we grasped each other's hands.

The selection

TREMBLINGLY, THE retired doctor adjusted the focus of his binoculars. The face in the circle of enhanced light blurred for a moment then sharpened. There could be no mistake now. A few minutes earlier, as the older man in his sights had walked along the street, he had looked achingly familiar, and despite the passage of more than half a century. Amazingly, his height and bearing had barely altered. But could the observer at the window of his first floor apartment be absolutely certain it was the right man? After all, the unaided eyesight of a seventy-year-old could play some strange visual tricks.

Now, as the man from the street sat at the window table in the café directly opposite the apartment building, the watcher knew for sure. The binoculars had confirmed his recognition. He understood from past experience that almost everything about an individual's features could be transformed: by the passing of time, by the weather, by plastic surgery and by disfigurement, self-inflicted or otherwise. Everything, that is save the look in the eyes.

The eyes of the old man, probably well into his eighties, were something else. The observer would never forget them as long as he lived; though he had met their chilling glare for only a few, panic-stricken moments on that freezing, hideous, howling night. That terrifying night when, as a shivering teenager, he stood huddled with his family on the platform ramp at Auschwitz-Birkenau, the Nazi's most notorious death camp in Poland. The eyes. Yes, the eyes … the eyes of a shark, black, pitiless, murderous. It was the man all right. The arrogant, swaggering young SS officer whose duty it was to decide between a continuing existence as a slave and liquidation by gas that icy night. The immediate fate of hundreds of terrified Jews, stumbling out of the stench of their cattle-truck transport, lay in this man's abominable hands. The power of selection was his and his alone.

★ ★ ★

Dr Leon Rozanski sat comfortably in his favourite chair by the window of his Tel Aviv apartment. Two years retired from his medical practice, and a widower for a decade, he enjoyed watching the people passing to and fro in the street below. Living just a stone's throw from Dizengoff, he took pleasure in a constant parade of citizens and tourists. He missed his consulting room; but observing closely the men, women and children ambling or hurrying beneath his alert gaze somehow instilled in him a compensatory sense of continued contact with the everyday world.

Not that the retired general practitioner lacked good friends and neighbours, many of them his erstwhile patients. Although he seldom ventured from his home now, he often welcomed visitors. Long-standing acquaintances would frequently drop by for a coffee in the morning or a game of chess in the evening. His plump and cheerful Russian home help, Martha, came in four afternoons each week to clean, dust and prepare a hot supper. Dr Rozanski and occasionally a couple of dinner guests were exuberant with praise for her delicious dishes from the old country, especially the Ukrainian stews.

Whilst the retired medic did not want for companionship, a wave of distressing loneliness sometimes swept over him. In part, this undoubtedly ensued from the loss of his beloved wife Silvia, but not entirely so. The depressing feeling of isolation had ebbed and flowed over many years and had been endured even when Silvia was alive. In fact, his late wife had shared the same emotion from time to time. The spouses were well aware of the cause of this deep emptiness that afflicted them. Their entire families, grandparents, parents, siblings, aunts and uncles, had perished in the gas chambers of Auschwitz. Leon and Silvia had been the only survivors.

Their own two children lived in New York: two sons, both medical men, with beautiful wives, wonderful children and very successful careers. All of them tried to visit Israel every few years. But they were always speaking on the telephone or writing Pops with the latest news and photos. Dr Rozanski looked forward to the calls from America; he loved chatting to the grandchildren about High School and their current crazes. He was so very proud of his sons, a psychiatrist and a paediatrician, and their respective families.

Dr Rozanski grabbed his walking stick, suspended from the chair back, and hobbled into the kitchen. An effort of movement lingered from a recent hip-replacement operation; but his medical advisers were encouraged by the surgical outcome, and their prognosis for a total recovery was good. He made himself a mug of instant coffee and returned with the steaming drink to his window seat. Placing the large cup on a adjacent occasional table, he settled back to resume his people watching.

Spring had arrived early in the city. The retired doctor gazed up at the sun-filled sky. The winter had proved to be much wetter than forecast by the weather pundits. Certainly, he felt, the rain had not assisted his post-operative recuperation. Small, fluffy white clouds drifted across the blueness like a flock of scattered sheep. He reached for his mug, took a sip of the hot liquid and put it down quickly. The tip of his tongue burned, just for a moment but the fleeting sensation of intense heat brought the flash of a dreadful nightmare to his mind. He squeezed his eyes tight shut; from his white-haired head to his toeless feet, it seemed to him as if his whole body had been seized by a searing pain.

After a few minutes, he opened his eyes and peered out of the window. A lukewarm globule of salt water trickled down his cheek and dropped onto the pocket of his white, short-sleeved shirt. He took a handkerchief from a trouser pocket and wiped the cloying mix of sweat and tears from his face. He stared for some seconds at the number tattooed on his forearm, shook his head slowly then continued his observation of the street,

Two young mothers, wheeling prams and gossiping animatedly to each other, sauntered by on the pavement opposite. They passed the hairdresser's salon, then Dr Rozanski's favourite café, with its huge picture window, crossed the road and disappeared out of his line of vision. He had recognised the two women, even remembered them from a time when they were as small as their own offspring. They had been brought to his surgery, he recalled, as they developed the usual childhood complaints, chicken pox … German measles. The old man swallowed hard and wondered why he had not recalled that illness in terms of the medical expression, Rubella. The adjective German was not one that he wished voluntarily to invite into his head.

He turned from contemplating the busy thoroughfare and looked across his living space to the cluttered mantelpiece. Along the length of the pine shelf were arrayed wooden-framed, sepia photographs of his grandparents and parents. He shifted his gaze to the heavyweight, oak desk in the corner of the large but prolifically furnished room. Smiling portraits of his wife, children and grandchildren, coloured images in silver frames, confronted his melancholy eyes. He turned back to the window and the street below.

A man was walking along the pavement opposite. He wore a light suit and a panama hat with a deep black band. The wide brim of the hat was pulled down, obscuring the top half of the man's face in shadow. Dr Rozanski felt a slight twinge of recognition. There was something disconcertingly familiar about the man's bearing and gait. He rubbed his chin with a questioning motion of his right hand. The sudden shock of wetness on his skin made him realise that his palms were sweating profusely. His eyes focused intently on the elderly man as he stopped, appeared to hesitate for a second or two, then entered the café. The retired medic wracked his brain. Despite not seeing the man's features clearly, he was almost sure he had seen him before … somewhere, some time. Frustrated by his failure to recollect where and when, he pressed his nose to the glass and peered intently across the road. He observed the man remove his hat and sit down at the unoccupied table by the window.

The doctor often popped into the café for a coffee or a cold drink of fresh Jaffa orange juice, though not of course in recent weeks. Now he spotted Tina, the pretty young waitress daughter of the proprietor, standing by the man's table ready to take his order. She scribbled on her notepad and turned away with her usual winning smile. As the man stared blankly through the window, Dr Rozanski's heart missed a beat. He began to tremble uncontrollably, his mouth became as arid as sawdust and the skin crawled at the nape of his neck. His head exploded with a solitary thought, "I know this man … I know this man."

His legs had almost turned to jelly. But with an indomitable effort of willpower, the old man reached for his stick and hoisted himself from his chair. For an instant as he stood shakily and slightly stooped, he experienced an unusual dizziness. He waited for a short while to recover his balance and composure. He made his way across the room, carefully negotiating a settee, two armchairs and a table, and finally leaned against his desk.

He removed a small bunch of keys from a trouser pocket and opened one of the left hand drawers. He returned the keys to his pocket and pulled out the drawer. Inside rested a pair of binoculars, a snub-nosed revolver and a tiny, silver box. The doctor lifted out the rubber-coated glasses and threaded a passage back to the window. He placed his stick against the wall and raised the telescopic sights to his eyes. Tremblingly, the old man adjusted the focus.

★ ★ ★

Dr Rozanski limped across the road to the café. The over-firm grip on his walking stick was the only outward sign of a profound inner tension. In the right hand, outer pocket of his jacket rested the gun, fully loaded, safety catch on. An inside pocket held the silver pillbox. Gently, he pushed open the glass-panelled door and entered. A few customers were seated at the rear of the informal restaurant. Although there were several unoccupied tables, the retired GP chose the one by the window. Here the older man sat with a cup of coffee in front of him. There were three vacant chairs at the blue cloth-covered table. On one of them sat a panama hat.

Sunlight streamed into the café, flooding the table with a warm glow.

"Would you mind if I sat at your table?" Dr Rozanski asked the man. "It's such a glorious day to be sitting by the window and, besides, my leg is playing up."

Without looking up, the man nodded.

"I hope it's okay."

The man looked up. The eyes. Yes, the eyes.

"It's okay … really, it's okay, please sit down."

The man gestured to the empty chair directly opposite to him. Dr Rozanski sat down, hung his stick on the back and pondered. The man had not said anything at first, just nodded.

Initially, the doctor had wondered whether the man understood what he was saying. His nod was equivocal. It could have meant no more than a guess at the request to sit down at his table. Now the medic knew that his table companion could understand, as well as speak, the language of modern Israel, at least simple Ivrit. Although the man's words had been few, spoken with a not uncommon middle-European accent, Dr Rozanski noted their idiomatic expression. The man was no tourist, no stranger in this homeland of the Jewish people.

Once again, the doctor confronted the older man's chilling eyes, a metre or so away from him. Just like that horrendous night on the ramp. The man stared through the window and Dr Rozanski shuddered at the still haughty profile. Without a shadow of doubt, this was the young SS officer on the milling platform. Although he never knew his name, the merciless eyes of the Nazi brute had haunted him in his worst nightmares for more than half a century. Now, a mere arm's length away, sat the man who had selected his entire family for immediate elimination. Dr Rozanski clenched his fists under the table and fought to control his heartbeat and breathing. He had to remain surface calm. Then Tina was standing by the table.

"We haven't seen you in ages, Dr Rozanski," she said brightly. "How are you?"

The doctor explained to the teenager about his operation, adding that he hoped to come in more often now that he was firmly on the road to recovery. He ordered a black coffee, and the girl moved quickly to the serving counter at the back of the café. She returned quickly with the piping hot drink and placed it on the table. The doctor allowed the cup to stand untouched. He shifted slightly in his chair to feel, reassuringly, the bulging outline of the gun in his pocket.

"I haven't seen you around here before," he said.

The sentence was half way between a question and a statement.

The older man did not respond, continuing to gaze through the window. The earlier, brief exchange showed that the man, albeit some years older than the doctor, was not deaf. The GP speculated on the man's failure to reply. Finally, he asked himself, What is this monster doing here … in Israel?

Accepting that the old Nazi was deliberately ignoring him, Dr Rozanski leaned across the table.

"I don't know your name," he said quietly, but with a distinct hint of menace. "But I know who you are."

The man turned from the window to face him. Three physical signs informed the doctor that his recognition had not been faulty. A nerve at the edge of the man's mouth began to twitch, his cruel, ruthless eyes became receptacles of a disbelieving fear and he started to rise from his chair, reaching for his hat.

"Sit down," the doctor ordered in a piercing whisper. "Now."

The man's eyes darted from the front door to the occupied tables at the rear of the café. None of the customers or staff seemed to be taking any notice of the two elderly men at the window table. The older man had noted the implied threat in the other man's voice. Now Dr Rozanski made that threat overt. He flashed the gun in his hand for a mere moment then hid it beneath the table again.

"If you don't sit down this very instant, and stay sitting down, I'll kill you right away."

The man sat down immediately.

"Y-you're crazy," he spluttered, nervously. "I've never seen you before in my life. What do you want with me?"

The retired medic stared into the man's hate-filled eyes.

"You are quite wrong on both counts," he said. "I'm not mad and you have seen me before. Oh, yes … and you've met my family, too."

"I know your name, also, thanks to the waitress," the older

man remarked, recovering his composure. "But you have surely mistaken me for someone else."

The doctor leaned back slightly, as if to attain a better visual perspective.

"No, I don't think so," he responded with a mordant smile. "Why don't you tell me precisely who you are, Dr Rozanski?"

The younger man shook his head.

"No, I sit here representing my entire family and the thousands of other Jews you selected for death."

The man, still clutching his panama, waved a finger of his free hand.

"You are insane!" he snarled, trying hard to keep his voice low. "I don't know what you're talking about."

But Dr Rozanski had detected the revealing beads of sweat forming on the older man's deeply lined forehead, each moist furrow bearing a guilty thought.

"But I believe that you do," the doctor emphasised, tightening the grip on his gun. "You converse in fluent Ivrit but you are definitely not a native of this country. I would suggest that you are German. Ironically, you look a bit Jewish in your old age. But you are most certainly not of our faith. I'll now state exactly who you are … a Nazi murderer."

The man was silent for a moment or two. Then he tried to laugh but somewhere in his throat the sound aborted into a strangulated cough. The attempt ended in a contorted half-smile.

"You're having some kind of joke with me, yes?" he persisted, hunching his shoulders.

His accuser leaned across the table again.

"Believe me, my gun is very serious, as are the bullets inside it. I'm giving you thirty seconds to admit that, in 1943, you were an SS officer at Auschwitz. If you don't, I'll shoot you dead. I'll have only one regret. The bullet that kills you will produce a faster result than the gas that suffocated the victims of your selection on the ramp. By my wristwatch, you have half a minute from now to decide your immediate fate."

The older man bit his lower lip and glanced desperately at the café's front door. Dr Rozanski made some quick play of moving his hand beneath the table.

"Don't even think about it," he warned. "And please don't labour under any misapprehension that I wouldn't have the guts to pull the trigger."

After some twenty-five seconds, the older man lowered his eyes and nodded slowly.

"Say it," the doctor demanded but without raising his voice.

The man with the panama looked at the doctor with resignation.

"Yes, you're correct, of course, I am German in origin," he began. "In 1943, as you say, I was an SS officer at the Auschwitz-Birkenau concentration camp. On several occasions, it was my responsibility to make selections from arriving transports."

"Now tell me how you come to be here, in Israel."

The older man sighed deeply.

"Okay, I will tell you. But, first, you must tell me what you intend to do."

"At this precise moment, nothing. Continue."

"In January 1945," the ex-SS man went on, far from reassured about his future, "we were hurriedly evacuating, no fleeing, the camp in view of the Russian army's rapid advance into Poland. In the confusion, I decided to implement a plan conceived some months earlier … when I realised that Hitler's war was lost. I adopted the identity of a dead German Jew, deserted into the countryside and somehow managed to survive until the end of the war. Eventually, I found my way to a displaced persons' camp in Austria. I was confident that I could pass myself off as a German Jew. Two factors, apart from the language, my physical condition at that time and some knowledge of the Jewish religion, culture and customs, assisted me greatly. First, I'd had my SS tattoo removed, painfully, very expensively but effectively, and the dead Jew's camp number tattooed on my forearm. Secondly, I was circumcised."

"You were circumcised?"

Dr Rozanski interrupted with surprise, turning slightly to ensure that other customers and the staff had no inkling of the bizarre conversation.

"Yes. I'd been circumcised as a child. For medical reasons, you as a doctor will understand. I thought this might've caused me real problems when I applied to join Himmler's SS. Naturally, my medical history was checked and my Aryan credentials were confirmed as impeccable."

The retired GP nodded coldly.

"After a couple of years in various encampments, I was approached by a man who said that young Jews were needed desperately in Palestine to fight a coming war with the Arabs. I'd originally intended to make for South America. But there were some problems. So, I thought, what better place to lose myself than amongst the very people who'd never credit a former member of the SS living in their midst. I agreed to go. In the end, I was smuggled past the British naval blockade in a rusty old tramp steamer packed with many hundreds of Jewish refugees. You may not believe it, doctor, but I actually fought on your side in the 1948 War of Independence. I was even awarded a medal for bravery. You could say that I helped to create the State of Israel."

Dr Rozanski remained silent.

"After the declaration of statehood, I opened a small, watch repair shop, here in Tel Aviv, though not in this district. Living in a tiny apartment above my work premises, I never married and kept very much to myself. I was accepted as an Israeli without question. I paid my taxes on time to the Revenue as a good citizen. I had no difficulty concealing my true identity. I didn't socialise that much. The chances of discovery by someone who might've recognised me from the war in Europe were very remote."

At that point in the narrative, the German stopped and frowned.

"You, Dr Rozanski, are that chance in a million."

The retired GP made no reply.

"In my heart ..."

At last, the doctor spoke.

"What heart?"

"In my heart, I suppose I knew that, sometime, this day would arrive.

The medical man held up a hand.

"You have no heart. Without mercy, you despatched my family, my late wife's family and countless other innocents to their choking, shrieking deaths in your gas chambers. They were utterly defenceless men, women and children. How dare you say that you possess a heart ... if you had one, it would be as black as hell."

"But I-I had no choice," the other man bleated, his eyes watery and begging.

The doctor moved an index finger to the trigger.

"So you had no choice," he said, his head nodding slowly. "Well, I will give you a choice now."

With his free hand, he removed the pillbox from his jacket's inside pocket and placed it in the centre of the table.

"The choice I will give you is this. Inside the box is a lethal capsule. One bite and death follows virtually instantaneously. In my right hand, as you are aware, is a loaded gun. You may choose, the capsule or the bullet. Once more, and for the final time, the selection is yours ..."

Commemoration service

TWO GERMAN speakers, a man and a woman in their twenties, sat talking together at the next table. The guttural language invaded my private thoughts and annoyed me. Tables from the Bohemian Café at the Grand Hotel Europa spilled onto sun-splashed Wenceslas Square. I sat alone sipping a Becherovska, the national herbal liquor. A tall glass of Staropramen pilsner stood handy to chase the more traditional, alcoholic concoction. Sitting amongst the tourists and mobile-wielding Czech yuppies outside the famous art nouveau hotel, I'd been thinking about the often-tragic events witnessed by this magnificent, elongated space in the vibrant heart of Prague, the so-called Paris of Eastern Europe.

Images came into my head of Soviet tanks lining the vast open space before me during the brutal occupation of the city in 1968. I recalled the fatal protest of student Jan Pallach, who immolated himself the following year. And then I remembered the vocal crowds of 1989, supporters of the non-violent Velvet Revolution that had heralded the demise of communism. But the hard, Teutonic sounds emanating from the neighbouring table shifted my reflections even further back, to the dark days of 1939. In April of that year, the German army paraded through Wenceslas Square to welcome the arrival of the Nazi Reichprotektor of Bohemia and Moravia.

I adjusted the black kippah on my head and recollected, from my Holocaust reading, that this event had foreshadowed the disastrous end of hundreds of ancient Jewish communities in the Czech lands. I'm almost fluent in German, a capability that stems from the Yiddish spoken by my parents and grandparents. However, I harbour mixed feelings about using it. Occasionally, the language has proved useful, especially in the Czech Republic where it is taught in the schools. I was distracted again by the voluble conversation of the two young people a couple of metres away. I turned to look at them. The man noticed my sudden movement and smiled at me through wire-rimmed spectacles. I did not respond. Instead, I swallowed the remnant of my bittersweet aperitif then grasped the glass of lager. The promising warmth of a Prague spring, as well as the honey-coloured Czech beer, filled me with a happy expectation, a kind of renewed optimism. I raised my face towards the bright afternoon sun and closed my eyes. Then I overheard the name, Terezin.

During the Second World War, Terezin or, as the Germans had renamed the town, Theresienstadt was a Jewish ghetto and transit camp. Between 1940 and 1945, more than 140,000 Jews, from many countries in Europe, were transported to this grim, former garrison fortress, some sixty or so kilometres north of Prague. Little did they know that their destinies had been finely choreographed by the Nazis, at the infamous Wannsee Conference in Berlin in January 1942, as part of Hitler's "final solution to the Jewish question". Although there were several routes into Terezin, there was just one road out. This led finally to the gas chambers of Auschwitz, the Nazis' notorious death camp in Poland. Of the 87,000 souls shipped out for "resettlement" in the east, barely three thousand survived the war. Thousands of others died in the town itself, from exhaustion, disease, starvation and general inhuman treatment.

My reaction, therefore, on hearing the name of this historically ill-fated town on the lips of two young Germans, was to pay a stern attention to their continuing conversation. The girl, whose long blonde hair cascaded over her white blouse, had her back to me. This had the effect of slightly muffling her voice and, to some extent, blocking that of her companion who sat opposite her. All in all, I caught only snatches of their exchanges. But my initial curiosity grew into indignation when I heard references here and there to the Gestapo, the SS and the Czech village of Lidice.

In 1942, the village was destroyed, and its inhabitants massacred, by the Nazis. This was a horrific reprisal for the assassination of the tyrannical Reichprotektor Reinhard Heydrich by two, English-trained, Czech partisans. Anger swelled up inside me as the German couple that had just started quaffing freshly delivered beers, began laughing. I could not believe my ears. Here were two, casually but smartly dressed, intelligent sounding, and obviously well educated, young citizens of the European Union. Not a pair of thuggish, neo-Nazi skinheads.

I had reason to hope that the new generation of young Germans had learned from the indelible stain on their nation's fairly recent past. I turned sharply but awkwardly in my chair, scraping its steel legs jarringly on the stone-paved sidewalk. The grating noise prompted the young German couple to stare in my direction. For an instant, the world around the three of us was silent and unmoving. Four light blue eyes focused on my head covering, then further south on what must have appeared a grimly hostile expression. In that frozen moment, like a paused, old video frame with blurred edges, the pair seemed struck by a shocked realisation.

It was the young man, his squarely chiselled features a

portrait of regret, who finally broke the spell that enwrapped the three of us. He leaned forward and murmured something to the woman. I was on the point of reacting in some way, when she rose from her seat and, to my surprise, stepped towards me. She was short, though willowy. Her pale, round and attractive face was filled with an expression I can only describe as repentant. For a moment, she stopped in her tracks and looked back, apparently seeking reassurance from her companion. He obliged by nodding purposefully.

It was as she came about to face me again that I noticed the gold chain around her neck. The centre of the chain, resting on her blouse, held what looked like joined up letters, also fashioned in the precious yellow metal. As the girl approached, and to my utter amazement, I could make out that they were Hebrew letters, spelling out the name Sarah. As I lifted my eyes to meet hers, my mind was the home of confusion.

When she stood silently before me, all I could think to say, in my obviously English accent, was, "Hello".

"Please excuse me, sir," she said in perfect English, "but my friend and I would be so grateful if you could join us at our table. We think you may perhaps have inadvertently misconstrued our behaviour just now."

Her demure demeanour was so disarmingly, yet sincerely, apologetic that I found myself accompanying the young women back to her table. Like a sprinter flying from his blocks at the starting gun's report, her companion sprang from his chair as I approached, holding my pilsner. He threw me a winsome smile and offered his hand, which I felt compelled to shake.

"My name is Karl," he said in English but with a pronounced German slant. "And this, sir, is my friend Sarah."

With a polite gesture, he beckoned me to sit in a vacant seat at the table. Once I had sat down and introduced myself, the couple resumed their places. At first, I felt unable to look at them directly; and a strained silence persisted between us for several seconds. The sun's reflection glinted brightly off our beer glasses as we raised them hesitantly to our lips. Then Karl spoke again.

"Please forgive us for intruding on your privacy."

I nodded neutrally, unsure of the situation I had walked into, and he continued.

"We are now painfully conscious that our discussion, or as much of our loud voices as you may have unavoidably overheard, could have given you, as an adherent to the Jewish faith, the wrong impression about us. I am a Gentile but Sarah is Jewish."

I glanced across the table at her and she smiled warmly at me. Karl noticed that I had almost finished my lager. He called over a waiter and, despite my weak protest, ordered another for me. The drink arrived almost instantly. I gripped the cool wetness of the fresh glass and watched the frothy head subsiding.

"I shouldn't have been listening to other people's conversations," I confessed, taking a gulp of the smooth, golden liquid. As I returned my glass to the table, I was disconcerted to see that the young couple were hand stifling childlike giggles.

"Please forgive us," Sarah said shyly. "But you have a moustache of froth on your upper lip."

Instantly, I knew why the couple had been laughing earlier. Suddenly, I felt very silly.

"Maybe I should ask you to forgive me," I said, grinning faintly.

It hit me forcefully that I may have made an impulsive and terrible mistake about this young man and woman.

Karl raised his glass and, totally unexpectedly, declared "L'Chaim!". For a split second, I was dumbstruck to hear the traditional, Jewish toast to life coming from the mouth of a German Gentile. When Sarah also lifted her glass, I recognised at once that the call for us to drink together was heartfelt and genuine. I swallowed some more of the refreshing lager and sensed my nervous system gradually relaxing.

"I think it's unfortunate that you may have misunderstood

some things we were saying about wartime events in this country," Karl said. "In what the Nazis named the Protectorate of Bohemia and Moravia."

I nodded, and he went on.

"I would like to explain something to you, about myself, which I believe you may find interesting."

Karl guessed that I was about to say he was not obligated to explain anything. He blinked in the radiant sunshine.

"Please allow me, sir."

What he related to me opened my eyes, humbling me for adopting a stereotypical approach.

"Actually, I am not German," Karl said. "I'm an Austrian, from Vienna."

Thinking back to the war years, I was not impressed by the national distinction.

"After graduating from university," the Austrian explained, "the time came for me to perform my deferred national service. Three options were available. I could serve nine months in the army, twelve months in the civil service or fourteen months devoted to what we term Gedenkdienst."

I made an unproductive, mental attempt at translating the word.

"I know your German is good," Karl said, bravely teasing me with amusingly mild praise. "But this is a technical expression, little known outside my country. It means, literally, commemoration service. The idea took wing in 1991 when the Austrian Chancellor admitted the role of our nation as a perpetrator in the Holocaust. Today, the programme sends delegates to Holocaust memorial facilities in Israel, the United States and fourteen countries in Europe."

Karl confirmed the choice I confidently expected of him.

"I opted for Gedenkdienst," he said. "And I spend my time now in Terezin, where I work in the ghetto museum and the associated educational and research facility."

He was anxious to tell me how difficult it was to be accepted on the programme. The young man also mentioned the rigorous eligibility and motivational tests of sincerity and commitment. I turned to Sarah, who had been patiently sipping her drink.

"I work permanently at the museum," she explained. "My late parents were children in Terezin, deportees with their parents from Berlin. All my grandparents were transported to Auschwitz towards the end of 1944. Miraculously, my father and mother, who knew each other in Terezin, were found amongst the survivors in the town. Much later, quite by chance, they met again in Germany, fell in love and married."

I had struggled to conceal my emotions as the pair described their work, and Sarah related the moving story of her family. Karl added, with a gentle pride, how he helped to run the International Youth Meeting Centre, created in former ghetto barracks and funded by the Czech Ministry of Culture.

"Mainly I assist in organising groups of mostly German and Austrian, but some Czech, High School groups," he told me. "They stay with us for a few days and attend a full schedule of lectures on the Holocaust, question and answer sessions, documentary film shows and meetings with concentration camp survivors. My other special work is to correct translations from Czech to German for pamphlets on the history of Terezin. It's all very satisfying work."

When Karl had finished speaking, I was at a loss to know how to react, either to him or to Sarah. I felt emotional and inadequate to the task. As we emptied our glasses in silence, a kind of invisible thread of understanding linked us closely together. The two young people began throwing guilty glances at their wristwatches. And I realised, equally culpably, that I had been keeping them from another engagement.

"I'm sorry," I said, studying my own timepiece. "I must be off now. I'm supposed to be meeting my wife in the Old Town

Square soon. Under that quaint Town Hall astronomical clock."

We all rose from our chairs at the same time. I shook hands with Sarah.

"Goodbye," Karl said, a broad smile on his face.

I pumped his hand and turned to go. Looking back over my shoulder, I raised my hand in a farewell wave and called out, "auf Weidersehen!"

Somewhere near Kiev

A TALL Jewish man in his mid-thirties leaned against the rail of the second-class passengers' boat deck. He surveyed in wonder the calm, sunset-lit ocean to the radiant horizon. Before retiring to the cabin where his wife and two daughters slept, he had decided to brave the deck to enjoy a small cigar. His spouse had objected to his smoking in their restricted accommodation. So he had donned his trilby, thick woollen scarf, fur-lined gloves and long, black overcoat and proceeded through the ship to the allocated deck space.

He had emerged into the chilling April night just below the great liner's fourth stack. There he had joined the few intrepid fellow passengers, mostly couples wrapped in close embrace, at the ship's side. All were prepared to suffer the freezing mid-Atlantic temperatures to witness the romantically dissipating, crimson glow. The Jewish man's gloved right hand held his cheroot awkwardly, as he inhaled then expelled smoke towards the fast disappearing western light. His own cold breath momentarily pursued the grey cloud then evaporated instantly.

The mighty, steel leviathan ploughed the sea westwards beneath a now starry but moonless sky. As he gazed into the darkening sea, the man retreated into himself, meditating on the life his family had left behind in Poland.

"Why do you want to go to America?" his mother had asked anxiously when he had first mentioned emigration. "I don't understand … you have everything here in Warsaw."

He remembered the strained atmosphere in his elderly parents' apartment that rainy Sunday afternoon. As his mother questioned him rigorously, his father continued to smoke his pipe and calmly read his newspaper in front of the fire.

"You'll be travelling around Pesach time," she said. "The family should be together for the Passover … and always."

He had tried hard to be a good son, like his three older brothers. But the nightmares had been coming to him more frequently. His mother should not seek to morally blackmail him. He could not tell her about the dreadful dreams that invaded his nights. She would never be able to comprehend their meaning.

"You've done very well in business," she went on, applying further pressure before assuming a slightly more conciliatory voice. "Why give it all up for an unknown future in a foreign land halfway around the world?"

He was about to respond when his father withdrew the pipe from his mouth and put down the journal on a side table.

"If he wants to go that badly, he must go, Mother," the old man said. "For goodness sake, he's old enough to make his own decisions … for good or, may the Almighty forbid peh, peh, peh, for ill. What right do we have to question his resolve to achieve even more for himself?"

"But he has family responsibilities, commitments," the mother urged. "How can he embark on an adventure like this?"

The couple's youngest son raised the volume of his voice, and regretted it immediately.

"I'm not going on an adventure, Mother!" he declared then softened his tone. "I've been writing to Uncle Aaron in New

York. There'll be a good job waiting for me, and a reasonable apartment for the four of us."

The white-haired woman threw up her hands in a histrionic display of aggravated frustration.

"I still don't understand you!" she cried, now shaking her head vigorously. "You already have a secure job and a decent house in a nice part of Warsaw."

The mother stared silently at her recalcitrant son, her eyebrows raised defiantly as if she expected her own logic to win an instant concession.

He threw his cigar butt over the ship's rail into the black water far below. He walked a short distance along the deck towards the third towering funnel. He was glad of the protection afforded by his warm and heavyweight, full-length coat. A slight movement caught his attention. Glancing sideways, he spotted a young couple huddled together in the private gloom beneath a lifeboat derrick. He smiled to himself. Probably newlyweds, he thought, maybe heading for a new life in the United States.

The inner smile faded quickly as the freezing ocean air bit achingly into the exposed flesh between his scarf and hat. The air, he thought, was almost as chillingly painful as his nightmares had been. He was thankful that they had been left behind in Poland, though, from time to time, their horrific images ripped into his conscious mind. He turned at the third huge stack. With some difficulty, he withdrew from his coat a gold watch, bequeathed to him by his maternal grandfather. The dial indicated a quarter past ten. He noted the late hour and slipped the precious possession back inside his pocket. He began walking in the direction of the nearest companionway that descended to his cabin deck. There his beloved little family were lying fast asleep, snug beneath their warm bedclothes.

"There's a war coming in Europe, Mother … and it's coming soon, believe me," he had said on that wintry Sunday afternoon. "The Balkans is like a tinder box and the Great Powers are spoiling for a fight."

Without looking up from the newspaper he had now resumed reading, his father nodded sagely. But his mother merely shook her head slowly.

"Always the pessimist," she moaned. "Have a little faith."

Her son frowned and shrugged his shoulders.

"What, in the jealous rivalries of useless politicians and despotic rulers? We're twelve years into the twentieth century, and we've still learned nothing from the past."

But it was not the war he knew was fast approaching that had formed the constant subject of his fearful nightmares. Although he believed such a conflict would be cataclysmic for the nations of Europe, the terrible dreams struck nearer home. His wife had anxiously witnessed him writhing on sweat-dampened sheets. She had seen the terror on his face as he suddenly came awake in the early hours, waking her from peaceful slumber, his eyes staring ahead, his lungs heaving with each gulp of air.

The first time he had revealed the content of his recurrent, subconscious visions, after constant urging by his wife, she had broken down and sobbed in his arms.

"I really do believe, my darling, that what I have seen will happen," he had said, stroking her long, silky brown hair. "Anti-Semitism is endemic in central Europe. I shudder to think it but, in the end, the Jews will suffer again. This time they may not recover from a tidal wave of violence and death."

He had convinced her that they needed to leave Poland, to leave Europe, forever and for the sake of their children.

"But what of your family?" she had said. "And mine, too."

Gently, he had raised her chin.

"They're all living a lie, my love. They're blinded by their comfortable assimilation."

His wife had gazed deeply into his eyes.

"But what if you're wrong?"

He had taken her small, soft hands in his own and kissed her tenderly on a wet cheek.

"Please trust me, my darling. I believe that I've been given a message that cannot be ignored. We cannot be certain of anything. But we must choose life for our daughters. Almost any unknown future will be better than the fate of Polish Jewry."

He quickened his step and passed the fourth black funnel. Suddenly, and for no reason apparent to him, he stopped, altered direction and made for the colossal ship's rail. He peered into the night's tranquil peacefulness, which prompted a feeling that here was a metaphor of hope for their future in a new country. He chortled inwardly, knowing that he was sufficiently realistic to acknowledge that nature's signs were often deceptive. Nonetheless, he enjoyed the moment of calm, dwarfed on the deck of the great ocean liner, which itself was a mere speck in the vast, undulating sea. To him, the contradiction was both comforting and frightening, something like the passage of life.

The images came to him, as they often did, unexpectedly. He closed his eyes and bowed his head, his hands gripping the wood and brass rail as if a sharp pain had shot though his body. There were the horrible images again. The same pile of twisted, skeletal corpses, their mouths gaping holes of terror. The same long lines of naked and shivering women, some holding the hands of small, bewildered children, others cradling babies in their trembling arms as they filed along the edge of a ravine. The same bearded men running naked through the forest, each following closely the one ahead, to the edge of the freshly dug pit. The same terrifying sounds of firing, the rapid stutter of machine guns, the ear-splitting rifle volleys. The same chilling screams of sudden realisation and disbelief, the same cries of horror, the same shrieks of pain, the same rivers of Jewish blood.

He slapped his hands against his ears, crumpling the brim of his hat. But the screams, the cries, the shrieks could not be stifled; they combined inside his head, a part of him now. Emotionally overcome with a disorientating grief, he moved in a sideways shuffle until he reached a lifebelt secured to the rail and held tightly to it. It was as if his senses had turned in on themselves, so that everything he was experiencing, seeing, hearing and feeling was of the world entirely within his own body.

Releasing his grip on the lifebelt, he stood back and looked at the name of the ship on its white surface. The black lettering stood out impressively. He began to trace each letter with the gloved index finger of his right hand, T-I-T-A-N-I-C.

At forty minutes past ten on that freezing night, the unthinkable happened …

Elijah's cup

I WAS six years old when I first saw the old tramp at our family Seder. It was the second night of the Passover festival. After the fourth cup of wine had been poured, Mum had left the table to open the street door. Dad began reciting the Shfoch Hamat'cha prayer from the Haggadah.

As Dad prayed for the downfall of our enemies, my bubbeh wrapped her arms around an ample body and turned towards the open dining room door.

"Can't you close the front door now, Helen, the draught's killing me," she called with a pained expression.

My Auntie Freda and Uncle Sam nodded their shivering agreement. As I sat frozen to my chair, though not because of the rush of chilled air from the street, Dad interrupted his davening.

"I'm not finished yet, Helen," he shouted. "Keep the door open."

Half the people around the table shook their heads disapprovingly, and hugged themselves with emphasis. They were too absorbed in their own discomfiture to notice the fear etched on my little round face.

"Please hurry, Michael," my zaydeh urged his son-in-law. "We're perishing here."

Paul, my older brother by three years, mimicked my maternal grandfather's East European accent.

"Hurry up, Dad," he echoed. "I'm perishing here."

The tramp was standing opposite me, behind my bubbeh's chair. He was wearing a grubby overcoat of dubious origin, the frayed collar turned up against a scruffy grey beard, and a battered hat of indeterminate age, colour and design. He grinned at me and placed an index finger upright against his closed and shrivelled lips. I pressed hard against the high seatback, my eyes popping with disbelief, my mouth gaping open in astonishment. Somehow, the room began to swim before my eyes and I felt really dizzy. Dad's disembodied voice seemed to come from a great distance … and then I heard the street door slam shut. It was like an explosion inside my head. I burst into tears and jumped from my seat. Mum had just returned to her place at the table. I fell on her body and buried my head in her apron-covered lap.

"What's the matter, darling?" Mum asked anxiously, lifting my head and planting a big wet kiss on a flushed, chubby cheek.

He's tired," advised Auntie Freda.

"He's drunk!" Paul screamed mischievously.

My bubbeh looked worried.

"Look how red his face is. Feel his forehead, Helen, he may have a temperature."

Gradually, I gained the courage to look about the room; and then over my mother's shoulder to the door leading to the hall. The grizzled old man had vanished. I remember feeling confused that nobody else had observed the strange, transient and poorly dressed visitor. At least my extrovert brother, sitting next to me, ought to have witnessed the tramp's presence. But if he had done so, he would have shouted his head off. I was too shy in company to ask my fifth question that Seder night.

"Is he okay?" Dad enquired, looking concerned.

I gazed directly at him, and he winked at me. He must have seen something in my eyes, or in my expression, that he recognised fleetingly. At that moment, I experienced the odd sensation of being alone in the room with him. His forehead creased and he tilted his head slightly. I thought he was about to ask me something, something important, but he remained silent. Instead, he gave me a unique smile that I have never forgotten.

"Can we get on with the service, Michael?" Uncle Sam muttered. "Time's marching on and the boy seems all right, now."

"Is he okay, Helen?" Dad repeated.

My mother nodded but sat me firmly across her legs, my back to her bosom and gave me a breathtaking hug.

"He's drunk, he's drunk!" Paul cried out.

I reacted quickly but in a tearful whisper.

"N-no, I'm n-not!"

Mum brushed some wayward hair from my brow with a sweep of her hand.

"He's only had some grape juice," she said.

"No!" my incorrigible brother insisted loudly. "Look at Elijah's cup. It's half empty!"

Everyone half-stood and stared at the large, silver goblet in the middle of the table. It was true. The level of wine, filled to the brim earlier by my Dad, was well down.

"He's drunk it!" Paul chimed, smirking at me. "That's why he's got the collywobbles."

My zaydeh winked at me.

"Did you drink it?" he asked.

I shook my head and began snivelling. Mum cuddled me. Even at my then tender age, I could recall a previous Seder and the discussion, certainly light-hearted, about who around the table had imbibed surreptitiously from the bulbous, silver becher. I glanced again at my father for the support I knew somehow I would receive from him. He pitched me a knowing smile.

"No, he didn't drink from Elijah's cup," Dad pronounced authoritatively, adding: "But we all know who did, don't we?"

Everyone around the Seder table burst into laughter.

"Elijah!" they sang in unison.

It was something of an annual ritual for our family gathering, though I was not fully aware of that at the time. Of course, everybody held fast to the belief that Dad had drunk from the mystical cup during the unwitting diversion I had created with my wailing outburst. You could always count on a distraction of one kind or another at the Seder.

"Why's it called Elijah's cup?" Paul asked Dad.

"I'm sure that I've told you before, son," he responded.

"Well I've forgotten," my brother groaned. "Tell me again ... please."

Uncle Sam gave my father a look of weary impatience, but Dad nodded towards Paul.

"How many cups of wine must each adult drink on Seder night, Paul?"

My brother had to think hard.

"Four," he replied finally, chuffed at knowing this was the correct answer.

"That's right," Dad confirmed. "But at one time the rabbis couldn't agree whether a fifth cup of wine should be drunk ..."

Paul interrupted.

"Why was that, Dad?"

Our father shook his head.

"I'm coming to that. To tell you the truth, son, I don't really know. The rabbis' solution was to fill a fifth cup with wine but not to drink it."

The family, including Uncle Sam but excluding me, nodded wisely.

"Over time," Dad continued, "the fifth cup became dedicated to the prophet Elijah. He lived nearly three thousand years ago. That's why we name the cup after him. According to our tradition, he never died. It's said that he will herald the coming of Moshiach."

I wanted to know who this Moshiach was, but I was too reticent to ask. Even though Paul looked as if he understood what Dad was talking about, I was sure he didn't really.

"Tradition also has it," Dad went on, "that Elijah will come on Seder night. That's why, after his cup is filled, Mummy opens the street door …"

When I heard that, I felt so scared that I nearly fell off Mum's lap. She grasped me in time and clasped her hands tightly around my waist.

"There's a legend," Dad said, with an odd look in my direction, "that Elijah will arrive dressed as a beggar on Seder night …"

Paul intervened again.

"Why's that?"

Uncle Sam looked like he was about to explode.

"All these questions," he grumbled loudly. "There's only supposed to be four tonight."

Dad acknowledged the need to conclude the service.

"It's said, Paul," he remarked finally, "that when he comes, Elijah will take note of how people react to him in deciding if we are ready for, and worthy of, Moshiach."

And when I heard that, and thought of the old tramp, I wet my pants.

⋆ ⋆ ⋆

Every second Seder night for the next seven years, I saw the old beggar. I was just as frightened on the second occasion as the first. But I did not run to the comfort of my mother's warm lap again, and I did not cry or wet my trousers. I was seven years old and trying very hard to be courageous. Even so, Paul repeated his accusation that I was drunk. After Mum had opened the street door, when Elijah is expected to be welcomed, my brother claimed he had seen me drinking from the prophet's cup. It was not true, of course. I would never have been brave enough to do such a thing.

My zaydeh passed away just before my eighth birthday. All of us were heartbroken. Mum was pregnant at the time and nearly miscarried from the shock. My sister was named Sally for my grandfather, whose name was Solomon, though everyone called him Solly. The following Passover, the old tramp appeared again. I was definitely not afraid of him now. He had become a familiar, expected figure to me. And, after all, I knew he would not hurt me and he always gave me a kindly smile. He never stayed for very long, just a couple of minutes. But it was obvious that no one, except me, could see him; though Dad usually gave me that strange, knowing look as soon as Mum had closed the front door.

As each Pesach came and went, I felt that I knew the unkempt old man better than the previous year. When Sally joined us at the Seder table, sitting in her highchair between Mum and me, the bearded tramp danced with joy to see her. When the annual visitor came to us on the second Seder night, and during the very short period between the opening and closing of the street door that he stayed, I never revealed to anyone that he was present in the room. In some years we had new guests, people that I had never seen before. Yet not one of them became remotely aware of my secret. It felt so good to be one up on Paul. Especially at the Passover following his barmitzvah when he considered he was an adult but did not act like one.

I saw the old beggar for the last time the year after my own barmitzvah. When the third cup of wine had been drunk and the fourth poured, I asked Dad if I could open the front door for Elijah. Sally was being sick; and Mum was occupied with her in the down stairs toilet. Even before my father had nodded assent, I had jumped up eagerly and run into the hall. With a pounding heart, I opened the door to the outside world. On the doorstep stood, to me, a now familiar old friend, dressed as usual in his tatty topcoat and peculiar headgear.

"Welcome," I said, with a confidence that surprised me.

"Who's that?" came my mother's voice from the toilet.

"It's only me, Mum. I'm just opening the door for Elijah."

The tramp stumbled across the threshold into the hall and I backed off a couple of feet. Unlike in previous years, when he would give me the predictable reassurance of a wonderful smile, the old man's features portrayed a look of melancholy. Then, for the first time, he said something. I was only thirteen but quite used to seeing him on a regular, annual basis. I was not at all apprehensive but I was surprised that he spoke. He did not say much and, initially, I could not understand what he was trying to tell me.

I thought he had said, "Not wet", which hardly made much sense, unless he was referring to the fact that it was not raining.

"Pardon?" I said, politely.

The old man drew closer to me and shook his head a few inches from my face.

"Not yet," he said quietly, but much more clearly now. "Not yet ..."

With that, he suddenly smiled at me. But it was such a profoundly sorrowful smile that I almost wept. He slowly turned away and shuffled towards the open front door, where he looked over his shoulder and waved meekly at me. Then he disappeared into the night.

I heard Dad calling from the dining room.

"You can close the street door now."

With a strange heaviness in my heart and, at that time, only a semblance of understanding, I returned to my seat at the Seder table.

* * *

It all seems so long ago. Now I am sitting at the head of the Seder table. It is the second night of the Passover festival and I have just poured the fourth cup of wine. I am about to recite Hallel. There seems to be a soporific, dreamlike quality about the room, a notion self-prompted by the remembrances of my childhood. Sitting around the table and waiting for my cue are my wife, our young children and our guests. At this moment, everything seems surreal. My wife moves, as if in slow motion, towards the hall and the front door beyond.

Now I can hear the door opening. A rush of cool air sweeps into the room. Our six-year-old son has a glazed, surprised look in his innocent, blue eyes, like a startled rabbit caught at night in the glare of a vehicle's headlights. Now his face crumples, he bursts into tears and I nod slowly and deliberately at him.

Clearing the mind

SHORTLY BEFORE one recent Rosh Hashanah, and its closely following Yom Kippur, I was strolling through the heart of London's West End. The city was enjoying a fine September morning, with warm sunshine radiating from a clear blue sky. As I ambled along the streets, it seemed like every other shop was a coffee house. Caffè Nero, Seattle Coffee Company, Pret, Aroma, Starbucks, Coffee Republic ... And the display lists of their various caffeine distillations appeared almost endless. Mochaccino, Americano, Doppio, Ristretto, Caffe Latte ... So I thought to myself, do we need this much coffee? It clogs our arteries, gives us heartburn and pumps up our blood pressure. It is hypertension in a cup! I dived into Costa and ordered a double cappuccino with extra chocolate sprinkle, to drink in.

The café was not very crowded. After all, it was mid-morning. Most of the local office workers were drinking at their desks, shoppers were licking the steam off department store windows and tourists were busy clicking their digital cameras. I settled myself on a stool near the huge picture window, and parked my large, steaming cup on the shiny steel ledge running its length. Taking a sip of the piping hot liquid through the white froth and clotting brown smudge, I gazed through the plate glass at the dizzily moving mishmash of traffic and pedestrians.

It felt like I was watching a DVD fast-forwarding on one of those huge, flat screen TVs. How did Wordsworth put it? "The world is too much with us …" Then another thought hit me. Do you know one of the most difficult things for anyone to do in the world today? Take two guesses. Okay, three. No? Well, I'll tell you. It has to be … clearing the mind. Try it. Try it right now, before you read another word. Do you see where I am coming from? Maybe we all drink too much coffee.

Sometimes, I pray that the myriad everyday thoughts that whirl electrically around the grey matter up top would cease and desist. Take five, maybe. And sometimes I pray for the freedom to concentrate on something really important, at least for a short while. To focus on a topic that will help me to become a better person, perhaps. I really do believe in the power of prayer. I believe that the Almighty does answer our prayers, though not necessarily in ways we might readily appreciate, or even comprehend.

Anyway, before the wad of chocolate sunk without trace, I ploughed my cappuccino's frothy topping with the long spoon supplied and savoured the sweet, viscous liquid. I heard a homeless guy selling the Big Issue, shouting at the top of his lungs in the street. It must have been a sign. Because I suddenly realised that, at this time of the year, approaching the Yomim Noraim, the Days of Awe, when Jewish people plead with the Almighty, I should really be thinking about the big issue. Clearing my mind, so that I can reflect more clearly on the meaning, shape and import of life … my life.

I was pondering the need to find cerebral space for some basic introspection, when I felt a hand on my shoulder. I swivelled round on the stool, expecting to see someone I knew. The expectation was fulfilled one hundred percent. But not in any way that I could have foreseen in my wildest imaginings. I could not help but recognise the individual holding a large espresso and smiling in my direction. It was … me!

Apart from the paralysis of shock, what can enter your mind when you seemingly confront yourself? Reflecting surfaces aside, I would say this was something as likely to happen as me levitating. Yet standing before me was a person who appeared to be my spitting image, my double … my doppelganger! Out of the corner of my eye, I noticed a street-side passer-by staring at the two of us with mild curiosity. The young woman grinned knowingly; and I knew instinctively that she thought we were twins. So let me make this absolutely clear once and for all. I do not have a twin!

As my initial trauma subsided, and I gradually recovered a normal heartbeat and pulse rate, my astounding look-alike pointed to the vacant stool next to mine.

"Okay if I sit here?" he asked me.

I nodded in a bemused sort of way and turned to my coffee for reassurance. Unthinkingly, I swallowed a mouthful and burned my tongue on the hot brew. At least the heat pain jolted me into a clear, though uncomprehending, realisation of the situation.

"Who am I? Sorry, who are you? Who are you?" I ventured, apprehensively, whilst studying the wholly familiar features of the middle-aged, grey-haired, not too bad looking man sitting beside me.

Facial characteristics, physique, demeanour and voice were unbelievably identical to my own. And the smart casual clothes looked remarkably similar to those I had put on that morning. I did note, however, the absence of a pimple on the guy's chin. From time to time, I still receive a small legacy from my days of adolescent acne. I had observed the nasty little red spot in the shaving mirror that morning.

"I don't think you need to ask, do you?" my living image responded.

"But what are you doing here? What do you want from me?" I fired back.

He brought the cup of concentrated, black coffee to his lips, sipped and replaced it on the ledge.

"I want nothing, save one thing."

I sensed my clammy hands trembling. Instinctively, I grabbed my cup for a touch of warm support. I needed to steady my reeling nerves. It is strange to say now but, with a mixture of patent inquisitiveness, misplaced hubris and impatient anticipation, I looked myself straight in the eyes.

"And what might that one thing be?" I enquired with emphasis.

My companion hesitated for a moment then chuckled unnervingly.

"The truth, my friend, just the plain, honest truth."

Now I hold the truth to be very important. But I know it can be a slippery commodity. So let me give you an example then perhaps you will get my drift. Two boys, let us call them A and B, witness a mugging. When interviewed by the police, A recalls that the robber was wearing a blue sweatshirt. B swears it was green. Both youngsters honestly believe that they are telling the truth. Only one of them actually is. It is boy A. Boy B is colour blind but does not know it. Nor do the police. But the Almighty does.

"All right," I said. "But what truth do you want? Is it the truth as you see it? Is it the truth as I see it? Or is it the truth as the Almighty sees it?" My new and mysterious acquaintance considered this for a few seconds, his expression enigmatic.

"I know you're an honest man and a true believer," he remarked. "In light of your question, I trust you."

Hey, wait a minute, I thought. Who was this guy to say that he trusted me? I was just about to think that I had never set eyes on this man in my life, when I thought … mirror. I gained the quick impression that my look-alike was starting to act like some kind of father confessor. Wrong religion, my friend, I chortled to myself. Besides, any T'shuva would be between the Almighty and me during the Days of Awe.

My hovering sidekick must have read my mind.

"Look, I'm not here to receive your confession, repentance or atonement for any sins or transgressions you may have committed," he said, a serious look spreading across his face. My face? "I know that's not my business. I'd just like you to appreciate that, if you want, you can talk frankly to me. I realise it may be difficult. I understand, truly. Maybe you'd find it simpler, easier if you did, well, communicate with me. Perhaps I can help you to prepare yourself."

Prepare myself? I cannot really explain what happened next. But, somehow, I found myself adrift on a tranquil ocean, metaphorically I assume. The shimmering, blue-green sea, soothingly rippling around me, was so comforting, so therapeutic … to hear, to see, to touch. I had the oddest sensation that the cool, translucent water was washing over and through my body and clearing my mind.

The feeling came in three waves. First, I sensed the washing away of my immediate environment's numerous distractions, the harsh, grinding noise of the traffic, the pleading, sardonic cries of the Big Issue vendor and the sterile conversation of fellow coffee drinkers. Next, all the stultifying, extraneous, everyday thoughts floated out of my head like flotsam from a floundering ship. Finally, with a newfound capacity to focus with a crisp clarity, I knew what I wanted to say to the character occupying the neighbouring stool. After I had done so, I felt unburdened, relieved, cathartic, primed.

I turned to drink some more coffee. When I swivelled back to face my freshly acquired pal, an empty seat confronted me. I glanced quickly around the room and then towards the glass entrance door. I believe that I caught a glimpse of a familiar figure disappearing into the street. I pressed my nose against the window, looking to right and left. But I could not spot him. Or should I say … me? So I sat up straight and contemplated the vacant stool beside me.

Sensing some sweat beads on my forehead, I pinched out a tissue from a mini-pack and wiped my brow. Then I noticed an empty espresso cup sitting on the ledge. Two words entered my head … alter ego. Being a bit of a wordsmith, I remembered the Latin tag's equivocal definition: an intimate and trusted friend and a person's secondary or alternative self. The dual interpretation seemed to reflect remarkably accurately the ambiguity of my recent experience.

I left Costa, bought a copy of the Big Issue (for the first time ever) and walked through Soho to Oxford Street. I hurled myself onto the platform of one of a convoy of Routemasters heading west, flashed my one-day travel card at the conductor and bounded upstairs to the top deck. Alighting opposite Selfridges, I crossed the road at the traffic lights, entered the huge department store through its art deco main entrance and hastened through the overwhelming, aromatic mist of its perfume gondolas. I lingered fairly aimlessly in the men's wear section on the first floor before exiting onto Baker Street and making my way to a nearby kosher restaurant. I gave my order to one of the guys behind the counter, waited for the chopped liver on rye, new green cucumber and a Diet Coke, then paid at the till. I found an empty table at the rear and sat down.

I opened my Big Issue haphazardly at a report on the dearth of affordable housing for teachers, nurses and other public service workers in the capital. But I was too preoccupied to read the article carefully, or even at all. When I suddenly felt a hand on my upper back, I nearly jumped out of my skin. I looked up startled into what turned out to be the face of one of the servers from behind the counter. His smile transformed in an instant to an expression of bewilderment. He stepped back slightly.

"Your French fries, sir," he said, gingerly placing the bowl of potato chips on the table.

The young man backed further away, bearing a look that owed more now to pity than confused amazement. One more tap on any part of my anatomy, I thought, and I would need to call a plumber.

As it turned out, I did not need to wait long. I was chomping on my tasty, well-filled sandwich when I sensed fingers drumming tentatively on my upper arm. This time, my reaction was not so volatile. I suppose that was because it came as no surprise to me. I knew at once who the drummer was, and his voice was instantly recognisable.

"May I join you?" the voice requested politely.

"Why are you following me?" I quizzed, albeit a mite tetchily.

My dead ringer from Costa had sidled into the padded leather, bench seat opposite me.

He now placed a plate with a salt beef sandwich and a latke, and a glass of lemon tea, on the table between us.

"I could ask you the same question," he responded with a wry smile. "But please don't worry. I'll be gone before you know it. I just wanted to make sure you were still on the right track."

Strangely, I started thinking about railways and locomotives. Maybe it was just a semantic association, like being asked by a psychoanalyst the first thing that comes into your mind when a particular word is mentioned. Who knows? But what occurred next was even more peculiar. I was back drifting on the ocean again, the water as placid as a lake. I was floating on some kind of raft, propelled along quite pleasantly by a light surface current. Just as well, because I am a non-swimmer. I wondered why it was so dark, until I realised it was night. I lay stretched out on my back, fully clothed I might add, gazing up at the billions of stars scintillating against the black, eternal depths of the heavens. I felt really at peace with myself, the first time in a long while, as I trailed my fingertips in the consoling sea.

Do not ask me why, but the advice of Polonius to his son Laertes, in Shakespeare's Hamlet, seeped into my head: "This above all – to thine own self be true ..." I closed my eyes and, quite oddly, sensed my emotions and intellect as tangible objects. When I opened my eyes, I saw that my lunch companion had disappeared. I finished my meal, left the restaurant and, deep in contemplation, walked quickly towards Baker Street Underground Station. It had started to rain.

★ ★ ★

On Yom Kippur, the Day of Atonement, with heart and mind, I made my peace with the Almighty. Somehow, I experienced a more intense and satisfying yet, truth to say, more humbling one-to-one with my Creator than at any time in the past. As I stood in the synagogue striking repeatedly the left side of my chest with a bunched fist, in the time-honoured way of showing repentance, I thought that I heard something very familiar. It was the echo of small waves lapping against the rocks of a distant shore.

Stopping time

ON HOW many occasions have you thought to yourself, "I wish this day, this hour, this moment would go on for ever"? Maybe they were times when your parents made lovely birthday parties for you as a child. Or times when you were tipsily ecstatic on receiving a brilliant examination result, a university degree, a professional qualification or an early promotion at work. Perhaps you recall having the thought when you kissed on your first date, fell in love or wed the person of your dreams. Could be the thought arrived on some simple and insouciant times, on days fishing from a tranquil river bank with pals from school, walking hand-in-hand with a lover along a romantic stretch of coastline or relaxingly bantering in the beer garden of a country pub with good friends.

Even now, the thought may come when you are drinking local red wine by a sun-splashed villa pool in Tuscany, strolling somewhere deep in the age-old forests of the English countryside, bronzing yourself in a steamer chair on a Caribbean cruise liner or chatting cheerily in the garden at home with a loving family or dear neighbours.

These are the times when you feel gloriously alive and

happy, amazing worry-free days when you experience a supreme elation or a deep contentment, hours, minutes, seconds when you wish that time would stop, forever. You should not be surprised if I tell you that your wish can easily come true. I do not mean by taking the battery out of your quartz watch or pulling the plug on a bedside, digital clock radio. And, for the avoidance of any doubt, I do not mean calling a sudden halt to the passage of time by doing anything remotely morbid or nefarious!

I wonder whether you would be interested in stopping time. I really mean stopping time, for all time. Maybe you are fascinated by the notion. Just a little? Well, if I can do it, so can you. In fact, like me, you have probably done it a thousand times, possibly quite a lot more and without even realising it. How? Photography. Yes, photography. Just think about it. On every occasion that you click your camera at family, friends or scenery, you are stopping time from running. Your spouse, partner, children, grandchildren, uncles and aunts, colleagues and friends are crystallised, frozen in time, at the moment you press the shutter release button.

Many of us relish the idea of pouring over old family photo albums on a cold, winter's evening at home. What better way to spend such a night when there is precious little of interest on the television, curled into your favourite armchair in front of a crackling fire (okay, central heating radiator) with a glass of Rioja and slowly flicking the illustrated pages of your own family's history books. Turning these precious leaves, with cherished images ranging maybe from sepia tone to the digital print, you are comforted in observing that time, the poetic old gypsy man, has been halted once and for all.

Here is a very old photo of your bubbeh and zaydeh taken in der Heim: she with her dark, modest bodice and severe hairstyle, he with his waistcoat and lofty, embroidered skullcap with a tassel. In another volume, there is a picture of your first baby smiling in his or her cot. Turn a few pages and neatly arranged are some snapshots of a holiday at the seaside, the kids playing ball on the sandy beach, pier in the background, and their grandpa snoozing in a deckchair with his trousers rolled up to his knees.

Choose another album, flip a few pages and witness you and your other half celebrating joyfully a major wedding anniversary with loved ones, sadly no longer around. Prepare for your eyes to well with tears from time to time. After all, it is only natural that watery pearls should trickle down your cheeks. Time may well have been stopped but long-term memories will have been born.

I was clearing out some unwanted junk in the attic of our North West London home a while back. In an obscure corner of the large loft I discovered an anonymous shoebox. I removed the dusty lid and, inside, I found a dozen, black and white, postcard-size photos. Later, I showed the pictures, which must have been decades old but in surprisingly good condition, to my wife. Like me, she had no idea where they had come from. It was just possible that we had forgotten acquiring them from our late parents or other family members. Though it did occur to us that we might have inadvertently inherited them from the middle-aged, childless, Jewish couple that had sold the house to us many years ago. In any event, we did not have a clue about their provenance.

After dinner that evening, we examined the images very closely.

"Twelve copies of the same, well-posed, formal images of a family group," my wife said.

"Yeah, a bit strange," I muttered.

"Not if they were for distribution to relatives and friends," she added, sensibly.

"Maybe it was taken on a special occasion," I offered.

My wife nodded.

There were five people in the identical pictures, two adults and three children, two boys and a girl. We went on to assume, quite naturally, that here was a father, mother and their trio of offspring.

"The clothes being worn suggest that the photo was taken some time in the 1930s," my wife said. "And the sitters appear to be a fairly prosperous, middle class, obviously Jewish, family."

I concurred.

"Any idea where it might've been taken?"

"You mean country?" I queried.

She nodded and I pondered for a moment or two.

"Somehow, I don't believe it was produced here in Britain. They don't look English, though that's not particularly relevant. If I'm right, I suggest it could've been taken somewhere in central Europe."

"Why not, say, the United States?" my wife countered. I studied the photo again.

"I really don't know. But it seems a bit too formal for New York in the thirties. I just have the feeling it's more in cultural keeping with Europe. The style of clothing being worn, as well as the studio backcloth, seems sympathetic to that geography. Unfortunately, there's nothing on the reverse side to give any clues."

The parents were seated in high-backed chairs against a painted, idyllic backcloth of trees with mountains beyond. We estimated the couple to be somewhere in their mid-thirties.

"The father's really quite handsome," my wife noted, somewhat predictably.

The man boasted what we believed was called, by then contemporary filmgoers, a Ronald Coleman moustache. And he possessed, according to my fellow scrutineer, rather nice and probably blue eyes.

"I think the mother's an extraordinarily good-looking woman," I pronounced, not to be outdone by gender attraction rivalry. "Just look at those fantastic high cheekbones."

The wife ignored my comments and advised, with an air of expertise, that the children appeared to range in age from about five to nine years.

The older children, the two brothers, were smartly attired in sailor's uniform and, my wife conjectured, "were most likely separated in age by about three years". They stood upright to attention, rather comically I thought, flanking their proud parents like nautical bookends. The younger boy was posed holding the outstretched hand of his sister across the lap of their mother. The daughter was dressed in a pretty, frilly frock and was standing shyly centre stage holding a dainty little handbag.

Later that night, I was about to stuff the old shoebox, which had contained the dozen photos, into a dustbin bag for disposal. Quite by chance, I noticed a small, grimy piece of card stuck against one of the shorter, interior sides of the box. Very carefully, I prised the snippet away from the cardboard until it was free, and flipped it over in the palm of my hand. Unluckily, and despite the care I had taken peeling the card from the box, some of the side paper had adhered, obscuring several printed words. My tentative efforts to scrape away the stubborn scrap with a fingernail proved unsuccessful.

On close inspection, however, I was excited to discern most of the word "Fotograf", the German word for photographer, though the actual name was indecipherable. In a corner of what appeared to be a business card, I noticed a tiny printed part of what had once been an address. I could just make out a few of the letters at the end. There were gaps between the characters. But I was able to discern enough for me to deduce, with a fair degree of confidence, the name of a German city that, coincidentally, I was planning to visit on business in the near future.

As I lay in bed that night, I speculated about how the photos came to be in our loft. But, more specifically, I was curious to know why twelve pictures portraying the same family image still remained together. Then I recalled something that could be significant.

"How could we have forgotten?" I whispered to myself.

The Jewish couple we had purchased the house from had both spoken with a residual, mid-European, probably German, accent. My sudden recollection seemed to confirm that the images belonged to them and possessed, therefore, a central European link. I wanted to wake my wife and tell her but had second thoughts about that. I would mention it in the morning.

A few weeks later, in October, my early Friday flight from Heathrow took little more than an hour and a half. A westerly tailwind sped the jet across the North Sea, above the flat landscape of the Netherlands and over the German border. In my flight bag were three of the photos I had discovered in our attic. After quickly negotiating passport control and customs, I exited the Arrivals door and checked the overhead signs for the S-Bahn entrance. I bought a machine ticket for the suburban train that would take me, in fifteen minutes, to the city's Hauptbahnhof, the main railway terminus.

Once out of the station complex, I pushed my compact suitcase onto the backseat of the first, cream-coloured, Mercedes taxi waiting at the cab rank, jumped in after it and was whisked to my hotel in a few minutes.

"Danke … Stimmt so … Ja, der Rest ist für Sie," I said, handing over a crisp, ten-euro note to meet the nine-euro fare; and telling the grinning, unshaven cabbie, doubtless of Turkish origin, to keep the change.

After I had checked in and taken the lift to the fifth floor, I entered my room with the key-card, scanned the bathroom for takeaway, toiletry goodies, switched off the TV screen with its ersatz welcome from the hotel manager, glanced at the busy street scene below my window, hurled my case onto the

Queen-size bed and unpacked. In all, it took me ten minutes from entering the building. I must be slowing down.

I opened up, and spread out on the crisp white duvet, a large-scale city map that I had bought at Stamfords earlier that week. Before leaving home, I had marked on the plan the location of the synagogue. And from information obtained on the Internet, I learned that it had been constructed on the site of a shul burned down by a rampaging Nazi mob on Kristallnacht, the night of broken glass, 9th/10th November 1938.

After an excellent buffet breakfast, and just before nine the following morning, I looked again at the 1930s photo. Then I set out on the twenty-minute walk to the synagogue for the Shabbat service. In recent years, I had davened at shuls in many German cities where, today, Russian immigrant Jews generally constitute about eighty percent of the 200,000 Jewish population of the country.

Invariably, the synagogues are housed in attractive modern buildings, usually financed in substantial measure by Federal and State authorities. Some of the architecturally superb structures contain a community centre, a school, a library or museum and often a professional kosher restaurant. Where a pre-war synagogue had miraculously survived the Nazi regime, more or less intact, it has often been beautifully restored to its former glory.

Generally, the local police force and community members provide the security around German Jewish institutions on Shabbat, and other days. Inside the well-protected buildings, visiting strangers are politely questioned. Quite often, airline-style security has been introduced. And hand-held, Shabbat-friendly, frisking machines are frequently in use. The synagogue I entered that morning was no exception. But after passing through the meticulous screening, and brushing aside with a smile the proffered apologies, I donned a tallit, plucked a siddur and Chumash from a bookshelf (both printed in Hebrew and Russian) and settled into an aisle seat in one of the many empty beech-wood pews behind the bimah.

My first impression of the décor was of tall pillars and brightness, a grille-fronted ladies' gallery, a high-vaulted ceiling, deep blue carpeting and a magnificently fashioned Aron Ha'Kodesh. Gradually, as the orthodox Ashkenazi service progressed, I absorbed the detailed embellishments. The chazan in a black gown, and wearing a bulbous black kippah, intoned nasally from the bimah; while a youngish, black-bearded man, also in a black robe and seated in the rabbi's position on a platform to the left of the Ark, bent reverently to and fro towards a prayer book on the stand in front of him.

As the service continued, more worshippers, men, women and children, entered the shul. I needed to shift seats three times to allow a regular to take his rightful place. At the start of leyning, the reading of the week's Torah portion by the rabbi, there were some one hundred congregants in the synagogue. The shammas approached me, confirmed that I was neither a Cohen nor a Levi (who have priority in being called up to the reading of the Law) but an Israelite, but nevertheless elicited my Hebrew name. Shortly afterwards, I was called to the bimah. On returning to my seat after the aliyah, I studied the generally friendly and welcoming faces of the men whose hands I was shaking. An ulterior motive lurked behind my observations, as I sought to identify those who appeared to be around the age of eighty. As it happened, there seemed to be just one elderly gentleman who fitted my specification. I perceived an intellectual vibrancy in his compelling eyes, which somehow belied my estimate of his age.

After the service, at the wine and vodka Kiddush in the spacious, adjoining hall, I introduced myself to the man. He was shorter than me, quite slim with grey wispy hair. He carried himself well for his age, which he told me was seventy-nine. Although my German is reasonable, his English was impeccable. As usual, I thought, a "foreigner" was putting my linguistic skills (such as they are) to utter shame. And so we conversed in English. Prost! Shalom! L'Chaim! Almost everyone, including me, shouted uninhibitedly after the young minister had made the requisite blessing.

Like many of the men present, me included, the old man downed his shot glass of Russia's national spirit in one, throat-arching gulp.

"You know what?" he said, holding out his empty glass to be refilled by the shul's beadle, "I'm one of the few German Jews left in this community."

He glanced around at the noisy throng tucking into plates of pickled herring, potato salad and cake.

"Mind you," he added with an endearing smile, "I'm not averse to their favourite, alcoholic beverage, even though my own tipple is schnapps."

Against a background buzz of Russian voices carrying on animated and vociferous discussions around the long, white cloth covered, trestle tables, the old man and I struggled to hear each other speak. But it proved impossible, and I did not want him to strain himself. After establishing that he had been born in the city in 1927, and that there was an excellent kosher restaurant in the Jüdische Gemeinde, the Jewish community centre attached to the synagogue, I invited him to have Sunday lunch with me. He looked overwhelmed but readily accepted. We arranged to meet outside the building at one o'clock the next day.

Sunday was really cold. Anticipating the wind-chill factor, I put on my topcoat and Russian, faux-fur hat. I left my city-centre hotel at 12:30, in good time for my rendezvous at the restaurant. My wife and I have been to several kosher cafés and restaurants in various German towns. Almost without exception, they are very professionally managed with really superb central European cuisine temptingly presented. I happily anticipated a culinary treat.

I arrived outside the community centre ten minutes early but the old man was waiting for me at the entrance to the building. As I expected, there was a police vehicle parked on the opposite side of the street with two uniformed officers observing us from the front seats. My newfound friend was chatting to one of the community's own security men who, when I approached, recognised me from the day before. Acknowledging me with a thin smile, he stepped aside from the front door to allow both of us to enter without the customary formalities.

My companion was very glad to see me again and shook my hand warmly. He led the way along a wide corridor, stopped halfway and pushed open a frosted glass, double door. Above it, I noticed the name of the restaurant in light blue, neon tube lights. We entered a large room with a pleasant, neutral décor and about twenty tables, of varying sizes, covered by brilliantly white tablecloths boasting a set of sparkling wine glasses and gleaming cutlery. A few of the tables were occupied, one or two seating seriously bearded men wearing broad-brimmed, black hats, and their modestly dressed, long-skirted wives in attractive sheitls.

Having been greeted warmly by the owner/manager and the headwaiter, the old man introduced me to them. In fact, they remembered me from the previous morning, doubtless my conspicuous call-up aiding their recollection. We left our overcoats and headwear on hooks near the door, and were seated opposite each other at a table for two by the heavy net-draped window. As we settled into our comfortable chairs, the old man pointed to the curtains.

"They're specially designed to protect against bomb and grenade shrapnel exploding through the reinforced glass panes."

I did not say so, but I knew this.

We ordered from the wonderful choice of meals on the menu; and my companion agreed to my selection of an Israeli cabernet sauvignon from the wine list. The bottle was brought, opened expertly and poured after tasting. Our starters of smoked trout and red onions, for me, and boiled gefilte fish with carrots and chrayn, for my lunch guest, arrived even before we began a conversation.

The old man grinned.

"Teutonic efficiency, you understand. Now eat, my friend … enjoy."

We spread the white linen napkins on our laps, and started eating in silence. I lifted my glass and proclaimed, "L'Chaim!"

He raised an eyebrow and nodded slowly, which made me feel a little self-conscious. We drained our glasses and I refilled them. When we had finished our hors d'oeuvres, I spoke of the photos I had discovered in my loft, and my belief that they were taken at a studio in this very city in the 1930s.

"Since meeting you in shul yesterday," I said, "I've been wondering. As you were born and raised here in this city, and would've been a contemporary of the children in the photo, I've wondered whether you might've known the family."

My lunch companion seemed keen to peruse the studio portrait. I took a copy from the inside pocket of my jacket and handed it across to him. Before he looked at it, the waiter came to clear away our empty plates. After he had moved away with the used crockery, the old man gazed at the image in his hand.

What happened next astounded me. His face crumpled into a frightening, skull-like mask of horror. At the same time he emitted what I can describe only as a shocked cry of anguish. I thought he was on the point of fainting, or about to suffer some fit or seizure. I rose quickly and rushed to his side, in my haste carelessly knocking over my glass of wine. A red stain spread out across the snow-white cloth like an expanding pool of blood, and the thin-stemmed glass rolled off the table onto the tiled floor and shattered. Everyone around me seemed to move as if in a slow motion film, the anxious faces of startled diners turning towards the source of the clatter and commotion, the owner and waiters running in our direction.

As I reached out to my apparently sick guest, he got up unexpectedly from his chair, brushed past me without a word, grabbed his hat and coat and hastily left the restaurant. I picked up the photo, explained hurriedly to the bewildered manager what had occurred, without really understanding the cause, stuffed some euro notes into his hand sufficient to cover everything, reclaimed my outdoor clothes and chased after my erstwhile companion. As I swiftly exited the building, dashing past a bemused security guard, I looked right then left and spotted my lunch guest hastening along the street. I raced after him against a freezing, blustery wind. As I drew level, he looked askance at me but did not slow down. Quite a pace he was setting, I considered, especially bearing in mind his advanced years.

"Please stop," I begged him. "Please tell me what's wrong. I don't understand. I'm really sorry if I've offended you in any way."

He pulled up suddenly, so abruptly in fact that my momentum carried me ahead of him before I halted, turned round and drew back alongside him. He was breathing heavily; and though his features had recovered a certain calm composure, his eyes betrayed an inner turmoil. He looked at me directly, scanning my face, his own softening slightly.

"I-I regret my behaviour just now," he said, panting volubly and placing a hand on my arm. "I-I'm afraid I was overcome. But my conduct was unforgivable. When I get home, I'll telephone the restaurant manager and make my apologies."

I opened my mouth to speak but he raised a hand as his breathing steadied.

"No, it wasn't your fault at all. My lapse was nothing to do with you."

A little bravely, I thought, I asked whether he would like to talk about it.

"Not now," he responded, quite brusquely, but adding quickly:

"There I go again. Please forgive me. I'm not thinking straight at the moment. Yes, I would like to speak to you again. I owe you that much, at least. Perhaps we could meet tomorrow morning sometime."

We arranged to see each other mid-morning in front of the train station. He knew of a pleasant konditorei nearby which, he promised, served excellent fresh coffee and delicious apfelstrudel. On shaking hands, he forced a smile, which I hoped represented some sort of absolution for whatever misdemeanour I had surely committed in his eyes. We said our goodbyes and trudged our separate ways, both deep in thought. In my hotel's bar that evening I favoured several tall glasses of one of the city's first-rate, local lager beers. As my body relaxed, cocooned in an all-embracing Chesterfield, I meditated on the extraordinary and unpredictable events of the day. Little did my imagination anticipate the astonishing story I was to hear on the following day.

As agreed, we met outside the Hauptbahnhof. He greeted me, surprisingly, in a very friendly fashion and I was gratified to detect a sort of considered resignation in his demeanour. For me, it was a refreshing contrast to the nightmare scenario of the previous day. He did not mention it and, of course, neither did I. At the coffee house, which possessed a very cosy ambience, lively with chatter, he threaded his passage with familiarity to a booth at the quiet rear.

The crisply uniformed young waitress took our order for coffee and strudel. Almost by silent concurrence the old man and I did not say a word to each other until our piping hot beverages and kuchen had been set down on our table. We began to munch the warm, flaky pastry, the soft apple pieces tasting absolutely heavenly. He noticed the agreeable look on my face as I quickly devoured the scrumptious confection.

"I told you about the strudel," he said, grinning. "And now I'm going to tell you about something quite different."

The story he narrated that morning at the café was almost incredible. I was so hypnotised by what he was relating that time seemed to stand still. No, that is not quite accurate. It was more like entering an infernal Wellsian machine and travelling back to another time.

"You must've wondered, if I may say so with all due modesty, why my English is so fluent," he began.

I nodded.

"Well, I lived for many years in England, in London actually, your own home town. I'll tell you where precisely very soon. I arrived at Liverpool Street Station on one of the last kindertransports from Germany in the summer of 1939. I was twelve years old. That is how I managed to survive the Holocaust. One and half million other Jewish children were not so fortunate."

I nodded solemnly, knowing from my reading about the thousands of youngsters who had escaped the Nazis before the war; and the terrible scenes on railway platforms where the children had to say what would be a final goodbye to their doomed parents.

"The photograph you showed me yesterday came as something of a jolt to me …"

I tried to say something but he stopped me.

"And it may come as something of a shock to you," he continued, "to learn that I am in that photograph."

I leaned back and gulped.

"I thought as much," my companion said with an ironic smile. "You see, I'm the oldest child, posing alongside my brother and sister and our beloved parents. The picture, as you guessed correctly, was produced in a well-known photographic studio in this very city, where we lived. I believe it was taken around 1937. I was ten, my brother six and my sister almost five at the time."

Hats off to my wife's fairly accurate estimation, I thought.

"I've wondered, of course, how the dozen copies came to be in our loft," I said.

"I'll come to that shortly," came the reply. "First, you may want to know what happened to the rest of my family."

I nodded, this time a trifle apologetically.

"I'm sure that I don't need to tell you about the evil history of Nazism, and its gradually but inexorably up-scaled persecution of the Jews in Germany during the 1930s. Suffice it for me to say that, following Kristallnacht in November 1938, my parents saw very clearly the writing on the wall. They told me that my siblings were too young to be accepted on the rail transports to England. That may've been the case, I really don't know. But, in truth, I don't think my brother and sister would have been able, at their young ages, to leave mother and father. I learned later from the Red Cross that my parents and siblings were transported to Theresienstadt, near Prague, in 1942. Subsequently, I discovered from other sources that my parents had been shipped to Auschwitz-Birkenau later during the war and gassed on arrival. What can I say? At least they died at the same time and maybe in each other's arms. I like to think that."

"What about your brother and sister?" I asked as sensitively and sympathetically as I could.

"It wasn't until the early 1960s that I learned of their fate. I went to a special, commemorative Holocaust conference in Tel Aviv, and took the opportunity to study the archives at Yad Vashem, the memorial museum in Jerusalem. I'm sure you know it …"

"Yes, I've visited on a few occasions."

"The reports indicated that my brother and sister had been separated from our parents and despatched to the children's laager at Bergen-Belsen concentration camp. But I also found out, to my great delight, that they had miraculously survived the horrible privations and diseases in the camp, where the famous diarist Anne Frank had died. They had been liberated by the British army in 1945, shortly before the end of the war against Germany."

I reached out to pat the old man's hand as it rested on the table.

"Armed with this information," he went on, after silently acknowledging my simple gesture of compassion, "I was determined to locate their whereabouts. To cut a very long story short, I found them living together ..."

He broke off suddenly, his chin trembling, his eyes glassing over. It was a minute or two before he continued.

"They were living as husband and wife in a small apartment here in this city, our old home town. What could I say to them? What did I have the right to say? Naturally, my emotions were confused. But I kept shtum! I said nothing. Thanks to sympathetic business colleagues, I was able to stay with them for several weeks. The stories they told me about their bare existence in Theresienstadt, and later in Belsen, were horrendous. Frequently, we broke down together, sobbing uncontrollably and hugging each other for long periods of time. But, having said that, I cannot begin to convey to you the joy we felt on being reunited. Sadly, their dreadful experiences had resulted in an inability to hold down any job. They lived on social security handouts, welfare payments of one kind or another and a miniscule government pension for Shoah survivors. They each spoke English quite well, having learned the language from British soldiers during their prolonged, recuperative stay in Belsen. I struggled to understand, but finally accepted, how my brother and sister had become very close to each other ..."

I ordered two more cups of coffee when the narrative ceased for a brief interval. I could perceive that the old man was trying desperately to come to terms with his revived emotions, for which I was culpably responsible whatever he had said to the contrary.

"In view of their plight," he went on, "I invited them to London, to live with me. I was a confirmed bachelor and would have welcomed the opportunity to live alongside what remained of my family. To my delight, my brother and sister agreed. Now I can tell you that, amazingly, my home in London eventually became your home. The pictures you found in my, sorry your, attic were given to me by my parents before I boarded the train bound for England. They'd intended to distribute them to our relatives but I'm afraid the Nazis' murderous activities had stymied that objective."

From my expression, the old man would have noted how absolutely dumbfounded I was by his revelation. The fresh coffee arrived. I certainly needed mine.

"But when we bought the house, your siblings were the owners," I observed. "I don't recall any other vendor named on the transfer deed."

My companion sipped a little of the hot black liquid in his cup.

"You're right, of course," he said. "Well before you and your wife purchased the property many years ago, I'd moved back to Germany, back to this city of my birth. I transferred ownership of my house jointly to my siblings. Indeed, I continued to support them financially."

"Why did you move back here, if I may ask? Surely, the town couldn't have held very many good memories for you?"

"You're right and you're wrong. There were some very good memories from my childhood before disaster struck the Jews, and the world. But the reason for my return was simply business. It's another long story with which I needn't bore you."

I raised the cup to my lips. The coffee felt good, and its heat was soothing.

"But tell me," I asked, "where did your siblings go after they'd sold their home to us?"

"They returned to Germany to live with me here. You see,

they had missed me, and I had missed them. Though, evidently, they had failed to completely clear out the loft space. I suppose the wheel of life had come full circle for us."

I took some more coffee as the old man correctly anticipated my next question.

"Sadly, they both passed away a few years later, actually within a couple of months of each other. I think you may now understand why."

I took an envelope, one from my hotel room's information folder, out of my inside jacket pocket and handed it across the table.

"Here are two copies of the photograph. Please take them, they're yours, anyway."

His eyes glassed over as he grasped the envelope.

"Thank you," he said softly. "This is the only photograph of my family I'll now possess and, of course, treasure."

That night, as I lay awake in my hotel room, I wondered whether the old man was then holding and looking at a fragment of crystallised time … as I was.

The stone setting

AUNTIE BLOOMA'S plump frame squeezed, with a practiced expertise, between the knots of people in the through lounge – dining room of the semi-detached house in North London. She aimed for the jostling crowd of humanity surrounding, and virtually obscuring, the refreshments table by the large bay window. Men and women swayed and dipped, in a kind of ritual bird dance, over the traditional, post - stone setting fare. Or was it more akin to vultures hovering above a freshly abandoned kill?

Auntie loved stone settings. She had attended so many in the last few years that the actual number eluded her. She had even received an invitation to one of them. But by no means did she consider herself a gatecrasher. After all, she would often think, it is a small Jewish world and everyone must be related in some way. And it was something useful to do on a lonely Sunday afternoon, an outing to get dressed up for, somewhere to meet and talk to other people. Funerals definitely did not appeal to her. They were far too depressing: all that weeping, and the cutting of the mourners' clothes by the rabbi, as the black-draped coffin stood on its sombre conveyance in the centre of the prayer hall. No, a levoyah was just too sad and miserable at her time of life.

She would always telephone around the cemeteries early on a Sunday morning to ascertain whether any memorials were to be dedicated that day. If there were a few positive responses, Auntie would select the grounds that seemed the most convenient to her. Of course, she needed to take into account the distance to be travelled by Underground or bus; and any information she could retrieve on the location of the family's home, where the customary, post – stone setting reception would be held.

A small boy, dark hair tousled and spectacles awry, emerged from somewhere within the feeding frenzy at the food table. With both hands he held an empty plate. In an instant, the item of crockery was seized from the lad's loose grip.

"Thank you, Michael, sweetie ... I'm your Auntie Blooma."

The boy looked up and frowned at the middle-aged woman in the long fur coat and funny hat with its peculiar veil.

"I haven't got an Auntie Blooma, and my name's not Michael," he squealed. "Gimme my plate back, you ..."

The woman's ample body easily thrust the child aside, stifling the whining sound in the process.

"Who's a silly boy, then?" she chuckled, propelling the boy still further away and making her determined way towards the scrum around the table.

Almost bowling over an elderly couple leaving the melee with plates piled high with smoked salmon bridge rolls, fried fish balls and honey cake, Auntie speedily plugged the gap they had opened up. Without her glasses, Auntie Blooma was at some disadvantage in making accurate selections from the generous spread. And the flanking elbows did not help, either. After extracting herself from the crush, she scrutinised her eclectic range of acquisitions. Two chocolate truffles she had clearly mistaken for fish balls, a squashed banana, some pickled herring on a cracker, a slice of cheesecake and an empty cigarette packet stared up at her morosely from the plate. Never mind, the attempt was good fun, she reflected philosophically.

Absentmindedly, Auntie picked up the finger of cheesy confection and began to nibble it through the fine net mesh suspended from the brim of her best millinery offering. The veil, which she now quickly lifted, was already sticky red from the glass of cherry brandy she had earlier taken from the array of drinks in the lobby. She sidled away from the table area, ever watchful for the lady with the tea tray and dying for a hot cuppa. It had been freezing at the burial ground that November afternoon. But still worth the long bus journey, she considered. And that nice young rabbi had given another of his wonderful speeches. It had brought tears to her eyes.

Pity about the mud, she mused. Auntie bent forward awkwardly and peered over her amply protruding midriff at her chunky boots. They had certainly been required footwear today, she thought, chortling quietly at recalling the inappropriate high heels worn by some of the younger women. In her time she had witnessed more than one of the stilettos snapping and breaking off on frost-hardened earth or sunk deep into the brown ooze. Having rapidly consumed the items on her plate, except for the fag packet, Auntie dumped the crockery on the convenient sideboard.

A short, thin, waxy-faced man with a balding head and a vague excuse for a moustache suddenly popped out of a tight mass of bodies. Almost breathless, he clutched an empty plate in one hand and a mug of steaming beverage in the other. Tiny fragments of schmaltz herring clung to his sparingly hirsute upper lip.

"That's very kind of you, Morris, love," Auntie Blooma declared with a broad smile that bunched her heavily rouged cheeks. "I haven't seen you for years, my dear."

Adeptly, she relieved the startled little man of his mug, without spilling a drop of the hot tea.

The helpless little creature had been no match for the ample woman hovering above him. He blinked twice, his forehead creasing like a concertina.

"But I'm not ..." he began, meekly.

Without more, Auntie took two steps back and allowed the space between her and this pathetic adversary to be filled by the milling throng of guests.

Protectively, Auntie tightly grasped the large cup then spotted a miraculously vacant chair by the double-glazed, patio doors. With the agility of a woman half her age and weight, she meandered through the multitude and claimed the seat in the name of her aching feet. While sipping her tea, she noticed that, propped like a waxwork in the neighbouring chair, was an elderly, silver-haired woman. Her small, hollow-cheeked face was almost entirely buried inside a heavy-knit, bright yellow cardigan. The wool was so luminous, Auntie thought, that it could have guided fog-bound fleets back to safe harbour. Tight against her canary ensemble, the old lady held a huge black handbag with contorted, arthritic hands. The whole black and yellow package suddenly shifted in Auntie's direction.

"Didn't I see you at a stone setting a few weeks ago?"

The squeaky, disembodied voice, accompanied by a rattle of false teeth, seemed to emanate from somewhere inside the ill-fitted cardigan. It was as if the item of woollen clothing was itself speaking.

Auntie mentioned a particular cemetery.

The cardigan nodded.

"My grand-niece's husband," it said, surprisingly coherently. "Terrible tragedy."

Auntie gestured sympathetically.

"I'm just a friend here, though," the wool muttered, a little guiltily. "Are you family?"

"I'm Auntie Blooma."

There was an indistinct mumble.

"Oh, I see."

Auntie nodded.

"He was very big, wasn't he?" the yellow wool queried.

"Pardon?" Auntie said, a little confused.

The cardigan appeared to wriggle irritably.

"In the community …" it added. "In the community."

"Who?"

The small, white-topped head rose curiously from the cardigan like a tortoise from its shell.

"The deceased, the deceased!" it cried repeatedly with annoyance. "That's why there are so many people here."

"Of course," Auntie confirmed, rising from her seat. "He must've been very big, indeed."

The miniscule and wizened head, which appeared to be perched precariously atop an impossibly scraggy neck, emerged completely from the formless yellow morass.

"Very nice talking to you," said a startlingly red-rimmed mouth to Auntie's retreating back.

The large, elongated room was now stiflingly warm and stuffy, filled with the noise of increasingly voluminous exchanges of family news and gossip. Somehow, Auntie felt, you could not quite beat the amiable atmosphere at the house after a stone setting. Everyone made a real effort to be friendly, sociable and talkative, at least after the food had been demolished. In winter, she relished the especially cosy atmosphere. Of course, she appreciated that, occasionally, there would be tears. That was to be expected. It was all part of the day. She herself could be bright and cheery or empathetic and understanding. Whatever was required, Auntie was more than willing to oblige. She certainly owed her hosts that much. And she was most respectful, always putting great store by her demeanour even though, thankfully, she hardly ever knew a soul.

Auntie edged her stout way back along the lengthy room towards the bay window. Outside, she noted, beyond the skeletal trees in the front garden, the winter sky was darkening. Her next task was to locate that marvellous, retired doctor who had very kindly given her a lift from the grounds. He had also offered to drop her home, too. Her one-bedroom flat was not that far away, but a car ride could save her a long Sunday wait for a bus. She shivered at the chilly notion.

"Hello, do I know you?"

A dark-haired, seriously made-up woman with a short, pointed nose blocked Auntie's path. She was probably in her forties, Auntie conjectured, but trying desperately, maybe with surgical assistance and not entirely unsuccessfully, for thirty-five.

"I don't know," Auntie replied, rather taken aback by the woman in a smartly cut, black, mini-skirted suit. "But you do look very familiar, my dear."

"I'm Karen, poor Harry's niece."

"Oh, yes."

The younger woman fingered an elegant string of pearls hanging from her neck.

"You know, I've not been to a stone setting for ages. Then one last week, and another this."

Auntie shook her head solemnly.

"I seem to remember seeing you at the cemetery last week," the woman recalled.

Auntie took a large white handkerchief from her handbag and dabbed gently under her nose.

"Unfortunately, I've had a spate of them too of late," she whimpered, eyes downcast.

How she hated this play-acting, though thank heavens it was rarely needed. The dark-haired woman placed a hand on her shoulder.

"Oh, I am sorry.

"Not to worry, dear," Auntie sniffed. "That's life, as they say. They all seem to be going now."

The pearls were toyed with again.

"I am so sorry."

"Oh no, dear, I mean the guests. They seem to be leaving now, and so must I."

The younger woman looked round the room. People were indeed gravitating towards the door and spilling into the hallway and lobby. Areas of floral-patterned carpet could now be detected between small knots of close family and friends lingering in the living room. Another well-groomed woman in her sixties, accompanied by a younger, equally manicured woman with the shared facial features of a daughter, approached Auntie and her short-nosed companion. Karen greeted the pair with a smile.

"Paula … Melanie," she said. "Are you going now?"

"Yes," said Paula, the older of the two. "But introduce us to your friend," she added forcing herself not to be tonally judgemental about the middle-aged woman in the ancient fur coat and unbelievable hat.

"I overheard you telling someone earlier that you're Auntie Blooma," Melanie said.

"And whose Auntie Blooma are you then?" enquired the mother.

Becoming seriously flushed at the concerted attention she was receiving from the three pseudo-sophisticated women, the questionable relative hesitated for a moment. These were always embarrassing times, on the odd occasions that they occurred.

"I'm poor Harry's wife's aunt," she lied.

"But Harry never married," Paula asserted sourly, a hint of victory twisting her thin glossy lips.

Auntie swallowed hard, her mind racing.

"This is the Harry Klein stone setting, isn't it?" she asked, with an expression of supreme innocence.

"No, it's not," Paula responded indignantly. "It's the Harry Baum stone setting."

"Oh, dear," murmured Auntie. "It would seem I've tagged on to the wrong stone setting."

The fur-coated woman backed away slowly from the trio of grimacing women, turned on her heels and hurried towards the street door. Maybe she should be taking her time at leaving, Auntie felt. It might have supported her unjustified claim of mistaken identity. Now it looked like she was fleeing the scene of some terrible crime. Melanie made an attempt to pursue the fast departing figure, but her mother held her arm.

"The chutzpah!" Paula exclaimed, scowling. "Tagged onto the wrong stone setting? Pull the other one it's got bells on! The pathetic old woman's probably a serial, stone setting, gate crasher."

Karen played with her pearls again.

"Come on, Paula, let's be charitable," she said. "What has she gained, a few slices of smoked salmon, a piece of cake and a cup of tea? Assuming you're right about her, the poor woman must be pretty lonely and desperate if she's seeking companionship at a stone setting ..."

Outside, in the street, it was now black enveloping night and starting to rain. Auntie Blooma turned up the deep collar of the fur coat that had belonged to her beloved late mother. Then she quickened her step, heading purposefully for the main road and the bus stop.

Echoes of the soul

IMAGINE YOU are alone inside a soundproofed room. There are no windows and just a single door. A table stands in the centre of the room. On top of it sits a state of the art compact disc player capable of finely reproducing the most wondrous and inspiring music ever composed. You insert a favourite Mozart CD into the machine. The otherwise empty and silent room is instantly overflowing with such sublime sounds that your heart trembles with joy and your mind sings with ecstasy.

You leave the room and close the door. Outside, your ears convey nothing of that miraculous music to your brain. But your heart continues to palpitate, reflecting the profound emotions of the harmony. And your mind still revels in melodious contemplation. Through the open windows of your heart and mind, you hear even now the reverberating echoes of your eternal soul. Like the faint, residual sounds of the Almighty's Creation, now receivable by modern science's most sensitively tuned instruments.

An enclosed and confined space like a room or, more relevantly, the human body can never be other than the temporal, or worldly, home of the immortal soul. Our ancient and sacred Torah speaks of the neshomah as the breath of life. We can sense this; for the soul, endowed by the Almighty, pure and vital, is the essence that can lift and enable Man to fulfil his ultimate destiny. Outside the transient bodily realm, the essential spirit is timeless and beyond the natural order of things.

According to reports, a scientist seeks apparently to explain the soul. He attributes human consciousness to a set of neurones generating bio-chemical reactions in the brain. He claims to have found the group of cells responsible for human consciousness and an individual's "sense of self".

* * *

A wise friend asked me once, "If an alien from another galaxy disembarked from a spaceship in front of your synagogue, what would he see?" I expected a joke to follow. But this was no frivolous, disingenuous question. I could see that from my friend's earnest expression. He afforded me a few moments to consider my answer.

The kind of creatures from other worlds that I have read about, or seen, in sci-fi novels and movies do not appear to lend themselves readily to intellectual, as opposed to technical, excellence. The mobile Martian technocrats on stilts, in H G Wells' War of the Worlds, did not have the sense to infer, before their invasion of Earth, that our blue planet was alive with bacteria and the viral infections that finally destroyed them. So I pondered my friend's question. What would the alien see gazing at my shul? I replied simply, "A pile of bricks and stones." My friend grinned meaningfully and nodded. We were clearly on the same wavelength. "But it would miss the point, eh?" he observed, rhetorically.

I cannot claim to have read the scientific research in detail.

And maybe I am resting too much on neo-sensationalist newspaper headlines ("Scientist locates 'cells of our soul'"). But, to my mind, locating the brain function that gives rise to consciousness, or the "sense of self", does not really address the existence of the soul.

We can accept that the concatenation of cells that constitute the brain produces signals that enable us, as human beings, to act and react. And we can understand that they also provide us with the capacity to think, so that we are aware of our existential selves. Indeed, it is our consciousness that gives us the ability to contemplate, though not to comprehend, the soul. Nonetheless, the neshomah is a hidden, ethereal and mysterious quality or essence that exists apart from the conscious mind, and with which it should not be confused. There can be no room for perplexity. Our brain cells, and thus our minds, cease to function when we pass away. But our spiritual souls, when no longer trammelled by this mortal coil, are free to return to another dimension …

★ ★ ★

Swirling eddies of autumn leaves, like miniature spiral galaxies of knotted brown matter, twisted ahead of us on the rough concrete path between the gravestones. My friend and I walked at the rear of the long column of mourners, bent against the biting wind and following slowly the black-draped coffin being wheeled on its final journey. A few minutes earlier, after leaving the crowded prayer hall, we had huddled around the rabbi as he intoned the requisite blessing before entering the burial ground.

As we wound our solemn way towards the allocated rectangle of excavated earth, the last resting place for our mutual friend's Earthly body, my companion turned to me. He held firmly to the brim of his fedora in the wild, unpredictable gusts, pulling it downwards to meet the raised collar of his dark overcoat. His features were almost invisible but I caught his words on the icy breeze. He was about to continue a discussion we had begun in the car while driving to the cemetery.

"I've been thinking about that scientist you mentioned," he said. "I thought about him when the rabbi referred to the Shema in the hall just now."

I recalled the moment during the minister's eulogy when he had quoted from Judaism's well-known prayer showing Jews the way they should commit themselves to the Almighty. My friend went on.

"As you know, the Hebrew words he cited translate as, "And you shall love the Lord your God with all your heart, and with all your soul and with all your might ...". It seems clear to me that the Torah separates the soul from the heart and the body."

As we bowed into the chilling gusts, brushing away the annoying flurries of dead foliage, I indicated my agreement.

"But sometimes, in modern siddurs," I advised, "the English word for 'might' is given as 'resources'. I think this helps to clarify the distinction even more."

"Why?"

"Because I believe it includes the notion of a strength of will or mind, as well as fervent muscle power."

We trudged between the long rows of irregular, marble headstones. As we struggled on, each line of memorials, some inclining at severe angles formed by time and the elements, reminded me (as always) of men curved to their devotions in the synagogue, particularly during the Yomim Noraim, when the house of worship is full. Wrapped in their fringed tallisim they bow and lean, forwards and sideways, in devout supplication to the Creator of the universe. Over the years, the bone white monuments in the cemetery have moved in the mud and clay of their earthy domain.

Ahead of us, I made out the straggling line of mourners leaving the pathway for the less secure earth. I could see the coffin being lifted and taken from the wheeled cart. Caringly, it was borne away through a milling knot of sobbing family members and grey-faced relatives and friends. Treading onto the murky soil behind them, we negotiated a trail between the groups of memorial stones and eventually joined the assembly at the tomb-side. Here the gravediggers, assisted by the cemetery superintendent and overseen by the rabbi, slowly lowered the raw wooden box into the open mouth of the grave. The holding ropes were withdrawn and the standing planks removed from across the excavated hole. A long queue of men waited patiently to take their turn in shovelling the ochre hill of lumpy and cloying earth into the gaping orifice.

After the recitation of the Kaddish, the mourners' prayer in praise of the Almighty, my friend and I walked silently back to the hall. Isolated patches of blue sky suddenly appeared as the sombre clouds retreated. The whipping wind had now calmed appreciably. Outside the low, grey-stone building we formed a line, as customary, to wash our hands at the large, white enamel sink affixed to the external wall. Quickly, we poured the freezing tap water onto our palms from a chained plastic mug after reciting the appropriate blessing. In the draughty hall, the reunited gathering was invited back to the shiva at the house of mourning. Afterwards, we joined the winding column of relatives and friends comforting the weeping family with their gently offered condolences. Grasping limp, moist hands, we added our own brief words of solace and reminiscence about the deceased and our sincere wishes for a long life.

We walked to our vehicle, waving departing acknowledgements to familiar faces in the car park. My friend clambered into the front passenger seat and, as I fired the ignition and followed the procession of vehicles leaving the grounds, he asked me another question, almost in a reverent whisper.

"Where do you believe our dear friend's soul is now? The minister referred to the olam haba, the world to come."

I drove through the cemetery gates and waited for a break in the traffic before turning onto the road. When I was ready, I did a very Jewish thing. I answered my passenger's question with another question.

"Do you know what a burial ground is called in Hebrew?"

I had no doubt that my friend knew the answer, but I continued before he had the chance to reply.

"It's known as a beth chayim, the house of life."

My companion nodded.

"Sometimes," he said, "it's also referred to as a beth olam, the house of eternity."

I nodded in turn.

We were both silent for a few moments as I negotiated a busy roundabout.

"Those names," I said, straightening my car into the road ahead, "they sound paradoxical, don't they? But I do think they convey the Jewish tradition and belief that death is not the end of everything. And that the soul is the quintessence of our physical life's spiritual continuation in another place."

I could sense my passenger reflecting on what I had just observed.

"I was trying to remember what the rabbi said about this in the prayer hall. I think he was quoting from the Talmud when he said, something like, the righteous will sit with crowns on their heads, reunited with loved ones who have passed away and delighting in the Almighty's presence. Doesn't this answer your question about where our late friend's soul now rests?"

Traffic in front began crawling towards a major intersection. My friend seemed restive.

"But I asked where *you* understood the deceased's soul to be now," he pressed.

Without turning away from the windscreen, I knew his expression was benign.

"Our friend was a righteous man," I said. "Who am I to say that the learned tenets of our Talmud don't provide the sense of his final, spiritual resting place?"

"That's very comforting to the bereaved. But maybe we shouldn't take what's written so literally."

I braked lightly until the car stopped. It was now gridlock on the highway. I turned to face my friend.

"Hold on!" I retorted, faintly irked. "We're talking about the soul, after all … a mystical entity beyond the physical world, beyond the confines of time, beyond the limits of space and well beyond our frail, human comprehension."

My weary passenger nodded with resignation.

"Then you obviously believe that each of us possesses a soul?"

"Yes, that's my clear belief," I responded. "Indeed, as I think you know, that's the Jewish conviction. Remember, because we can't see, hear or touch something doesn't mean it hasn't any existence, whatever form that existence may take. Think of the very air we breathe, the breath of life. But, as I'm sure you appreciate, understanding the nature of the neshomah is truly something that we, as mere mortals, can never do."

I switched on the car radio and tuned it to my favourite classical station.

"Let's just try to relax now," I pleaded, "and listen to some beautiful music."

It happened to be Stravinsky, who once said, somewhat viscerally, I don't understand a word or a note of music, but I feel it …

The angels' share

"IT'S GOOD of you to be here, rabbi," she said. "Come in, please. It's an awful, winter's night outside."

The grey bearded, middle-aged minister of the local synagogue nodded in agreement, as the woman quickly closed the street door behind him.

"How is your husband?"

The elderly woman shook her head, on the point of tears.

The rabbi removed his overcoat and wide-brimmed, black hat and placed them on the hallstand. Then he adjusted his large, black kippah.

"The doctor's just left," the woman murmured, her eyes red-rimmed, her face sallow. "He says it could happen at any time. He's given him another shot of morphine, so there's hardly any pain now. Though his breathing's very laboured, as you'll see."

The woman bowed her upper body and clamped both hands to her head as a distraught sob wracked her slight frame. The minister, who had known the elderly couple for many years as regular shul-goers, offered some gentle words of comfort as she led him into the living room.

"He didn't want to be in bed," she said, sighing deeply. "I've made him as comfortable as possible in his favourite armchair and covered him with a blanket. He sleeps most of the time, anyway."

The living room was very warm and dimly lit by table lamps. The dark, heavy drapes at the window were drawn against the cold, black January night. On entering the gloom, the rabbi became conscious of people sitting around the shadowy periphery. Vaguely, he heard the wife quietly introducing a son, a daughter, a sister-in-law, a cousin and one or two close friends, though he could barely make out their faces. He walked towards the armchair in the centre of the large, square room.

The minister had spoken to the husband regularly over recent months, finally in a hospital ward. Sadly, he had charted the man's gradual decline and suffering submission to the inexorable illness. The old man's head, a yellowish mask in the subdued light, was framed by wayward wisps of grey hair as it rested against the white pillow. His eyes were closed, and the blanket covering his chest rose and fell, like a heaving sea. The wife tenderly smoothed away some errant strands from her husband's brow, and whispered into his ear.

"The rabbi's here, my darling."

She beckoned to the minister, a man much respected and admired in the community. He drew up a vacant chair close to one of the dearest and kindest members of his congregation. As he placed a forearm on the back of the armchair and leaned forward, the faithful congregant opened his eyes. He turned slowly to face his visitor and forced a smile to his dry, cracked lips. The rabbi returned the gesture with as much warmth as he could muster, but with a heavy weight of sorrow in his heart. He had seen that vacant look many times before, in the eyes that held the mirror to imminent departure from this world. The old man opened his mouth. The rabbi moved even closer.

"Yes, my dear friend?"

Breathing rhythmically but heavily, the dying man made a further effort, straining to raise his head. This time the minister heard the question.

"Where am I going, rabbi?"

The old man's head succumbed to the pull of gravity and fell back onto the pillow his eyes closed again, the acceptance of his destiny implicit. The minister sighed and shook his head. Then he noticed, on a coffee table close by, a cut crystal glass of what he knew to be malt whisky. His congregant was well known to be a connoisseur of the famous Highland spirit. And they had often shared a wee dram together at Kiddush after the Sabbath morning service. The community stalwart frequently referred to the golden liquid by its Gaelic name, uisge beatha … the water of life. The glass stood in incongruous juxtaposition to its rapidly fading aficionado. The man's wife had anticipated the rabbi's thought processes.

"Doctor says he can have anything he wants, it doesn't really matter now."

The minister nodded. He heard the muffled sounds of her renewed sobbing combining with the groaning wind shaking the winter-gnarled trees outside.

The rabbi moved close to the man's ear, while still gazing at the whisky.

"Remember, my dear friend, you told me once about the angels' share?"

The minister waited for a short while then perceived an almost imperceptible nod.

"I recall you saying that, over time, each cask of malt whisky in a distillery's cellars releases a natural evaporation of part of its goodly spirit into the atmosphere. And that this is known as the angels' share."

Again, the rabbi noticed a slight inclination of the man's head in distant recollection.

"Well, in answer to your question, it seems to me that, throughout your life and by your deeds, you yourself have released part of the goodness of your own Jewish spirit, your neshomah, your dear soul. I know you and your courage well enough to state that your timeless and eternal soul will return to the Almighty. And that you will sit in the Holy Presence, and in the midst of his angels, for ever more."

The man stirred and shifted with respiratory awkwardness, opened his eyes and stared at the rabbi with whom he had enjoyed so many interesting conversations across the years.

"I hope you are right, rabbi," he murmured throatily, the effort to speak painfully evident on his pale, shrivelled face. "But, really, I do believe … I do believe."

The minister nodded, fighting back the tears.

"I know that very well, my dearest friend," he said, recalling a debate they had engaged in a few years back.

It was just prior to Shabbos. They were both waiting for some other regulars to make up a minyan in the synagogue. Unusually, there had been a local power cut; and the caretaker had lit several large candles and placed them strategically around the bimah and the Aron Ha'Kodesh. The flickering lights infused a macabre, yellow glow. And the ghostly shadows they cast around the shul had given it an almost mystical atmosphere. One of the members felt like a character in The Dybbuk, Ansky's frightening, supernatural play about demonic possession. Another supposed that there had to be evil in the world for us to know what good is.

The rabbi looked sorrowfully at the dying man and remembered his heartfelt contribution to the exchange of views during that strange, Friday night discussion. He had striven to forge a link between the human mind and the soul, the universe and the Almighty. To him, they seemed to share the same intangible and eternal timelessness, the incomprehensible infinite. To him, there was no doubt about the Almighty's omniscient existence. The ordered universe revealed it, the mind beheld and knew it and the soul felt it. The thoughts appeared to help the man towards his strongly held faith.

As he now observed the irregularly breathing body in the armchair, the rabbi was glad that his congregant had a determined belief in the afterlife. Not for him the wretched, nihilistic concept of oblivion and the utter lack of meaning it gave to some lives and to the Holy One's hallowed purpose in Creation. The misguided atheist who preferred the theory of accidental happenings, his unassuming congregant had contended with surprising passion, could not truly contest the plain evidence of the Almighty's being, displayed for all to see in the limitless miracle of the heavens.

The dying man emerged again from semi-consciousness.

"My dear friend, do you want to recite the Shema with me?"

Arid lips parted, as the old man began to follow the Hebrew prayer that daily declares the everlasting Oneness of the Almighty.

"Hear, O Israel: the Lord our God, the Lord is One.

Blessed be His name, Whose glorious kingdom is for ever and ever ..."

The prayer seemed momentarily to rally the man. His eyes moved from left to right and back again in an unmoving head. But he seemed slightly agitated, as if disappointed at not catching sight of an object he was hoping to see. The minister understood immediately.

"Would you like a sip, my friend?"

The man nodded jerkily.

The rabbi reached out and picked up the glass of malt whisky. He inclined it to parched lips, gently supporting the man's head, as some of the golden liquid drained from the crystal tumbler. Soon the eyes closed again and the head fell back against the pillow. The man's breathing was now less fitful, his chest rising and falling at a more temperate rate. The minister knew from experience that the climax was not far off.

In the background, he sensed the close family and friends moving quietly towards the armchair. The wife took up a position on the right side of her husband, the children arraying themselves at the feet of their father where the blanket splayed onto the carpet like a deathly train. With what appeared to be a supreme, final effort, the old man opened his eyes again and freed his right arm from the swathe of bedclothes. He turned slightly towards his weeping spouse and slowly raised a skeletal hand. She clasped it between her palms. Her beloved husband finally allowed his eyelids to fall. With a terminal sigh, he whispered, "I can see the angels … they're smiling at me."

Glossary

Afikoman *The half of matzah hidden during the Seder*
Aliyah *Literally, a going up; a call to the reading of the Torah; settling in Israel*
Aron Ha'Kodesh *The Ark or cupboard in a synagogue holding the Sefer Torah/s*
Ashkenazi *A Jew of Central or East European descent*
Ayen hora *The evil eye*
Bagel *Circular bread roll with a hole in the middle*
Barmitzvah *A Jewish boy's coming of age on reaching thirteen*
Becher *A drinking cup, often made of silver, for wine*
Bensching *Saying grace after meals*
Beth Din *Jewish law court*
Bimah *Raised platform in a synagogue from which the service is conducted*
Borscht *Beetroot soup*
Bris *The circumcision of a Jewish boy eight days after birth*
Bubbeh *Grandmother*
Chai *Life/Hebrew letter representing life*
Challah *Plaited loaf used on the Jewish Sabbath and festivals*
Chametz *Products that cannot be consumed during the festival of*

Pesach/Passover
Chassid *Extremely orthodox Jew*
Chazan *Cantor in a synagogue*
Cheder *Religion school for Jewish children*
Chol Hamoed *The days during Pesach/Passover when a Jew is allowed to work*
Chrayn *Strong horseradish sauce*
Chumash *Volume containing the Five Books of Moses*
Chutzpah *Cheek*
Davening *Praying*
Erev Yomtov *The night on which a festival begins*
Frum/frummer *Very orthodox/ a very orthodox Jew*
Galus *The exile or Diaspora of the Jewish people from the Land of Israel*
Gefilte (fish) *Boiled or fried rounds of minced fish*
Gelt *Money*
Gevalt *Disturbance or commotion*
Gutte neshomah *A good soul*
Haggadah *The book relating the story of the Israelites' Exodus from Egypt*
Halachah *The body of Jewish laws*
Hallel *Collection of psalms recited in the synagogue on Jewish festivals*
Heim/der Heim *Home/The Homeland*
Heimische *Friendly/informal/warm/cosy Jewish atmosphere*
Holocaust *The murder of six million Jews by the Nazis*
Ivrit *Modern Hebrew as used in Israel*
Kaddish *Prayer recited by a mourner*
Kiddush *Blessing recited over wine and bread on the Jewish Sabbath or a festival*
Kippah *Skull cap*
Kishkes *Guts*
Kosher *Food and drink that can be consumed under Kashrut (Jewish dietary law)*
Kreplach *Meat in dough parcels served in chicken soup with noodles*

Kuchen *Cake*
Kvelling *Brimming with pride*
Latkes *Potato pancakes*
Lavoyah *Funeral*
L'Chaim! *A toast "To Life!"*
Leyning *Reading from the Torah in a synagogue, usually by the rabbi*
Loch in kop *Literally, a hole in the head; crazy*
Lokshen *Noodles*
Lox *Smoked salmon*
Magen David *Star of David*
Mah Nishtanah *The four questions asked by the youngest child during the Seder*
Matzah *Unleavened bread required to be eaten during Pesach/Passover*
Mezuzah *The prayer container affixed to the doorposts of Jewish buildings*
Mikveh *Jewish ritual bath*
Minyan *The quorum of ten Jewish men required for prayer*
Mishegass *Madness; stupidity*
Mishpocheh *Family*
Moshiach *Messiah*
Neshomah *The soul*
Noch *Also; yet*
Olam haba *The world to come*
Parve *Relating to food comprising neither meat nor dairy products*
Passover/Pesach *The Jewish festival commemorating the Exodus from Egypt*
Purim *The Jewish festival celebrating the rescue of the Jews in ancient Persia*
Putz *Idiot; nincompoop*
Rabbi *Jewish religious leader and teacher*
Rebbetzen *The wife of a rabbi*
Rosh Hashanah *The Jewish New Year*
Rosh Yeshivah *The head of an advanced, religion college for Jewish men*

Sabra *A person born in Israel*
Seder *Literally, order; the Pesach service, generally in the home*
Sefer Torah *The scroll containing the Five Books of Moses*
Semichah *The qualification required to become a rabbi*
Shefoch Hamat'cha *A prayer recited during the Seder*
Shabbos/Shabbat *The Jewish Sabbath*
Shalom *Peace*
Shammas *The beadle in a synagogue*
Sheitl *The wig worn by the wife of a very orthodox Jew*
Shekoach *Literally, strength; usually said to a person who has performed an aliyah*
Shidduch *An arranged marriage*
Shiva *Period of mourning*
Shlaff/Shlaffing *Sleep/Sleeping*
Shlemiel *Fool*
Shlepping/Shlepper *Carrying a (usually heavy) load/Person carrying such a load*
Schmaltz herring *Fatty, and often salty, herring*
Schmooze/Schmoozing *Chit-chat, gossip/Passing the time with chit-chat, gossip*
Shoah *The Nazi Holocaust of six million Jews*
Shtetl *Jewish village or township in the Eastern Europe and Russia of yesteryear*
Shtum *Silent*
Siddur *Jewish daily prayer book*
Strudel *Cake usually filled with apple*
Shul *Synagogue*
Synagogue *Building used for worship by Jews*
Tallit *Prayer shawl generally for use during services in the synagogue*
Talmud *Collection of Jewish laws, commentaries and traditions*
Toches *Buttocks*
Torah *The Five Books of Moses*
T'shuva *Repentance*
Yarmulka *Skull cap*

Yeshivah *Advanced, religion college for Jewish men*
Yeshivah bocha *Student at a yeshivah*
Yiddish *A language originated by Central and East European Jews, basically a German vernacular with words formed in Hebrew letters*
Yiddishkeit *Jewishness*
Yomim Noraim *The Days of Awe, Rosh Hashanah to Yom Kippur*
Yom Kippur *Day of Atonement, the holiest day in the Jewish year*
Yomtov/Yomtovim *Jewish holiday/Jewish holidays*
Zaydeh *Grandfather*